Can tragedies have a happy ending in Storybook Lake?

Every town has one—a mean girl, hell-bent on taking down everything in her path—and Danielle Ranier played the role to a tee. She broke up Storybook Lake's most beloved couple and to save herself from a lifetime of lectures on morality, she hopped on the first plane out of town. Six years, one child, and a big secret later, she's back, fleeing from her abusive husband, who isn't quite willing to set her free. Now on trial for a murder she didn't commit, Simon Hunter, the only man she's ever loved is offering her a lifetime of love and security. If she could only reveal the secrets long-held inside her, a family that never was might finally come together . . .

I0524994

Books by Melissa Shirley

Storybook Lake Series
Here He Comes Again
Falling Grace
Breaking Hearts

Published by Kensington Publishing Corporation

Breaking Hearts

A Storybook Lake Romance

Melissa Shirley

LYRICAL PRESS
Kensington Publishing Corp.
www.kensingtonbooks.com

First Electronic Edition: August 2016
eISBN-13: 978-1-60183-613-7
eISBN-10: 1-60183-613-9

First Print Edition: August 2016
ISBN-13: 978-1-60183-614-4
ISBN-10: 1-60183-614-7

Printed in the United States of America

For Gina and Diana

Acknowledgements

Very special thank you to the best CP in the universe.

Chapter 1

Opening Statements

"All rise!"

Being on trial for my life taught me two things. One, when the bailiff says "all rise," everyone in the courtroom should immediately shut up and stand; two, the business end of being on trial and the tremors associated with it did not couple well with coffee drinking and silk blouses.

I blotted at my shirt while my lawyer leaned in close to advise me, yet again, of the possible outcomes of the case should I lose. Grace Wade turned to face me head-on and recommended I at least consider the prosecutions deal of life in prison with the possibility of parole in twenty-five years. *Twenty-five years?* I decided to gamble on a jury trial and a possible life sentence. Surely, at least one of the twelve people would realize I didn't kill Sean, no matter how badly I wanted to, and no matter how much unwavering gratitude, trial talk taboo, I harbored for the person who'd actually done the job.

The jurors filed into the courtroom, seven women between the ages of thirty and late sixties and five men from early twenties to late forties. A school teacher, bus driver, street sweeper, an accountant, landscaper, college student, and three food service professionals--translation: waiters and waitresses--a dog trainer, boutique owner, and a hairdresser, all had been chosen as my peers. Somehow, being accused of murder changed how I evaluated my *peers*, especially since I had no choice but to put my life in their hands.

Calvin Coolidge Connor, the prosecutor and apparent love child of Beetlejuice and Mr. Frodo--dark black hair, a slender waist, and a suit swallowing him almost whole--looked over at me with slits for eyes and a grim smirk on his lips. As green as any other small town thirty five-year-old prosecutor eager to make a name for himself, he probably jumped at the chance to take this case. He'd been an opportunist in high school, too, but as friends back then, I'd overlooked it. In this moment, with a gallery full of TV cameras, former friends, and reporters with pens poised to capture every detail, I hated him for it.

My attorney, the only lawyer I'd ever met, had been my best friend growing up, and though ten years had passed since we did more than make small talk on the phone, she took my case, no questions asked. Even though Grace had been career dormant as of late, I sat next to her not at all worried. She'd always been wrapped in some karmically blessed aura of greatness. At least, that's what I told myself in the morning before I dressed for trial.

She smoothed her skirt as we sat and waited for the prosecutor to begin his opening statement. At seventeen months older than me, Grace had movie star beauty. Along with her dramatic good looks, she capitalized on her porn star figure by wearing short, mostly respectable skirts, and blouses opened at the throat, thoroughly enhancing her pushed up C cups.

Without looking at me, checking her notes, or picking up a pen, she stared at the troll and waited. To anyone else, she appeared calm, poised for battle, but her fingers trembled as they sat idle against the table. A light sheen of sweat dotted her forehead and upper lip. We ignored the whirring of cameras, crinkling of papers, muffled coughs, hushed whispers in the court room, and most of our childhood friends on the witness list. For a former glory hound like Grace, ignoring it all said something.

As much as I'd come to love Storybook Lake over the last year, we weren't holding the trial at home. Storybook Lake would never let something so tainted as murder touch its cobblestoned, gas-lit streets. The proceedings had been transferred to neighboring Bloomington and my friends and former neighbors, all with ready-formed opinions as to my innocence or guilt, elbowed for space in the tiny courtroom.

Cal, whose grades in high school mirrored his initials, stood and walked to the center of the room, facing the jury, his back to me. While I understood he had a job to do, it irked me he'd been able to start without as much as a glance at the pile of notes on his table. Executing a perfect military turn in his too-shiny clown shoes, he took three paces toward the judge parallel to the jury, pulled in tight, turned a hard left and stalked to his original spot. He stopped abruptly, facing the twelve people instructed to hang on his every word.

"Good morning, ladies and gentlemen. My name is Calvin Connor and I represent you, the good people of the State of Illinois."

I nudged Grace and mouthed the words, "suck up." She shot me a glare and then went back to ignoring me.

"Storybook Lake, Illinois is an innocent little tourist town with a quiet character based on works of literary greatness. Its existence celebrates the lives of those who let us borrow their words to transport ourselves through whatever carefully woven life they have created in their pages. On June fourth, this woman"--he pointed at me without turning his head or body--"shattered the calm normally floating over the quiet little city. She lured her husband away from his home in California with the promise he would get to see the son she kidnapped."

I scanned the room for the Academy Award presenters and shrugged when no little gold statue or red carpet actress appeared.

Grace leaped to her feet. "Objection, Your Honor. Mrs. Turner had, and continues to have, sole custody of the child. There was no kidnapping involved and absolutely no evidence she lured her husband here. In fact, all evidence points otherwise." Grace turned to me, eyes wide and the hint of a smile on her lips.

The judge turned her attention to Cal. "Mr. Cooper?"

He simply lifted one shoulder, cocked his head toward it with an off-handed smile, offering no explanation.

"Sustained."

The judge shot him a dirty look.

He refocused on the jury and continued. "This woman, the defendant, is a cold, calculating killer who involved herself in a relationship with another man while still married to Sean Turner. She knew in order to be with the love of her life"--*Air quotes?*--"and raise her son with him, she needed to get rid of her husband. She had to make sure he didn't have the ability to interfere. So, what did she do? She took a knife and stabbed Sean Turner, not once, not twice, but seven times. And, in a matter of seconds, her burden of marriage disappeared."

He shook his head and clucked his tongue. "But then, Sean turner refused to die, to let her take his son away and live with another man. He refused to give up his hold on his wife and on life. She couldn't let him live, especially not now. Attempted murder? She would have lost her son, anyway. So, she ran to her purse, took out the gun she stole from her boyfriend, a former chief of police, and shot Mr. Turner in the face." He made a pistol with his fingers, flicked his arm out in aim. and *shot* me. "She lied to investigators, not once, but three times. She lied to her friends, her family, and to her son."

Grace rocket-launched out of her chair again. "Objection, Your Honor. May we approach?" Without waiting for an answer, she stomped to the front of the courtroom and stood, hands on hips, feet apart. Grace Wade, princess warrior, ready for battle.

After an animated discussion--her hands flailing, his head bobbing and the judge jerking her head back and forth ping pong style--she returned to her seat next to mine and picked up her pen. She scribbled, *No worries. I got this.*

I aspired to worried.

The judge glanced at Cal, then the jury. "The objection is sustained. Ladies and gentleman, there is no evidence the gun used to shoot Mr. Turner was, in fact, the gun belonging to Simon Hunter." Cal received his second stink-eye from the judge in a matter of minutes. "Proceed, Mr. Connor."

"The point isn't who this defendant lied to or whose gun she used, or why Sean Turner turned up in Illinois. The point is she lied and she lied a lot. She left Mr. Turner in his hotel room bleeding to death."

Nope. By the time I arrived, he'd been stabbed and shot and died alone. The way I always knew he would.

"The relationship between the defendant and Mr. Turner was born in the back of a limousine where the defendant conceived the couple's child. After trying unsuccessfully to dupe Keaton Shaw into believing the child belonged to him, a DNA test proved her a liar. Another lie in her long list. With no other choice after being chased out of Storybook Lake in shame, she sought out Sean Turner and married him, then quit her job."

I hadn't quit my job. My job didn't require a desk or an office, just a pen and piece of paper. I designed kids' clothes for a living.

"Then she moved to California to be with her husband. After a few thousand arguments over money, she left the marital home, taking the child with her. When she returned over the Christmas holiday, she visited Storybook Lake with her husband, and while they were there, together, as a couple, she flaunted her desire to be with Mr. Hunter in Sean Turner's face."

We had been fighting over my money and the way Sean spent it in big fat wads, but the tone of Cal's voice turned the greed around on me. And, for his information, during the trip in question, Sean found me talking to Simon for the sum total of one minute, hauled me back to the hotel, and hit me with such force my eyes rolled back. I thought he'd literally broken my face. The next morning, he'd cried like a baby, said he couldn't stand the thought of losing me. I went home with him because he'd been *sorry* and because he promised to start over with me and make a life with me and Kieran. Plus, Simon went to the New Year's party with Kelly Devlin, the big shot magazine writer he'd broken up with me to date.

"Mr. Turner, by this defendant's own admission, cried, begged, and pleaded for her to return to him so he could share in the life of their child. Reluctantly, by another of her own admissions, she returned home to Mr. Turner where the real fighting began."

Rage at the injustice behind Cal's half-truths welled up inside me. Grace covered my fingers with her own, squeezing hard, probably to stop the drumming against the table top. The fighting started because Sean slept with every stripper in his employ, as well as some who worked for other clubs. *Jeez!* Where was a tiny-headed voodoo doll when I needed one?

"By the time she finished with him, Sean Turner couldn't wait for Danielle to leave, but he wanted his son. Within hours of her leaving, he filed papers for custody of his child."

Sean had used custody as leverage to lure me back. I resisted the urge to roll my eyes. Grace had been forthright about how I should behave, and eye rolling topped the no-no list.

"But did this defendant cooperate after the police found the body? Did she ever tell them she had, in fact, been in Mr. Turner's hotel room? No. Did she tell them she stalked him to the hotel, fought with him? No. Instead, she pretended she'd had no contact with him since she'd taken their son and run home to Storybook Lake months earlier." He shook his head and his pacing in front of the jury continued.

"When investigators discovered otherwise, her story changed again, tailored to fit the evidence. She finally concocted this story of abuse toward not only her, but the child. She, in her desperation to stay out of jail, involved their four-year-old son in her web of lies." He stared down most of the time, presumably to make sure his clown shoes didn't catch on one another and cause him to topple head over feet. "Danielle Turner is the worst kind of predator. She uses her beauty"--he stabbed a bony finger through the air in my direction and gazed up at the jury--"to snare men into her web of lies."

His words curdled my blood.

"She used her over-average intelligence to try to outwit cops and investigators. And she used her son as a weapon to get her way. In this case, to get her way she had to kill Mr. Turner. Otherwise, she couldn't embark on her new life with Simon Hunter. In a town which celebrates its fiction, don't lump her in with the likes of Shakespeare, Mark Twain, or even Dr. Seuss. *Her* fiction is as unbelievable as the evidence will prove it to be." With a smirk, he raised one eyebrow at Grace and went back to his chair, needing a copy of the yellow pages on his seat to properly see over the top of his table. Without it, he seemed to have tucked himself almost underneath the smooth, flat surface holding the mountain of notes and binders on the case.

Grace stood and smoothed her skirt. "Mr. Connor." She shook her head, long, blond hair swinging along her back, soft curls dancing. "Shame on you."

"Your Honor." Calvin shoved his legs against the fabric of his cushioned chair, shooting it backward into the short wall dividing us from the gallery. The clatter echoed throughout the high-ceilinged room. "Ms. Wade needs to speak to the jury, not the prosecutor."

The judge smiled at Grace. "Miss Wade, you know better."

Grace nodded, her lips pursing as she tried to wipe the smile from her face. "Yes, Your Honor." She turned back to the jury and introduced herself, then began. "Mrs. Turner didn't lure her husband to Storybook Lake. She didn't want him anywhere near Storybook Lake or her son. Since the day of their wedding, Sean tortured Danielle, beating her and later Kieran. There is irrefutable evidence to prove it."

She turned to Cal, with another quick shake of her head as though reprimanding him for his lie. "As soon as the private detective Sean Turner hired to hunt Danielle found her, bad, scary, dangerous things started to happen. He had her home vandalized, then broken into. She received countless texts on numerous cell phones indicating Sean knew exactly where to find her and exactly how she spent her days. The week he died, Sean bought a plane ticket and flew to Storybook Lake to step up his efforts to intimidate my client, her friends, and her family. The evidence will show you Danielle did not kill Mr. Turner.

"Instead you'll see how Sean Turner taunted her, threatened her life repeatedly, not only over the last week of his life, but during the entire course of their relationship. What the evidence will not show you is that she had a single thing to do with his murder. The prosecutor has no murder weapon, no eye witness, not a single, tangible thing to prove Danielle had anything to do with Sean's murder. She admitted to seeing him. She admitted to being in his hotel room, but no matter how hard they tried, they couldn't shake her story about what happened after she got there."

She paused for a moment, her eyes pivoting from me to the jury. "You are going to hear things about Sean Turner which are going to make it seem as though he's the one on trial, about his behavior, his job, and his sex life. Make no mistake. We're not trying to smear Sean Turner's name, but this is all information you need to walk into the jury room with a full picture of the events leading up to the night Danielle left her husband and returned home to the safety of Storybook Lake.

"Danielle had the most to lose and nothing to gain by Sean Turner's death. When he died, she inherited an almost bankrupt strip club and a pile of debt he ran up in the months since she left. She had an army of friends surrounding her to keep her safe from Sean and his henchmen. The fact is, many, *many* people had a reason to want Sean dead. Danielle didn't kill him, and Mr. Cooper cannot prove otherwise."

Grace smiled once more at the jury, then came to sit beside me as Calvin stood. "Your Honor," he said, with enough glee in his voice I imagined him about to spring into cartwheels. "I call Mr. Keaton Shaw."

Ugh. Keaton's *debt* to me had been repaid, and no matter what he said about forgiving me, I had no idea what he would say or do on the stand. He raised his right hand, swore to tell the truth, and took his seat to the left of the judge. After he stated his name for the record, he shot me a half smile. I hoped against all other hope it was a good sign.

When he tightened his tie, adjusted his jacket, then pointed a straight-forward gaze at the jury, several of the female jurors sat up straighter. His beauty inspired the same reaction wherever he went.

"Mr. Shaw." Calvin walked from his seat to the podium, almost wringing his hands together in evil merriment. This had to be his nerd dream. He had the captain of every sports team in our graduating class sitting in front of him testifying against the homecoming queen. It played out like an after school special gone wrong. "How do you know Mrs. Turner?"

Keaton's eyebrows moved toward the center of his forehead as though he'd never heard a question more stupid. "We all grew up together." His tone clearly indicated he included Calvin in the group.

Calvin chuckled. "Right. We did."

Though I'm sure Cal remembered growing up outside their circle a little differently than Keaton remembered growing up surrounded by Gatlin, Joss, Simon, Kelly, and Luke.

"Growing up, how well did you get to know Mrs. Turner?"

Keaton smiled. "We were friends, then we dated in high school. After high school we lived together for a while."

"And when you were living together, was it while you were still married?"

Uh-oh.

"I was in the process of getting divorced."

"But you were still married?" Cal's question left Keaton no room to wiggle out of the answer.

"Yes." He ground out the word as one eyebrow cocked on his forehead, daring Cal to take it further.

A bubble of anger formed in the pit of my stomach as Calvin asked, "And your divorce stemmed from your involvement with Mrs. Turner?" *Oh, good Lord.* I nudged Grace. *Object, dammit.* She'd never been good at hearing my mind messages, so I kicked her shin. She whirled to look at me and tilted her head. "Stop."

"My wife thought I was having an affair." *Explain, explain, explain.* I hoped Keaton had the gift of telepathy Grace did not. Unfortunately, he remained sitting, hands clasped in his lap, waiting for the next question.

Calvin continued grinding his ugly little axe to a razor sharp point. "During the time you lived with Mrs. Turner, did either of you use drugs or alcohol?"

"Yes." Keaton looked at me and frowned.

"Both of you?"

"We didn't do drugs."

I closed my eyes as memories of those days washed over me...dim, alcohol-fogged memories.

"And during your time away, Mrs. Turner became pregnant?"

I wanted to smack Cal's self-satisfied smile right off his smarmy, thin lips. If eye rolling topped Grace's no-no list, I had to assume smacking the prosecutor was off-limits, but the desire itched inside my palm.

"Yes."

"And she let you believe the child belonged to you for how long?"

"She didn't do it on purpose. We lived together like couples live together."

I guessed that was his way of saying we'd had some sex. Knowing Joss had a seat a few rows behind me, I couldn't decide if his lie helped or hurt either of us.

"He could have been mine." Keaton frowned.

Calvin peered up at the judge. "Your Honor, the witness is non-responsive."

The judge glared back at Calvin. "And your question was leading. Rephrase." She shot a lifted brow look at Grace.

"How long did Mrs. Turner let you believe you'd fathered her child?" Grace stood up. "Objection. Relevance and foundation."

The judge looked at Grace, a half smile crooking her lips. "Sustained."

Calvin clarified the details. When had we lived together and where? How long after we began living together did I become pregnant? How long after I told him did I have the baby?

"And how long before you discovered he belonged to someone else?" Grace stood again. "Objection, relevance."

"Your honor, it goes to her motive for seeking out Mr. Turner in the first place."

Grace almost popped her hip out of place coming around the desk, and for a split second, I thought she might wrap her hands around his neck instead of punching them against her waist. "Your Honor, we believed Mr. Shaw was going to be called because he was a first responder to the scene."

"She can't tell me what to ask my witness." Calvin's voice climbed to a child-like whine.

The judge cocked her head. "Approach, please." They walked to the front of the courtroom, and I sat back in my chair, remembering.

Chapter 2

How it all started.

Since the moment I first noticed boys in fifth grade, Simon Hunter was the boy I saw myself growing old with. He had the best smile, the most expressive honey-colored eyes, and a way with people that made an entire town love him. Even when he didn't know it, he was everything to me. Any minute I could sneak into his presence was a minute I savored and cherished.

When we got around to the business of being adults, our schedules seldom coordinated, but we spent most Fridays together. I'd skipped out on the last three, wanting him to see what it would be like without me. I wanted him to miss me with a desperate passion.

The missing only happened on my end, and I had the phone log to prove it. As it went to voice mail, I glared at my phone and left my tenth message…a pitiful, I-miss-you-please-call-me-and-let-me-know-you're-okay kind of message. Since high school, he'd been my reason for waking up in the morning, the hero in the dreams I had every night, and the focus of all the moments in between. And damn it. Friday was our day.

After a quick makeup check, I left my apartment, the one we'd planned to share up until a few months ago when he started making all those trips to LA with Gatlin. I kicked the jealousy away with the toe of my shoe against a rock on the sidewalk.

For three full blocks, I took my frustration out on chunks of concrete until I strolled past the bakery. It took every ounce of my will not to press my nose against the window to see if he'd decided to loiter inside while his sister worked, or if he'd just run in to get some free pastries. His car was parked out front, so I leaned against it for a few minutes, waiting… remembering the first time he kissed me…the way his hand cupped the side of my face, the brush of his lips so softly over mine. Had we been sixteen? Seventeen? It was a lifetime ago.

Thousands of kisses followed the first one, and I always wondered when that feeling of perfection would wear off. I guarded against it, always creating new ways for Simon and me to retain everything we had going for us. Maybe we needed to take a trip, somewhere tropical where bikinis and board shorts were the required wardrobe until the sun went down. *Yes.* He'd been on the Storybook Lake police department long enough he could wrangle a weekend off to be with me instead of Gatlin. My schedule would be much easier to rearrange. I worked at the resort. No one would miss me if I didn't show up for a month much less a weekend.

All I needed was a plan, and since I had one and the confidence that came with it, I pushed off the fender I'd been lounging against and strolled into the bakery. Simon glanced up from the table he occupied with Jocelyn. After a long moment, he stood.

"Good luck, bud."

Her smile confused me, but I ignored it in favor of the euphoria of knowing Simon and I would be vacationing together very soon--as soon as I could get to a computer and book a trip. I bit my tongue to restrain an insult over her dye stained uniform and waited for Simon to join me by the entrance.

"You too. I'll expect to be an uncle soon."

As he followed me out, I looked over my shoulder at him. "What was that about?"

He let the door swing shut behind us and shoved his hands in his pockets. We stood staring at each other on the sidewalk. "It's their anniversary, and she's going to meet Keaton at the bar tonight."

"How lovely for them."

He met my sarcasm with his usual shrug. "I need to talk to you. Can we take a walk?"

Something about his body language was off. He hadn't touched me, kissed me, or so much as looked in my eyes. Instead of turning to walk beside him, I took a step closer, then blew out a quick puff of air when he stepped away.

"Simon?"

Finally, it dawned on me...the downcast gaze, the nervous stutter step, Joss wishing him good luck. He was going to ask. After all this time, all these years of waiting, he'd finally decided to make an honest woman of me, and I was ready.

"Let's go for a walk, Dani." Without waiting to see if I'd follow or fall in step beside him, he started across the street to the park. Bypassing the picnic tables and chess sets, he veered over to the playground equipment and sat on a swing. On any other day, he would crook his finger and we would engage in a public display of affection that could be considered inappropriate by most non-porn watching individuals. This day, he stared off at something far away only he could see. Probably getting the words organized in his mind to make it the proposal I'd always dreamed of.

I clasped my hands in front of me. Waiting. Heart beating a few thousand thumps a minute. I swiped my palms down my jeans. No way was I having sweaty fingers when he went to slip that ring on.

"Take your time, baby. I'm not going anywhere." For as long as I lived, I'd be right there by his side, until death did we part. "This is *the* Friday." I would have clapped as an exclamation point to my sentence, but I didn't want to interrupt his thought process. This moment was one I would cherish. It needed to be perfect. I couldn't stop the smile spreading across my face when I plopped down into the seat beside him.

"Friday?" He shook his head and continued staring at his shoes.

"Our Friday. The Friday I will remember for as long as I live, so you better make it good." After a few minutes of staring at everything but me, he met my eyes, and I wished he hadn't. There wasn't happiness in his whiskey-colored gaze. It was something far different and it scared me.

"Simon, what's wrong?" My heart stopped. This wasn't a proposal. No. It had to be. We'd been together for more than eight years. It had to be a proposal. I wouldn't survive anything else. "What did I do?" I couldn't fix what I didn't know I'd broken. I might have blamed him, but historically, the mistakes in our relationship belonged to me, so I went with the odds.

"It's not you, Dani." He ran his hand through his long, golden hair. "I didn't want this to happen."

I stood, hoping my weakened muscles would hold me. "What happened?" Okay, maybe it was nothing. Not the images I imagined, anyway.

His tongue ran over his bottom lip, and my normal flutter of attraction skittered through me. "I never wanted…I mean… I don't want to hurt you."

My throat closed and the air in my lungs evaporated. No conversation that started that way ever meant anything good and I knew it. This couldn't be happening. "Then don't." Had manipulating him into missing me backfired? My stomach churned at the thought. What had I done? More importantly, what had he done?

His gulp echoed on the eerie quiet of the park. It was as though everyone in town had shut themselves in to avoid the devastation our break-up would leave behind. In the romantic notions of my mind, it made sense the town would suffer through my broken heart right along with me. The truth, however, was quite different. No one would care but me. No one would even know unless Simon or I wanted them to, or he told his sister. Then it would be picking a side. Who would dare go against the golden Simon? Devastation was not too strong a word. It didn't even come close.

"I've... I haven't seen you at all lately."

When I opened my mouth to explain, he held up his hand.

"Please, just let me get through this."

I snapped my jaw closed, but he didn't continue speaking.

He blew out a breath instead, scrubbed his palm over his face, and held a single blink for ten or fifteen seconds. "You know I went to California with Gatlin, right?"

"Yeah." A ball formed in the pit of my stomach, then went for a roll trying to make its way out my mouth.

"Maybe we need some time apart."

A piece of my heart froze and an image of ice cracking flashed through my mind.

"You're the only girl I've ever been with, Dani, and when I talked to Kelly, she suggested..."

I didn't give a damn what she had to say. "Kelly Devlin? That-that"--I scanned my brain for an insult I could apply to her and came up empty--"Kelly Devlin?"

"We think--"

"As if it's not enough that damned Jocelyn is always trash talking me, now I have to worry about Miss Congeniality, too?"

"Don't, Dani. This is about us. Not anyone else. Kelly and I talked for a long time and she, I mean, we"--he shook his head--"I think we need some time to figure out if we belong together or if we're just comfortable."

I pictured him and Kelly, perfectly wonderful Kelly, lying on a beach, running through the surf, holding hands... The longer I stood, the worse the pictures became. "Time? It's been eight years, Simon."

"Dani, this doesn't mean we're finished. It just means we're taking a step back to make sure."

"A step back." Another piece of my heart chipped off. "Go. Be with Little Suzy Happy Pants if you want. We don't need a break. We're finished."

I spun away, then whirled around, anger and pain warring inside me. I never let blind fury beat me, but I couldn't stop it. The sharp stabbing was too intense, and I clung to my rage to escape the grief already killing me, one aching cell at a time. I wanted to scream at him, to hold him accountable for my heartbreak, but I couldn't summon enough anger to overpower the grief. "That's what all the trips to California have been about, right? Not surfing with Gatlin, but screwing Kelly."

"I didn't sleep with her. I would never cheat."

I laughed, the sound as bitter as the taste. "No? You keep going out there behind my back to see her, to be with her when you belong here with me." Oh, God. The tears were coming, threatening to spill with just one more blink.

"You told me to go whenever I asked you."

"Because I thought absence would make your freaking heart grow fonder." I shook my head. "I was giving you space. I didn't think you'd go out there and fall in love with someone else."

He held out a hand, and I jerked away, lifting my hands in the motion for surrender as I backed up a few steps.

"Dani, we can still be friends. I don't want to lose you."

I bit my bottom lip. "When you brought me over here, I actually thought you were going to ask me to marry you."

He reached out again.

This time, I sidestepped to avoid the touch I longed for, but my pride wouldn't let me accept. "Don't. Just don't."

"You're gonna find a great guy."

I swallowed the lump in my throat and took three steps, then a fourth. "That's a great idea. I'm gon-gonna go home and get ready to go ou-out or something." I stumbled over a divot in the grass and caught myself before I could do any more damage to my flailing self-respect.

"Are you okay?"

"Oh, yeah. I'm great." I turned and fled, literally ran away from the scene of the crime. Only when I found myself alone in the dead silence of my apartment did I let the tears break free.

Chapter 3

I would have liked to have been the hero in the aftermath of our break-up, or at least the person taking the smallest amount of blame, but looking back, I had moments which should have made me hide my head in some sort of windowless box so no one ever had to witness my shame.

Case in point...

"So, what happened with Simon?" Keaton Shaw bent over the pool table to line up his shot. A blue button-down stretched tightly over broad shoulders and tucked in at his narrow waist. He'd flipped his tie over his shoulder so as not to interfere with his already lousy pool skills. His jeans fit snug, hugging his long legs and slightly rounded ass. The denim appeared as though it had been smoothed by time and a few hundred machine washes. I didn't exactly tingle to touch it, but I admired him with the healthy kind of respect, which would earn me a few extra Hail Mary's for coveting someone else's stuff. And there was no mistaking--Keaton Shaw belonged to someone else.

He'd been beautifully perfect since he arrived on the scene in eighth grade, but the sadness in his eyes lowered his total handsomeness score. Not by much, but enough. I knew Keaton--worked with him, dated him in high school, then dated his BFF for the last eight years--and he'd never admit to sadness or validate the idea of trouble in his perfect life with the equally flawless Jocelyn. Only someone who knew him well or suffered the same affliction would be able to tell.

We had the same shoulder slump, identical too-much-sadness glances that tried too hard and came away weak. Yeah. I could tell.

We shared a hurt delivered by people who'd divvied up their DNA to become two halves of a matching twin set. I'd been tossed away earlier in the day, but Keaton's agony was much fresher, deepening the lines of his face, hunching his spine in a way I'd overcome already...until I had to breath the words, "Simon wants Kelly." Then mine burned anew.

I coughed to hide a pending sob, and my feigned strength faded. Simon's words had broken me into a thousand tiny shards of gloom and despair, each one labeled with a happy memory I would have to drink myself into oblivion to forget. Hence, my reason for being in the bar. That was what I told myself, anyway.

"Little Kelly Devlin." Keaton zinged the six-ball into the corner.

I nodded and concentrated all my energy on draining the cold beer in my hand to block out the intensity of the stinging in my stomach. I couldn't lash out at Simon. Well, I could have, but it wouldn't have been fair. He'd been honest. More so than I cared for. He couldn't help if his heart wasn't as emotionally invested as mine. Probably.

In a desperate effort to end my suffering, I'd called Grace, master plotter and revenge seeker, to lay out my tragic tale--complete with mistaken hope for a proposal--and in true best friend style, she said to hit him where it would hurt. And that meant going after *Jocelyn.*

If we'd been in a superhero comic, *she* would have been my arch nemesis, my kryptonite, the anti-me. The idea of taking *her* down made me smile. On the flip side, it would involve Keaton, the boy who'd been my friend even when it hurt him. Vengeance would never be more than a pleasant, daydream kind of fantasy. Grace's plan would destroy *Jocelyn*, but it had the potential to kill him. I couldn't do that.

And Speaking of *her*… "When did Joss say she'd be here?" Saying her name made my beer bitter. She wasn't just anyone. She'd been Keaton's wife since he graduated college. Most interesting to my cause, she was Simon's sister, the person he loved more than himself.

I'd spent eight long years tolerating her, calling a truce to our war because I loved him. Yeah. The idea of hurting her sounded better by the minute, and I almost went with it. Then I caught a glimpse of Keaton… broken, drunk Keaton, whose eyes glittered with tears.

He was too wrapped up in his misery and probably the rumors of his doomed marriage circulating Storybook Lake to notice me right in front of him.

"About an hour ago." The pool stick clattered across the felt cloth covering the table and rolled to a stop resting against the eight ball. His shoulders slumped. "I don't know why I'm so anxious for her to get here. She's going to ask me for a divorce…leave me, anyway."

I imagined the pieces of his heart fracturing more by the minute.

Life hadn't been kind to them recently. They'd lost a baby. His picture perfect dream crumbled, but so had mine. Still, chatting about his heartache, helping him, felt infinitely better than wallowing in my own. "You want to talk about it?"

"No. I want to drink until the words won't hurt anymore." His half smile slid into a grimace, and he lowered his head as his shoulders shook. He really loved her, and I almost picked up my bag and went out to find her. I would have loved to unleash my last twenty years of frustration in a butt-kicking she needed. Instead, I handed him one of the hundred proof shots I'd bought on my way in. When he finished his, he handed me his empty glass, snatched mine, and smiled as he tipped it back.

"You better slow down, golden boy. The she-bitch isn't gonna wanna come in here and find you all drunked up."

"Don't you get it, Dani? She doesn't care enough to come in here and find me at all or she would have been here already." A lone tear fell. "She's gonna leave me."

"No, Keats. You're her Romeo." They were the original star-crossed lovers, doomed to eternal misery.

"Not anymore." His tears came freely, and I took three steps closer invading every square inch of his personal space. He rested his ass against the wooden edge of the table with one hand braced on each side of his hips. Before he could shrink completely away, I cupped his cheek, forcing him to look at me.

"She's a fool, Keats. I would fight for you with every breath in my body." I gave him a little shove. He swayed, then hunched forward, putting us at eye level. His head dropped again, and I moved between his legs, then leaned down to press a kiss to the nape of his neck. "I hate seeing you like this. If she doesn't realize what she has, then it's her problem. You deserve someone who will love you for what you are, not what she wants you to be. Let's get out of here."

He didn't flinch, but tilted his chin slightly to the left and looked at me from beneath droopy eyelids. "Yeah?"

I couldn't be sure whether he meant it as a question or encouragement, but I knew which way I took it and continued nipping, then soothing his sensitive skin with kisses. To be held, to share the freshness of my suffering with someone eased my broken heart. Every fiber in my body needed someone to look at me, to see *me*. No matter how wrong, Keaton was there.

"Love isn't supposed to hurt, Keats." I lowered my hand to his belt, then his zipper, ignoring my conscience as though its screaming warning was no more than a whisper. He squinted up at me with wild eyes, glassy from the alcohol, then lifted me onto the pool table and kissed me like no one else existed in his world. Before it occurred to me to reconsider, I threw myself into kissing Keaton, holding him, running my hands over his skin.

I didn't need to see her walk in. Her anger charged the air in the room and her shouted threats fell on deaf ears as I climbed off the pool table. Instead of paying attention to her, I hurried out to the bar to get another drink from Scotty. If I could drown my hurt, maybe my shame would die an equally alcohol soaked death. Somehow, Grace's plan had come to life and I'd done nothing to stop it. Nothing at all.

I slid onto the stool, ordered a new beer and a shot. As Jocelyn stormed out the door, Keaton stumbled behind her. Scotty pushed a bottle in front of me. "What did you do, Dani?"

I swallowed hard, pasting on my mean girl smile--the one I'd practiced in front of the mirror until I had it just right. "I don't get mad, Scotty. I get even."

And so the reign of the evil Danielle began.

Chapter 4

Once the story of how I broke up Keaton and Jocelyn grew legs, the new rumors spread in sheets on the wind. First, they said I had sex with Keaton right there on the pool table. Then they added a fist fight with the poor, brokenhearted Jocelyn. It didn't help that she worked in the bakery and everyone saw her dragging herself to work with eyes swollen from crying and wrinkled uniform shirts from ignoring her iron. Her telling anyone who would listen how I destroyed her marriage also did considerable damage to my reputation.

It took a while for the *entire* town to shun me, but my long-standing feud with Jocelyn made the rumors more believable than I cared to fight. The ladies who played bridge with my mother started it. They turned up their snooty noses when I walked through the kitchen during their regular Tuesday night card and wine fest. The guys who sat outside at the barber shop jumped in the bridge-lady boat, concentrating way harder on their chess games when I walked past, avoiding so much as a semi-sociable hello. All the animosity only added to my bitterness, and I didn't bother concocting a defense.

Because he'd lost his golden boy status, landing with a thud into my realm of shame, Keaton waited a couple months, then turned tail and ran. After he left, I didn't waste much time booking my own flight out.

He went west and proceeded to lose himself in whatever bottles of alcohol he could get his hands on, trying to drown his sorrows over losing his precious Jocelyn. When his mom told my mom where he'd ended up, I changed my flight from destination-anywhere-but-here to Arizona. Not quite finished with the job of ruining my own reputation, I decided to take it a few steps further and make sure Simon and Jocelyn found out my exact endgame. They'd hurt us and deserved a taste of the pain.

Instead of using one of those private Internet search sites, I booked my flight through the Planes of Passion travel agency, which sent out a weekly newsletter to the entire town. The column, *Who's Headed Where*, arrived on Jocelyn's doorstep on a Wednesday, and the name calling reached an epic high on Thursday. As a side note, and also on Thursday, Simon and Kelly very publicly announced their relationship, before she tootle-ooed her way back across the country to her job in LA. I'd finally lost the boy of my dreams for good.

I couldn't leave soon enough. Breaking their hearts went a long way to healing mine, but I would never be healed in Storybook Lake. Besides, drinking with Keaton was better than drinking alone in the stable with only the horses to chat with.

Mom and Dad wouldn't even look at me, and took trips of their own to get away from the embarrassment of having the town harlot for a daughter. In the six months it took me to decide to leave, they went on four vacations. My parents were probably the only fifty year olds in the world who insisted on a yearly trip to Disney World and left the kids at home--another week of sun and sand for the over-worked psychologist/house wife and the international banker. Maybe they left because of their love for the beaches or the draw of the giant man-sized mouse and all his merchandise, but that year, they couldn't take enough trips to Florida.

They didn't postpone their latest holiday even after I told them when I was heading out, and my overwhelming and somewhat surprising guilt gave way to relief they wouldn't be around to witness my escape. I'd heard enough long, disappointed sighs from my mother, and I didn't need any more stern looks from my dad to send me on my way.

Whenever they jetted off on a new adventure, they asked Simon to feed the horses, so I spent a lot of time hiding in the loft watching his muscles expand and contract as he scooped feed and shoveled stalls. He never tried to come in the house or see me, but once I'd heard him talking to a horse about me.

Why'd she do it?

I'd waited too long to tell the truth for anyone--most especially him--to believe me now, so I pretended I hadn't heard and went on ogling him in secrecy.

I spent the night before drinking with Gatlin Reid, the town salon owner. By drinking, I meant I'd invited him out for a hair-coloring house call. We drank a gallon of homemade wine; then one innocent kiss turned to two, and we fell into bed as though he hadn't spent the last two years pretending to be gay and I wasn't pining for Simon. I piled shame on top of sin, blamed it all on Simon, then tried to drink it away. Aside from the daily hangovers, I had no friends left, no one who cared enough to save me from myself.

I walked down to the barn for a last ride. With any luck, I could saddle up and get the hell out of there before Simon showed up for morning feeding time.

* * * *

As I cinched the saddle, Simon strolled around the corner whistling some happy tune that aggravated the not-my-first-wouldn't-be-my-last hangover pounding in my frontal lobe. My vision clouded and, in true evil Danielle fashion, I blamed it on Gatlin for answering my invitation, then regrettable sex with Gatlin, and finally the homemade wine, which inspired both.

Why couldn't he wait twenty more minutes to show up? And for the love of God, did he really have to whistle like one of the fairy tale dwarves off to work?

I peered through the wooden slats of Buttercup's stall. *Damn.* Where had all those muscles come from? I'd just seen him the previous week, but to my Simon-hungry eyes, he looked better and better every time I ran across him. He'd let his hair grow out, and it blew back on the wind slicing through the barn. He had a walk, a way of being that glowed with something I could only describe as happiness for life…and his clothes hugged all his fun spots. Months of pent-up longing stirred in my stomach. *Fool. He left you.* The desire rolling in my belly volleyed its reply, *but he looks so good.*

I stepped out of my far stall hiding spot, and he jumped, shaking his head, his mouth hanging open. "I didn't know you were here."

"Don't worry. I'm leaving." I had to work at it, but I couldn't have injected more venom in my tone without a snake and a syringe. Ignoring my saddled horse, I stomped and stumbled through the tall grass alongside the barn. *Left foot, right foot, left foot, right foot.* The pounding of my heart kept a perfect tempo with my feet. I concentrated on walking to keep myself from focusing on him. I couldn't blame him for his anger, but damned if I wanted to look it in the eye, either.

"I heard you're heading out west." The soft tone of his voice stopped my forward motion.

I turned to find him leaning against the white painted siding of the stable, arms crossed, shoulder holding the wall in place. My ponytail whipped across my eyes as I squinted at him, waiting for the more nasty words I figured would come. Surely, he would have mentioned if Gatlin told him about our one wild night. "I'm flying out tomorrow."

"To see Keaton?"

"Why do you care?" I had a burning need to know if it mattered to him--if I mattered to him, at all. It didn't take long for my high hopes to crash. A second grader could have deduced he'd only asked because Keaton belonged to Jocelyn, and because the whole town blamed me for destroying their happily ever after. And no one in history had become more a part of the town than Deputy Sheriff Simon Hunter. "Because you're killing Joss. This is actually killing her." If he expected sympathy *for her* he'd hopped on the long, lonely disappointment train.

"Well, isn't she lucky she has you? But he's out there with no one." I shook my head preparing for a battle I knew wouldn't end with a shiny ring and a proposal of forever. I'd ruined everything for myself, but I would be damned to burn for eternity before I'd let him walk away without a bit of his own shame. "And what's wrong with you, anyway? You're his best friend and this is killing *him*." Then again, if I was leaving, why not take one last memory with me? Everyone I'd ever met decided to believe all those horrible things about me, so why shouldn't I use it to my advantage? *Homewrecker, slut*--not quite an invisible label when the whispers started wherever I went.

I took three steps toward him. "Besides, there doesn't seem to be much reason for me to stay here."

A glimmer of something soft, sweet, in his gaze shot my hopes skyward. One inch forward and our bodies would be within groping distance, and nothing in the world made me happier than a good handful of Simon. "Does there?"

He went mute, standing there with his tongue trailing across the center of his lower lip. I didn't know if it ever occurred to him exactly how provocative his little move looked, but my pulse sped up every time his nervous habit kicked in.

I slipped my finger inside the collar of his shirt, tugging him toward me. "I mean, you're all wrapped up in Hollywood Barbie." She'd moved out to California to stay, and finally, something--their long distance relationship--worked in my favor.

Our breaths tangled together as my hands slid under his warm cotton T-shirt and my lips found the little spot on his neck that lit him up. "I'm just in the way here. Right?"

He stayed quiet as my hands attacked the button of his jeans and my lips continued tasting him wherever I could reach.

It took a couple more seconds of touching him before he pulled me in and crushed his lips against mine. When he took over, the game changed, and I lost sight of who played who. After a few minutes, he pulled away enough to let his eyes caress my face. My anger disappeared with each skim of his fingers against my skin and with the sheer strength in his arms as he lifted me against his chest and carried me inside the barn.

A roll in the hay was not actually the most comfortable way to say good-bye, but I tucked away the memory for future use, then hopped in my car and drove out of town before he had the chance to break my heart a second time.

Chapter 5

Finding Keaton hadn't been a problem. I'd stepped off the plane and hailed a cab to the bar closest to the address his mom gave me. We spent the first couple days drunk enough neither of us remembered why we were drinking. By the end of the week, though, his slurred whining began--he missed Jocelyn; he loved Jocelyn; I wasn't Jocelyn, could never be Jocelyn. I wanted to smack him with one of the empty bottles so I didn't have to hear her name one more time. Instead, I screamed at him and ran out of the apartment.

Six weeks later, after a straight month of exhaustion and nausea, I made an appointment with a doctor someone from my new job recommended.

Pregnant.

While I couldn't be even moderately sure who fathered my baby, I knew one hundred percent for certain who did not.

Once again, shame ate at me and I dawdled my way through cleaning up files that didn't need my attention, shuffling papers, and restacking them into a normal order. The last thing I wanted to do was tell Keaton about my impending motherhood. I'd never been able to talk him into my bed. Or seduce him into it. Or keep him sober long enough to find it. Even falling down, slobbering onto the sofa cushions drunk, it would take him about six seconds to figure out the baby couldn't be his.

I walked into our apartment a couple hours later than usual. Keaton lay half-reclined on the sofa, his eyes closed, an almost empty bottle of Jack Daniels fisted in one hand.

"Hey."

The sleepy way he dragged out the slur said the bottle had probably been close to full at some point during the day.

"Where you been?"

That he hadn't consumed enough to take away his concept of time caused a sliver of trepidation in my mind's eye. I kind of hoped he passed out before I got to the day's big headline.

"Work." No point in beating around the bush. Much. "I went to the doctor this morning, so I stayed a little later than usual to make up the time." I worked at a small law firm as a file clerk. Even if I walked home after my shift and didn't take the bus, I usually strolled in by five-thirty. I looked at the clock--quarter till eight.

"Are you sick?" He sat up a little straighter, almost seeming to care as he blinked once, twice, then again with three quick flutters of his lashes. Although Keaton had always been one of the prettiest humans I'd ever known, without Jocelyn, he looked beat up. The bags under his eyes were deep purple. His hair was too long to be cute and too short to be rock-star sexy; his clothes were wrinkled and his eyes lacked their usual sparkle. He took a long swig from his bottle less beautiful than I'd ever seen him.

I snatched it away, set it on the end table, and sat down beside him. "Why don't you call her?" I softened my voice in the hope maybe he would finally listen. I'd tried everything from bribery to badgering and he stood tough.

He stared off into the distance, probably imagining her perfect nose or her bright shiny teeth. "She made her choice, Dani. Life without me was better than life with me." The despair rolled off of him in waves, and he reached for the whiskey to take another drink. "I hurt her and I have to live with it."

I took his face in my palm. "Keats, you are broken without her, and if you don't figure out how to fix all of this, it'll kill you." Or maybe he would end up inadvertently killing himself, but in any case, he would be equally dead. He was really the only friend I had, and even though I hated Jocelyn, I hated what being without her had done to him more.

"You can't die from a broken heart, Dani." He poked his finger in the air in a Ben-Franklin-discovered-electricity motion as if the news were some big deal I should take note of. "I'd already be gone."

I gave him a shove, sending him face first into the sofa cushion, then helped him sit upright. "I hate to break it to you, golden boy, but you're pretty much already gone." I laid a hand on his chest and he covered it with his own. "I know it hurts. Trust me, I'm aware, but you haven't really lived in a while."

He opened his mouth and blew out a scoff. "I live."

No, he didn't. He drank until he couldn't stand, then passed out.

"I go to work every day." He swayed one direction, then the other before catching his balance and saving the bottle from tipping over.

I took it again and set it out of his reach.

"And I come home and drink because I miss her so much, but you drink too. Why do you get to throw stones when you're no better than I am?" He closed his eyes and blew out a potent breath. "I don't want to fight with you."

Being his second choice didn't bother me. If I couldn't have Simon, it didn't matter to me who I spent my time with, but I cared about his happiness and it had been quite a while since he'd smiled. I couldn't remember the last time I'd heard a real laugh out of him. Though the thought made me mentally wretch, *she* made him happy. Only her.

"Fight with me, Keaton. Do something that means you're still in there, and you aren't just some pathetic shell slogging through life on a bottle of whiskey."

"It's kind of mean to kick a guy while he's down."

In spite of myself, I smiled. A little part of the boy I'd known still lurked around in there. Little pieces of wit showed up every third or fourth moon phase, but it wasn't enough.

"Again, what about you? Are you saying you're not broken? Losing Simon didn't wreck you just a little?"

It wrecked me a lot, and it irritated me that, as drunk as Keaton stayed most of the time, he could tell. He couldn't have heard me crying. I only did it at night when his alcohol soaked dreams brought her back to him and he called out her name as he slept.

Maybe makeup didn't hide the sadness well enough. I shrugged and leaned my head against his shoulder. "I'm surviving. You're not."

"No, Dani. You're wrong. We're both surviving it, thanks to you. I'd be lost without you. You saved me." He kissed my hair and offered me a drink of his whiskey.

I choked back a new, more bitter round of guilt. I'd caused this whole mess. I was no better, maybe even worse, than all those people back home said. *Slut. Harlot.* Words I hadn't thought of since I got to Arizona rang through my head. I put my hands over my ears to block them out, but they were inside me now, a part of me. To top off the fuel in my self-loathing tank, I'd gone and gotten myself pregnant with no clue exactly who fathered the baby. I put the wreck in homewrecker.

The heat of shame rolled its way up my neck to my cheeks. He ran a hand under my hair, cupping my neck, and the human contact sent a different kind of warmth skittering along my skin. I turned to him, imagined the half-lidded eyes stemmed from desire, and pressed my lips against his, coaxing his mouth open with my tongue, deepening the kiss until his response overcame both of us and we fell backward on the couch.

He pulled away and threw his arm over his eyes while I rested my head on his chest. "Sorry, Dani. I don't know what came over me."

I wasn't Jocelyn and he wasn't Simon, but we were all either of us had. My thoughts overtook my mouth. "I'm pregnant."

"Huh?" He sat up, the abruptness of his motion pushing me onto the floor. In his defense, he'd probably been drinking most of the day.

I leaned against the couch, and my head fell against his knee. "I know. Shocking, right?"

"A baby?"

More guilt eked its way to the surface. I wanted to be the good version of myself--the one hidden behind my excuses and immaturity, the one who frowned when I blamed everyone else for the problems I created. She was the person my baby deserved, the person we all deserved. To be that person, I had to tell him the truth and pray he remembered it the next day. "I didn't mean to, Keaton." Maybe the truth would set us free in a way our life choices hadn't. "The baby isn't--"

"I'm gonna be a daddy." Nothing wide-eyed crossed over his face. No disbelief or shouted curse words condemning me for my sluttiness. Instead, he smiled, beautiful, real, for me.

I stayed still, mentally berating my whoredom and deception when he lowered his body next to mine and kissed me so softly I almost melted into the carpet. "I always wanted a baby."

"But Keats, you can't..." He had to know this baby belonged to someone else. We'd never done more in his bed than sleep. He had to know, right? *I always wanted a baby.*

The evil Danielle, who hid behind lies, protecting herself with a shield of apathy, would just go with it and let him believe the baby belonged to him. He thought we'd had sex. The girl I wanted to be would certainly stand up, push him away and tell the truth, no matter the consequences. In the absence of a well-needed eenie-meenie-miney-moe moment, I didn't make a conscious decision. I sat there and waited for a decision to be made.

"A baby, Dani. We're gonna have a baby."

The sheer awe in his voice, the wonder in his wide-eyed gaze... I went with it. "You really wanna do this?" And just like that, the guilt ebbed and I concentrated on the soul peeking through his normal droopy-eyed drunkenness. If he wasn't going to go home and restore his marriage, no harm could come from keeping quiet, right? A lot of relationships and two parent-households were based on less than what we had--friendship, kindness, mutual respect. I reasoned my deception away, locked the shame down and ignored the nagging voice in my head yelling at me to tell him the truth. I promised myself I would if he ever decided to go home and get her back.

He lifted me onto his lap and pressed his lips against mine. When he pulled away, his smile hovered inches from my mouth. "We're going to have a baby, Dani."

I pulled away and swallowed any trace of regret. Maybe I could be the better me in a different way. We'd fallen so far from where we'd once been as people. To be good at parenting, we had to work our way around to the basics...sober basics. "We have to get straightened out then, Keats. I don't wanna bring a baby home to us being all messed up all the time. It's not fair to the kid."

He spent the next thirty-three days in rehab, then came home sober and cleaned up. It was a good thing he'd gone away, too, because between the hormones, the lack of alcohol, and thoughts of Simon, I snapped at the refrigerator for running, the TV for playing the wrong shows, and my boss for saying, "Good morning."

Chapter 6

When Keaton returned, he came back the way I remembered him best--the old Keaton, the happy-go-lucky prankster who always smiled and did his best to make sure everyone else did too. He called Simon more often, trying to wheedle information out of his best friend about Jocelyn when he thought I couldn't hear, but I heard everything.

Even though he missed *her*, he did most of the right things to pretend he was happy with me. He kissed me--those chaste kind of kisses that worked equally well for an aging grandmother or a new born baby, the kind without emotion or feeling. Every so often, he held me, and more than once went so far as to talk to my stomach while he lay in my lap as I read. But *she* was always there, between us, to the point of making me resent her, him, and the fact the baby couldn't be his.

I only had to catch the smallest glimpse of him to see him regretting his decision to stay with me, but most of the time, Keaton saw me as a person with feelings and a heart. It had been a while since anyone I cared about looked at me with anything other than contempt. He still wouldn't sleep with me. Instead, he used an exorbitant amount of words to reinforce my worth. I deserved more than casual sex. He said it often enough I considered stitching it on a pillow.

Kieran made his way into the world on a ninety-nine degree day while Keaton was at work. After about a hundred calls to his voice mail, one to the ranch where he worked, and a few prayers to a God I had all but given up on, I finally got a hold of him as they wheeled me into delivery. He arrived in time to see Kieran take his first breaths, but just barely.

As soon as I looked at my boy, saw his whiskey-colored eyes, the perfect shape of his face, I knew who he belonged to, but more than that...I fell in love for real. I wanted redemption, to be saved from the person I'd been so my baby boy would be proud of me. More than simply wanting redemption, I needed it.

* * * *

A couple of months after Kieran turned a year old, we left Arizona and moved north--way north--to freezing cold Canada. Keaton took a job at a hunting lodge, and I began making and selling children's clothes on the Internet. Soon, I raked in cash by the handfuls and Keaton took on less hunts at work to give me time to sew and fill orders. During any number of conversations about my boy, I opened my mouth to tell him the truth. Every time, I chickened out. We had a good life together.

I told myself he chose not to go back to her, and I ignored the hurt inching its way into his every gaze. Pretending I didn't see him staring off into the distance at nothing wasn't easy, but I did it well. For three years, I didn't tell him the truth, rather I tried to convince him to go home. Even though it pained me to say the words, I couldn't watch the boy who'd been so full of life and fun disappear into the man who ached for someone who had left him because of me.

The afternoon before we left for home, he walked in without his usual fake smile. I sat folding Kieran's laundry on the couch and glanced up when he plopped down next to me and took my hand in his. With his thumb, he rubbed small circles in my palm while Kieran tossed toys out of the box we kept in the corner.

"The laundry isn't going to fold itself, Keats." I tried to pull away, but he held on.

His quiet moments were limited to his sleeping hours, but he didn't utter a word as he stared at our intertwined fingers. He'd finally decided. Though I'd talked until I had no words left to convince him to beg for her forgiveness, the reality of not being enough to hang on to him hurt. I'd given our relationship everything I had, and even though I'd pushed for it, all this time he hadn't gone home, and it gave me hope. Someday he would come around. *Nope.* I braced myself and waited. This was going to hurt.

He took a quick breath and blew it out. "Dani, I'm leaving. The resort has a job opening and Simon said they want me to run it again."

The part of me content to cling to a man for my baby's sake crumbled. He planned to walk away from Kieran? My heart ached for my baby's loss. It only took a glimpse of his face to know he'd made his decision, and it made him happy. His smile said it all.

Well, if I had to lose him as a friend, and I would have to lose him because Joss would never let him see me again, at least I would know he'd gotten what he needed. I nodded and continued folding the clothes as though my stomach hadn't started flipping and flopping like a fish in a net.

"You could go home, too, you know."

"There's nothing for me there." Canada didn't have a lot to offer, either, but at least I wasn't a slut internationally. Well, once I crossed the border, no one called me anything like it, anyway.

"Simon's there." He squeezed my hand.

"And he moved on." I pulled away. "Don't worry, Keaton. I know you need to go. It's okay." The words cracked as a vision of Simon invaded my thoughts. Going home would do more than cause a waver to my voice. It would shatter me in places that had only begun healing.

"What do you want to do about Kieran?"

My pulse dropped a notch. He had at least considered my boy.

I should have told him--just said the words--but I sat still, uncertain how to tell him he couldn't be the father to my child. "Keaton--"

"Please, Dani, come home with me. I know things are tough there, believe me, but don't you want to let Kieran meet your folks? And mine?" He followed me to the kitchen and stood behind me as I looked out the kitchen window. "If you show them the Dani you showed to me, all that mess before will be forgotten."

I spun around, the old me present and accounted for, begging for her moment in the light. "If *that* me is so damned great, why didn't I turn your head?" I didn't wait for an answer but shoved past him to stand in the middle of the floor. "I couldn't even make you forget *her* for a single minute. Seriously. How many nights in a row did you get drunk because *that* me didn't measure up? I. Wasn't. Enough." I stabbed my sternum with a pointed finger as I spoke. "I don't need to go home and watch Simon with Kelly and let him make me feel like crap too. Kieran and I can have a really good life here. I don't need anybody else to love me. Not you. Not Simon. Not anyone."

His voice did nothing to mask his confusion. "I thought you didn't want me to love you? You said just sex and friendship."

Yep. Even I thought my behavior fell into the slightly bi-polar category. Of course, our deal had included sex, and he hadn't given any of that up.

I couldn't stand there and pick a fight with him. He had to do this. I couldn't blame him for trying to be better, mend himself in ways I hadn't been able. "I didn't. I mean, I don't." I sighed. "I'm sorry. The thought of going back there makes me crazy." Just thinking of Simon with Kelly actually caused my stomach to ache.

"I know. But you aren't a runner. It's time to go home and face whatever"--he grinned--"or whoever you're running from." He leaned against the counter, his smug smile aimed at me. "Do you remember when we went out in high school?"

I rolled my eyes and nodded.

"I didn't break up with you because you'd done anything wrong. I let you go because I knew you two belonged together. You did then and you do now."

"Whatever. You broke up with me because you had a thing for Jocelyn. And I don't care what you say about me and Simon." I turned to face him, whatever I'd been pretending to see out the window as forgotten as my life before Simon. "I'm not going home, and even if I decided I wanted to be in Storybook Lake, it wouldn't be to try my luck with him again. We didn't work out, and that's the way it is. Unlike you, my friend, I don't live in the past or rely on it to make my future a happy one."

He shook his head and smiled his I'll-convince-you-one-way-or-another smile. "When Simon walked into a room, you were all over me like icing on cupcakes." He wrapped an arm around me, and I rolled my eyes at his bakery reference. *She* owned the bakery in town. "But when he wasn't around, we could have parked an airplane in the space between us. I see your face when I talk to him on the phone."

"It's lust. I haven't exactly been getting any since I got here."

He let that pass. "It doesn't have a thing to do with your lack of sex, and you know it. You are all Simon, all the time. Don't let him get away again."

"He has someone else." That was not the most fun thing I'd ever had to say. "He moved on. And so have I."

Keaton chuckled. Chuckled! "He might be dating someone else, but I guarantee if you go back, you'll end up with Simon." He put a hand on each of my cheeks to stop my headshaking. "Come on, Dani. You both deserve to be happy." His lips brushed the top of my scalp, and he rested his cheek against my hair. "Together."

"No." I didn't deserve to be happy. I'd lied my ass off for the last three years, and I stumbled through every single day with my deception staring me in the face. No. Happiness was more than I could ever hope for, more than karma or God would ever allow me.

The next day, we sat together on a flight to Storybook Lake.

Chapter 7

Coming home was a far different experience than I expected. I hadn't told them about Kieran, just strolled up the porch steps with him. Their surprise quickly morphed into a crazy kind of joy I'd never really seen out of either of them. Then the shopping began, and without much warning or expectation of repayment, Kieran and I had more stuff than would fit in my bedroom. Toys, books, clothes... If they sold it in town, or one nearby, Kieran and I received it as a gift.

My mom cleaned out her upstairs office to decorate a bedroom for Kieran. A dinosaur mural decorated one wall, and she'd ordered a bed designed to look like a rock cave. The carpet mimicked a stone path in the center of a grassy knoll. It took all of one minute for Kieran to fall in love with his new room and his new family.

For me, the fact they'd taken us in meant more than I could ever find a way to show. I tried to help out, to prove I'd reformed and changed my wicked ways, but my mean girl peeked out every once in a while. When she did, I hopped in the car for whatever reason I could formulate to make an escape. That was how I ran into Simon. Literally.

I didn't bump into him at the grocery store, the strip mall, or at the library where I'd spent a good many hours hiding from my parents' enthusiasm. No. Running into my ex-boyfriend took on a whole new meaning, or more precisely, the *Webster's Dictionary* meaning, and I did it with a fully licensed motor vehicle, plowing my mom's front end into the rear of Simon's patrol car as he waited for a stop light to turn green.

I couldn't claim distraction, since I hadn't taken my eyes off the light bar on top of his fully decaled police cruiser from the minute it turned out in front of me. I'd continued to stare at the roof rather than his taillights, then smacked into the trunk as he'd stopped and Mom's car kept rolling. He stepped out onto the pavement in a slow motion-unfolding of his long limbs. I blinked and swallowed hard as he strolled to where I white-knuckle gripped the steering wheel.

"Mrs. Ranier?" I wanted to crawl into the trunk before he had a chance to reach the window. When he got closer, a smile lit up his face. "Dani?"

Jeepers. His uniform inspired a quick bout of hot bonus fantasy--black cargo pants emphasizing every toned muscle, front and back, a T-shirt with the word POLICE between his shoulder blades and boots that could have belonged to a Hell's Angel. He had a gun on one side of his belt and a badge on the other. If I ever had to be arrested, I wanted this guy to pat me down.

"Hi, Simon." Heat flooded my pores. I tried to open the door and get out, but the hood and front fenders of the car crinkled accordion style, against the door.

"Are you okay?" He leaned closer, taking in the windshield, webbed where my head hit on impact.

"Yeah, but I think I'm stuck." I pulled the handle twice more to prove my problem.

With most of his top half bent inside the window, he held on to my shoulder for a second until I wriggled from beneath his electric touch. "Can you climb out?" His radio crackled as he called for a tow truck and an ambulance.

"I think so." Holding my dress with one hand and grasping the passenger headrest with the other, I twisted my body and shimmied over the window ledge. His bulging eyes said my attempt at modesty had been much more attempt than success. I tugged at the skirt.

He licked his lips, then brought his gaze to my face. "Oh, shit, Dani. You're bleeding." He dashed to his car, then jogged back to me. My eyelids fluttered shut as I inhaled the citrus-y scent of his cologne. I opened my eyes to find his face inches from mine while he investigated the gash on my head. "You're probably gonna need a couple stitches." With a gentle touch, he pressed a patch of fabric over the cut. "Does it hurt?"

"No." The tingling in the lower half of my body overpowered any northerly pain.

I didn't care that we were standing in the middle of the street or that he belonged to someone else. His soul-melting gaze held mine, and one hand cradled the nape of my neck as he used the other to stop the blood trickling in a thin stream from my hairline.

Another police cruiser pulled up, and Simon dropped his hands and stepped away. He sprung into action, giving orders to divert traffic to make way for the ambulance he'd called. All-business Simon stirred my pulse with his in-my-face hotness. After about an hour, the cars had been towed off, a deputy retrieved and delivered Simon's personal Jeep, and I sent the ambulance on its way. I could live with a scar if it meant leaving this whole humiliating experience behind me.

We stood on the sidewalk facing each other, grinning like a couple of goofy teenagers waiting for our first big kiss. He reached out a hand to once again touch my face, and I closed my eyes, savoring the whisper of his hands on my skin. "Are you sure you're okay?"

I nodded, still under the power of his special brand of magic. Any words I might have spoken stuck in my throat. Breaking the spell, he cleared his throat and pulled away.

I swallowed hard and stepped back from his car. "Well, thanks for not writing me a ticket." I shuffled from one foot to the other, waiting for something. "I sh-I should go." I turned and hurried away, past the jewelry store and the wedding shop. As I neared the beauty parlor his mother once owned, I slowed. Through the window reflection, I watched Simon's gaze follow me.

Probably thinking I'd turned into some sort of beauty parlor stalker, Gatlin waved from inside. The sight of someone friendly brought a small smile to my lips. Aside from Keaton, he'd been the one member of their little group I'd always gotten along with.

"Hey, Dani, wait a second."

I couldn't have walked another step if I tried. My legs went weak at the curiosity and the slight trace of urgency in his voice as he *Dukes of Hazard* slid over the hood of his car toward me.

"Wanna get together? Have some lunch? Maybe catch up?"

"Don't you have a girlfriend?" My heart pounded at the idea of *catching up* with Simon, but I'd turned over a new leaf, and boyfriend stealing had a big red line through the list of acceptable behaviors I kept on the keep-Kieran-proud Post-it in my mind.

"I asked if you wanted to catch up." A smile tipped the corner of his lips heavenward. "Not have an orgy."

Orgy? Hardly. If I ever got my hands on him again...one on one...for hours. Instead of voicing my thoughts, I cleared my throat and shrugged at him. "Well, you gotta clarify. Catching up with you could mean a lot of things, and it puts pictures in a girl's mind."

He chuckled as I tapped my forehead with my finger.

"Pretty pictures." I over-exaggerated my sigh. Okay. So, my reformation had a ways to go.

He ducked his head and color brightened his cheeks while I chewed my lip for a split second.

"Catching up sounds good."

With the gentle pressure of his hand at the middle of my lower back, he guided me to the passenger side of his SUV. After his chauffeur's flourish and bow, I climbed in and breathed deep. The car smelled like him, had little touches of Simon all over it--including a picture of Jocelyn with Keaton attached to his dashboard.

Almost before I knew it, we arrived at Hood's Hideaway, a new restaurant on the outskirts of Storybook that my mother raved about for an hour the previous evening. The glorified tree house bordered on the resort property where Keaton worked. It had a thatched roof over top of steel beams. Fake vines and plants "grew" inside. A trunk reached up through the middle of the floor, dividing the room into fours.

After our waitress served frothy coffee concoctions with whipped cream and sprinkles in primitive designed grog cups, she strolled away, leaving us alone, shielded by artfully placed foliage. I took a sip of the hot brew and swallowed quickly. My chest burned as the scalding liquid made its way down to my stomach. I sucked in a breath and blew it out. "Wooh. Wow." I cleared my blistered throat. "So, what happened with you and Hollywood?" I wasn't after the down and dirty details, but a bit of clarification would lighten the weight on my chest when I thought of them.

He smiled a little, and an old familiar longing bounced around in my chest. "She decided to stay in California and I decided to stay here."

What kind of girl chose a crappy magazine job over Simon? *The fool.* Blind fool. While Keaton might have been beautiful, Simon was more. More handsome, more sociable, more affectionate, more...everything I wanted in one finely muscled package.

He took a big drink of coffee, pulled his lower lip between his teeth, and smiled. "That's hot."

I nodded. "I could have told you to drink slow." I dialed the conversation back to his relationship status--the only information I cared about, anyway. "And now you're consoling yourself with a sweet from the bakery?" I gave myself a mental thumbs-up for the confidence with which I'd said it, for the wit, without a single hint of jealousy or malice for the friend of Jocelyn's he'd started dating.

"Such a way with words." He grinned. "And I'm not consoling myself with Lizette. I really like her." He narrowed his eyes and glared at me for a moment before his face relaxed.

I held up my hands in surrender. "Okay. You made a love connection. I'm happy for you." But my stomach turned at the thought of Simon--*my* Simon--with any other woman.

"And what about you? Anybody lighting your fire these days?"

I shook my head and ran my thumb around the rim of my cup. Keaton and I never discussed how or the amount of details we would give Simon about our time together. They'd been best friends for years. I didn't want to be the one to destroy such a lasting bond.

"So, you and Keats are finished?"

"What? I, um, I, what?" I knocked my coffee over in surprise, then quickly snatched my white linen napkin off the table and began sopping up the cooling brown liquid.

"*Simon says* you can't keep secrets from a guy like me, Dani." He chuckled and took another drink. Smaller this time. "I'm his go-to guy for everything. Plus, Joss is my sister and I don't want to see her get hurt, so I asked him."

"Oh." My hands stilled as the waitress wiped our table clean, then left to get me another drink. She'd probably put it in a sippy cup. "I should have figured Keaton already told you." These weren't guys who kept things from each other. "But yeah, we're over. To be honest, we never really began. He loves her too much to be with anybody else."

"Is your little boy his?"

I'd been keeping this secret for so long I almost spilled it right there behind the fake vines hiding us from the other customers. Since he had a vested interest in knowing what I knew, I should have told, but I didn't. I couldn't tell him now. He was happy with someone else, and Kieran and I had almost ruined one relationship already. "I don't want to talk about Kieran's daddy."

"Why?"

"Because you have your life and I have mine, and we don't share our secrets anymore." I looked down at the table. "So, sheriff, huh?"

He chuckled. All serious points of conversation came to a screeching halt. Instead, we chatted about Arizona's dry air, his mom's rekindling of her marriage to Alex Rogers, his move into Gatlin's apartment, my dad's new horses--everything except the one thing I wanted to discuss--us. Three hours and a couple pots of coffee later, he drove me back to my mom's and pulled up in front of the house. "This reminds me of the old days."

Me too. How many nights had we sat out in front of the house, steaming up the windows to his car? Just the thought of air-fogging activities with Simon had my blood pressure climbing. "Yeah."

My body without any encouragement from my brain, maybe responding to the nostalgia, or maybe responding to Simon, leaned closer and our lips touched. Every pent-up feeling and emotion I'd ever suppressed washed over me. I wrapped my arms around his neck, losing myself in him.

The kiss lasted forever and ended too quickly as he jerked away from me. "Dani, I can't do this."

An ache throbbed in my chest.

"I have a girlfriend."

I nodded. "I know." My eyelids fluttered shut, and I dug my fingernails into my palms.

"It's not fair to her. No matter how much I want to sit out here and kiss you, I can't do that to her."

Okay, already. No need to beat me over the head with it. "I have to go in." I hopped out of his Jeep and counted the thirty-nine steps up the walk to keep from running, my pride insisting I not look back as he drove away.

Three days later, Simon walked into a bank in the middle of a robbery.

Chapter 8

I knew the chances of being allowed in with Simon at the hospital hovered in the low-to-not-happening range, but I had to go. Knowing I might never see him again, drew me to the parking lot. It took ten minutes to talk myself into getting out of the car. Somewhere in the hospital, Simon lay broken, probably dying. My head pounded from the hours I'd spent crying. My heart ached at the thought the world--*I*--might never see his smile again.

I rode to the fourth floor with no idea how I would be able to manage the walk into his room. As the doors whooshed open, I inhaled the smell of antiseptic and death. A sob tore from my throat, and the doors started to close while I breathed in and out through my nose, trying to get my shit together. The last thing I wanted was to fall apart here, in front of his family, the waiting room full of his friends, and most especially, his sister. I walked in, and Keaton stood to meet me.

"How is he?"

He rubbed a hand down my back. "He's tough. He won't leave us, Dani."

Simon's mother put her hands in mine and tugged me in for a hug. "Thank you for coming." She barely resembled the always put-together, perfectly made-up carpool mom I'd seen so often growing up. Her hair, instead of hanging straight and smooth, fuzzed with curls, and her eyes were puffy and red.

I couldn't do more than nod around the lump in my throat. "Can I see him?"

She cupped my cheek with her palm. "Of course. Joss is in with him now, but when she gets back, you can go in."

Keaton led me to a seat next to him. Simon's mother sat beside me on the other side. She huddled with her husband while I leaned in to talk to Keaton. "What have they said, Keats? Is he going to wake up?"

He swallowed hard. The sound broke a little part of me. His eyes were shot with red from crying, and his hands shook as he reached out to comfort me.

After a minute, I pulled out of his embrace. For Keaton to look so devastated, Simon was worse than I thought. They'd been almost inseparable for the biggest part of their lives.

"They said he's hurt pretty bad, and every day he doesn't wake up is..." He looked down at his shoes, then lifted his head and dropped a hand on my shoulder. "He's tough, Dani."

Hearing it a second time--as though he needed to convince himself--didn't calm the trembling in my hands.

"And he has a lot of reasons to wake up."

"You doing okay?" A sob broke from one of us; I couldn't be sure who, but tears streamed down his cheeks.

"He's my best friend." His voice cracked. "I would trade places with him in a minute."

"He knows that. You guys are..." I couldn't bear the thought of what we would all lose if Simon didn't make it. "Just tell me he's going to be okay."

"He's gonna be great."

We sat quietly, wrapped in hope and grief until Jocelyn strolled around the corner from her visit with her brother. She stood in front of Keaton and her sadness drew him to his feet, guided his arms around her, his instincts taking over where his words could not.

After a few moments, she moved away and looked at me. "What are you doing here?" Her voice held none of its usual venom or malice.

"Can I see him?"

The whir of the overhead fan provided the only sound in the room. All breathing and speaking stopped. "Why?"

I blew out a breath and counted ten tiles in the floor before I could answer. "Because I love him too."

She opened her mouth. "Tha--"

Before she could refute the statement with her warped Jocelyn logic, I shook my head and lifted my chin to meet her gaze. I wouldn't hide how I felt about him to make her feel better. "And he loves me and you know it." She snapped her lips shut, and I softened my voice, calling on the more-flies-with-honey theory. "Come on, Joss. Please. Let me see him. Then, I'll go."

The tight lines in her face relaxed. Her fists unclenched, and she drooped in Keaton's arms. "He's only allowed visitors every two hours. It'll be a while before anyone can go back in."

Relief flooded every nerve receptor I had. I stepped around her so she could sit by Keaton. "I'll wait downstairs in the coffee shop."

She reached out and grabbed my arm as I started for the elevator. "You can wait with us." Keaton smiled at me, then leaned down and kissed the top of her head.

The clock ticked so slowly I checked and rechecked to make sure it still moved at all. No one spoke, and the silence in the room echoed louder than if we had all started screaming. I waited, praying for news, for a sign, for something to happen to bring Simon back to me.

When Joss stood, she looked over at me and nodded. Each step down the hall broke something inside me, and I swallowed a sob as she pulled the sliding glass door open. "You can't stay long."

She left the door open, probably eavesdropped outside, but I didn't care. I pulled back a curtain and held in a gasp, covering my mouth so the sound couldn't escape. After a moment, I leaned over and pressed a kiss to the only spot on his face still visible under the gauze and bruises. "Simon." I picked up his hand, brought it to my face, and closed my eyes, soaking in the warmth of it. "I miss you so much." An ache started in my chest and spread down the entire rest of my body. I'd blown all my chances with him, and I shook with the recognition I might not get another. "Please, don't die. I know things between us aren't right, but the other day, in front of my house, all I wanted was the way it used to be. Please, fight for me. I need one more chance. There's some stuff I have to tell you. It's about more than you and me now. You have to wake up."

I wanted to crawl into the bed with him and wrap myself around his body, absorb whatever kept him asleep. Instead, I leaned over to lay my head next to his. "I know you're in there, Simon. Just come back. If not for me, do it for Keaton and Joss…and your mom. You have so many reasons to wake up. If you only knew…" I couldn't tell him. The words wouldn't form. I sat quietly, listening to the sounds of his breathing. The monitors and pumps plugging him full of medicine whirred and beeped. I focused on those noises to block the sound of my heart breaking into pieces.

"Oh, for the love of God, Simon. Does every single thing have to be so hard between us? Just once, can't we do things the easy way? Open your eyes and let me know you'll be okay." When he didn't move and the beeps remained steady, I huffed out a sigh. "You are so stubborn. It's one of those things that drives me crazy about you and makes me love you so much more at the same time."

I brought his hand to my lips, then my cheek, and held it for a second against my heart. "I love you. Don't die." I turned to walk out.

A few days later, Simon woke up and I breathed my first sigh of relief in a while. Later, as I lie in bed thanking God for the miracle he'd given me, the pounding on the kitchen door started. I checked the window. Keaton.

"What are you doing here?"

"I blew it with Joss." His eyes were rimmed in red and his hair stood on its ends as though he'd shoved his hands through it a few hundred times.

"What happened?" I led him to the table and curled my body into itself as I sat next to him.

"She asked me if Kieran is mine and…" He dropped his head to rest on his forearms.

"He's not, Keats." Oh, Lord. What had I done?

He jerked his gaze up. "What?"

"He's not yours." There. I'd said it and I'd said it with enough conviction his head sat straighter on his shoulders. "I'm not proud of it, okay, but I had a couple one nighters before I left and a fling right after I got to Arizona." His frown deepened and the explanation tumbled out. "We had a fight, and you kept saying her name. I had to get out of there so I didn't have to listen to you anymore. I went out and got drunk and met a guy. Jesus, Keaton, I'm so sorry." I'd decided earlier in the day to tell him, and since he'd shown up already upset, I unloaded most of the whole story.

"You lied to me?" Keaton blinked rapidly as if trying to digest the information.

I didn't flinch at his anger. How could I? I'd kept a secret that cost him her, again.

"I didn't lie, Keats. I just didn't correct you, but we never had sex, not since that one time in high school, anyway." And we never spoke of that since neither of us really enjoyed much about it. "I mean, I wished we did. I wanted to, but you were so in love with Joss that even if you could have, I don't know if I could."

He rolled his eyes and plopped down in the chair across from me.

"Okay. I probably could, but it would have been wrong, and we would have both regretted it. I don't need any more of those on my permanent record." I sighed and continued before he could say any of the words I knew would be coming. "To be honest, I didn't think we would ever come back here. I thought you would be a great dad, and we could build the life you wanted, and it would all be okay. I couldn't be her or take her place in your heart, but for a while, after Kieran was born, I didn't think it mattered so much. I thought you would get over her, and I would forget about him, and we would have a nice life. I pictured white picket fences, carpools…you being the soccer dad."

He stood up, raking his fingers through his hair. "All this time, you let me think Kieran is mine when you knew damned well he couldn't be?" He shook his head and glared at me. "I told my family about him. My mom spent this week out buying kid toys…."

I didn't know what to say to make it right. Guilt inched its way along my nerve endings, heating my skin with shame. "I'm sorry, Keats. I wanted to tell you a thousand times, but I couldn't."

"Jocelyn hates me because of all this." He turned his back to me, clenching and unclenching his fists.

At the mention of her name, my vision clouded, putting a red tint on everything in my sight line. Instead of getting loud, I leaned back and crossed my arms, adding a hint of sarcasm to my tone. "Oh, that's right. The freaking world revolves around Jocelyn, doesn't it? And what Jocelyn feels, and how my having a baby with or without you affects *Jocelyn*. I can't believe I forgot such a well-known fact."

"You know what I mean. I lost her again because she thinks we made a kid." The hurt behind his words spoke louder than anything he said.

"I'm so sorry."

He glanced up, doubt turning his eyes dark.

"Really I am. I'll talk to her. I'll tell her what happened, or didn't happen."

He turned slowly, a ghost of a smile tilting his lips. "Take my advice. Stay away from Joss for a while."

I sighed. "All right. I could write her a letter. Send her a text or an e-mail if you want."

"I better handle this one." His shoulders slumped, and he leaned against the counter.

"What are you going to do?"

"Give her some time to cool off, I guess. I don't know." He yanked out the chair again and dropped his head onto his hand. "She's all I want, Dani. I can't live without her."

Oh, how well I knew. "Then don't, Keats. Fight for her."

"She doesn't take to that very well."

"Don't be a quitter now. I didn't come all the way home to watch you give up on the one thing you need, no matter how ridiculous I think she is."

"You have a way with words, Dani." He blew out a long breath and jammed his fingers through his hair. "God, I could really use a drink right now."

"Yeah. Getting drunk'll solve it." I went to the sink for a glass of water. "Here. Try this." The glass shook as I set it on the table. How many mistakes would I make before I finally got life right?

"Why didn't you tell me? I would've stayed, anyway. You didn't have to pretend with me."

I sighed. "I was ashamed. I wanted to be better than the person Jocelyn tells everyone I am, but instead, I keep proving her right." I hung my head, guilt and shame billowing through me. "I know I shouldn't have let you believe he's yours."

He shrugged, waiting for me to continue.

"The only way I can think to fix this is to get a DNA test."

"It won't prove I didn't sleep with you." He smiled softly. "For the record, I would be proud to have Kieran for a son."

I smiled softly. "You are going to be a great dad. Someday."

"I keep hurting her."

"Then stop."

His eyes widened.

"Okay, this one is on me, but I can't fix it with her. You have to do it."

"I know."

"And it has to be something big. Something extraordinary. Skywrite her name or take out a full page ad in the paper to say you're sorry or whisk her away to somewhere you can be alone to work it out." Simon had done all these things at one point or another. He might have acted tough and too cool for romance, but he'd been...perfect.

"She doesn't respond to the grand romantic gesture."

Boy did he have a lot to learn. "You're so dumb. Do you know where I got those ideas from?" I didn't wait for him to look up. "Your best friend did all of those things for me, and do you know who she loves more than anyone in the world...except herself?"

He frowned. "It sure as hell isn't me."

"Not today, but you can't give up. I did *not* come back here to watch you lose her for the second time." *To be turned down by Simon, yet again.*

He closed his eyes, leaned back in the chair. "She won't talk to me."

"She will. Just give her some time." I covered his hand with mine. "Keaton, she would be a fool to let you go again. Trust me."

Chapter 9

Amid Jocelyn's hatred and a new bout of my mother's intense scolding, I made the choice to get the hell out of Storybook Lake again. Leaving Simon hurt the worst, but I had no choice. I couldn't keep destroying the relationship Keaton desperately needed to be whole. By mere presence alone, I came between him and Joss without ever saying a word. Of course, I said several words, but even without my in-her-face sass, simply being there hurt her and, in typical Jocelyn fashion, she turned it around on him.

My leaving wasn't altogether altruistic. I couldn't bear for Kieran to ask every day where Daddy went. How could I explain my mistakes to a kid like Kieran? Absent a good answer, I stole a page from Mom and Dad's book and decided on a vacation that I intended as a more permanent move than a short-term holiday. I wanted to make up for the things I couldn't give him--a happy family life--with things I could. So, I loaded him into the car, hyped it as an adventure, then threw myself into his enthusiasm.

Traveling slowly across five states, we visited the Botanical Gardens in St. Louis, the Titanic museum in Branson and an Elvis Tribute Contest, the Spencer Museum of Art, the Topeka Air and Combat Museum, and the Garden of the Gods in Colorado. Even with a vocabulary rivaling some adults, he lost interest quickly. We traveled with only the GPS as our guide. When I wasn't concentrating on driving or when the long stretches of road went on forever, I was willing Simon to call. I spent a lot of time disappointed.

Traveling with an over-intelligent toddler and a broken heart tested my resolve, but we made it work. However, when we arrived at the Grand Canyon, Kieran took fate by the short hairs.

It started with a simple question inspired by a book Keaton purchased when we were out buying baby things before Kieran was born. We'd read it to him cover to cover every night after.

"Do you know about dinosaurs?" If he never asked me another question, I would always have remembered this as the one that started it all.

"Of course!" I played along with the hundred and twelve dinosaur questions he asked in a day. Any time he could find a way to sneak one in, he did. He asked me if I knew about fossils and the Jurassic and Cretaceous periods. If I answered wrong, he shared with me all he knew. I'd read him those books since birth. He knew a lot. I answered wrong on purpose.

"Did you know Brachiosaurus eats leaves off trees and he weighs as much as six hundred cows?"

"Wow. I bet he could eat a little boy like you in one bite." I couldn't help but smile at how smart my boy had become.

"Mom." A serious frown darkened his features. "I'm not a leaf on a tree. I'm a Kieran."

"Well, there's a museum about four hours from here where we can go see some dinosaur bones." Mesa had a museum exhibit he would love.

"How long is four hours?"

I smiled. "Two hundred and forty minutes."

"How long is a minute?"

This line of questioning I could roll with. "Sixty seconds."

"How long is a second?"

"Faster than you can say 'I have the best mommy in the whole entire wide world.'"

He giggled as I reached down to tickle his ribs. He looked up at me with the sunset reflected in his light brown eyes. "Do they have a Quetzalcoatlus?"

I tilted my head trying to picture which of the dinosaurs I should be imagining. Wings? No Wings? It didn't matter if I knew. He only cared if the museum had one. "Probably." I gave his hand a little squeeze. "But let's enjoy this while we're here. Look how big that hole in the Earth is."

"Do they have a T-Rex?"

His lack of attention to the natural wonder before us was my own fault. I'd mentioned the D word and he grabbed on with both mental fists and wouldn't let go. I sighed. "Maybe."

"And a Stygimoloch?" Thankfully, the books we had bought had been written with phonetic pronunciations and as I read them to him, we both learned to pronounce the names. His first word had been "dino."

I nodded and he smiled.

"I love fossils." And when he got stuck on an idea, nothing I did would shake him back to where I wanted or needed him to be.

As far as I knew, he'd never seen one, but his enthusiasm brought a smile to my lips.

"Did I hear someone say Stygimoloch?" A deep male voice, from off to our left had me gathering Kieran close to me. The words *stranger danger* flashed through my mind in bright red neon. Kieran looked up at me, and I turned to the owner of said voice.

Ignoring the don't-talk-to-strangers rule (probably because a dinosaur hadn't said it), he wiggled free from my grasp and stepped forward. "Me, Kieran."

A very tall man stepped closer from out of the sun's blinding glare. I blinked twice. *No. No way.* My skin grew warm. Of all the people in the world to be here, why him? Why now?

I said, "Sean?" at the same time he said, "Danielle?"

"How have you been?" He pulled me in for a hug. My arms stayed at my sides.

Kieran stepped between us, and I stumbled out of the embrace. "That's my mommy." He folded his arms over his chest. "You're a stranger. Don't touch her."

"Your mommy?" Immediately, Sean's face darkened. "And how old would you be?"

"Three." Sean held up his hand, counted on his fingers mumbling random words. "Arizona," then "limousine" then "shit."

Kieran looked up at me with all the confusion a kid his age could possibly display--wide eyes, open mouth, crinkled forehead. "What's he doing, Mommy?"

"Math."

A range of emotions danced across Sean's face before the equation morphed into an answer and his eyes popped wide open. He glared at the ground for the longest part of a minute, then turned his gaze back to my face and grabbed my arm. Before I could dig in my heels, he pulled me ten steps out of Kieran's earshot.

"Mommy!" He screamed a monster-under-the-bed kind of wail. He might have sounded all grown up, but seeing his mother manhandled brought out the baby in him. I shook free from Sean's grasp, rushed back, and knelt in front of my son.

"It's okay, buddy. He's just an old friend of Mommy's, and he wanted to talk to me for a second." I hugged him close.

He swiped the back of his arm across his face, pushed me away, and walked over to stand in front of Sean, hands on his hips waiting for an explanation.

Sean cocked an eyebrow at me.

"Mommy says it isn't nice to grab people."

Sean's incredible height made Kieran seem even smaller. "Your mommy kept a secret from me. Does that make it okay?"

"No."

"Should I say I'm sorry, then?"

Kieran nodded.

Sean grinned the most handsome grin I'd had aimed at me in a long while. "I'm very sorry."

Kieran hugged my leg.

Sean glared and lowered his voice to an almost whisper. "We need to talk."

I took a minute to contemplate the wisdom in that. I'd already leaped up to my eyeballs in this drama. What did I have to lose by going all in? "I rented a cabin for tonight. We can talk there while he takes a nap."

After ironing out a time to meet, I took Kieran to the car. My heart beat a thousand angry thumps a minute and my mouth dehydrated. I would just tell him the truth and let him be on his way. No harm done. Why I hadn't corrected him from the first moment he started calculating time in his mind, I couldn't imagine, but I promised myself to take care of it first thing when he arrived. I'd learned my lesson about keeping secrets, about letting men think they fathered Kieran. I put Kieran down for his nap and went out to pace the front porch while I waited for Sean to arrive. Leaning back against a post, I closed my eyes.

The night we met, he'd hired a limousine. Now, he pulled up in a shiny black Porsche that purred through gleaming silver pipes as it idled before he shut it down. He climbed out of the car, larger and more handsome than I remembered. His hair glinted golden brown with little shots of blonde, which meant he either worshiped the sun, or paid pretty good money for natural-looking highlights. His eyes stormed gray with little sparks of blue--a combination that reminded me of cool summer nights at the lake...with Simon... Simon who hadn't called...hadn't had anyone call on his behalf. I cleared my head and aimed a smile at the man approaching.

He took a seat next to me on the front steps. "I don't want my son to grow up in a single parent household."

I opened my mouth to spill the truth. "Sean, he's--"

"I think we should get married. Tonight."

"M-mar-married?" My mouth dropped open and any thought not revolving around white dresses and flower bouquets flew from my mind.

He grinned. "You know. Two people joining their lives together until death do they part."

"I'm familiar with the concept." I hadn't meant to snap the words.

"What if he isn't yours?"

"Are you in the habit of screwing random strangers?"

"Are you?" I didn't usually taunt people, but marriage? Really? Our relationship consisted of two five minute conversations, three tequila shooters, and a quickie in a car. Marriage seemed a little over-the-top.

"Is he mine?" He glanced over, leaned forward, and clasped his hands in front of him.

I kicked at a rock trying to formulate an answer to explain my behavior away.

His voice lowered to a desperate whisper. "You know what? It doesn't matter. I think destiny gives us certain chances in life, and you being here, in this place, on the two weekends I have ever been in Arizona in my life is destiny trying to tell me something. I would be a fool to let a family slip away from me when it's all I have ever wanted." He shook his head and took my hands in his, turning his body to face me. "I have a nice life, but without a family, none of it means anything. I'm lonely and fate is giving me this chance with you, with him." He jerked his thumb toward the door of the cabin. "I don't want to waste an opportunity I might never get again."

I should have asked him why he thought he would never get another chance at a family, or about his career, or even what kind of nut-job asks a girl he screwed in the back of a car and never saw again to marry him. But I didn't ask and he didn't tell. The next day, off to Vegas we went. Within a few hours of our arrival, we became Mr. and Mrs. Sean Turner.

Chapter 10

I thought of Simon every day and no matter how wonderful my life appeared, a part of me was back in Storybook Lake--the part that truly lived and loved. My mother kept me informed of his condition and the remarkable speed with which he continued to recover. For me, that had to be enough.

Sean and I settled in California, where he owned a night club and a house situated high on a cliff with only one way in and one way out. The first few days were fine, then Kieran had a tantrum when I made him go to bed. My entire world erupted. Suddenly, my new home was a riot of screaming and yelling. First Kieran, then Sean in response threatening to spank Kieran if I couldn't shut him the hell up. While Kieran's will outlasted mine, but mine outlasted my new husband's. Sean stormed to the garage, and with a roar of his engine and the squeal of his tires, left.

Sometime in the wee hours of the morning, he stumbled in the front door, tripped over a dinosaur toy, and hit his head on a marble table in the living room. I hadn't bought the table, dropped the toy, or forced him to drink so much he could lose his balance over whatever obstructed his path. He yanked me from the bed by my arm and dragged me through the house to show me the table, as though I'd pushed him. Three drops of blood landed on the floor, and he stood over me (more swayed over me), as I scrubbed the carpet before he let me go back to bed.

When Kieran woke two hours later, I got up and coffee'd my way through the day. That night, Sean went out, and I smiled at the relaxing peace. Earlier than ever before, I took Kieran to bed with me. All was forgotten.

Sean and I got along fine for a while. He even planned a trip home to Storybook Lake so he could meet my family. I booked flights for the Thanksgiving weekend, still under the assumption that he was the prince in my fairytale.

The day before our trip, Sean came home and decided we needed a bigger house, since I was "rolling" in money from my "little clothes business." I hadn't commented with the appropriate enthusiasm. Instead, I told him I liked our house. I must have liked it, anyway, as I'd paid off the mortgage only a couple weeks earlier. In his mind, though, stating a contrary opinion meant I questioned his judgment. I'd stepped outside the wifely box he believed I belonged in and humiliated him. As retribution for my 'bad' behavior, he slammed my head into the counter. Within minutes, a bruise and bump added a bit of new character to my face.

I couldn't go home looking like I'd been in a bar brawl. He left me no choice but to cancel our flights and make the appropriate apologies. Later, when he left for the club, I didn't waste any time packing bags for me and Kieran. We were leaving. I would go home to my parents and beg them to help me with Kieran if I had to. So long as my baby was safe, I could live through seeing Simon with someone else.

Kieran fell asleep during my packing, and I didn't have the heart to wake him. The morning would be soon enough.

The next morning, Thanksgiving Day, I woke to the sounds of dishes clattering against one another and the smell of a freshly baked turkey in the oven. I climbed from the spare bed in Kieran's room, wiped my eyes, and walked out to the kitchen. A woman in her early senior years stood at the counter peeling potatoes.

"Hi. I'm Danielle." I gave a quick glance of all the area I could see, hoping to catch a glimpse of my soon-to-be ex-husband, then turned again to face her. "Where's Sean?"

She dried her hands and extended one to me. "I'm so happy to meet you. He's told me so much about you."

"I'm afraid I'm at a disadvantage." He'd mentioned no one to me.

She grinned and winked as though we shared some great secret. "That boy. What am I going to do with him?" It seemed rhetorical so I stayed quiet. "I'm Sean's mother. He called me yesterday and asked me to join you for dinner today. He said you weren't much of a cook, so I jumped right in." She patted my hand. "After the holidays, I'll come by and teach you. Can't have my boy eating TV dinners. He works hard and deserves some home-cooked meals."

But I could cook. I didn't have my own show on the food network, but I could throw together a suitable dinner--Thanksgiving or otherwise--if the urge so struck.

She leaned close enough I could smell roses and baby powder. "Now, where's my grandbaby?"

She didn't mention the bruising and swelling on my face, but walked around me down the hall, presumably to wake up my boy or hers. Making a left, she went for mine, then stormed into the room like a paratrooper on patrol. I caught up just in time to see her yank back his blanket. She snatched him out of bed to hold his limp body at arm's length.

"Oh dear." She wrinkled her nose. "He wet the bed." She gave him a shake. "That's naughty."

"Hey!" I took him from her and held him close. "What are you doing?"

"Oh, you have to punish him. You cannot let a little boy as old as he is get by with this kind of behavior. Once a pisser, always a pisser."

Seriously. I had to get the hell out of there. It wasn't just Sean. Their family tree must have been struck by lightning.

She stood with her hands on her hips, apparently waiting for me to dole out a punishment. The previous day, he'd seen his father smack his mother around. For a kid who'd never known anything more than unconditional love and inside voices, he'd handled it well. If a little bedwetting was the worst I had to deal with, then I would deal.

"I'm going to give him a bath."

"He doesn't need a bath. He needs a whipping." She sniffed as I glared at her. "If you aren't willing to take my advice, I just don't know how I will ever be able to feel as though you accept me. I'd hoped we would be close." She turned on heel and walked out.

She could hope all she wanted.

* * * *

After Sean and his mother washed and put away the dishes, I waited for Sean to leave, but he never did. He sat beside me on the sofa. If I scooted away, he inched closer. When I went to look for my cell, it had magically disappeared from its spot on the dresser in Kieran's room.

His mother drank a bottle of wine and fell asleep in the recliner. I took Kieran to bed. While I read his dinosaur book to him, she came in to kiss him good night. He flinched and she pinched him.

Acting from sheer instinct, I shoved her away from him, putting my body between her and my son. "He doesn't know you. Don't you ever touch him again."

Without another word, she stomped out to the living room. A second later, Sean appeared in the doorway, arms crossed, eyes flashing with anger. "What the hell did you say to my mom?"

"Can we talk about this later, Sean?"

Kieran still fussed over the welt left by her nimble fingers.

When I walked out of Kieran's room an hour later, Sean's pacing had worn a trail into the carpet. His mother stormed out earlier when he couldn't make me apologize right away. She vowed never to return. At first, he stayed calm, the proverbial before-the-hurricane-kind-of-calm.

I jumped on the offensive, yelling at him over his mother, forbidding her from seeing *my* child. He jerked his head toward me. Rage reddened his face. His fists clenched, and before I could duck or react with more than a blink, he attacked.

By morning, the right side of my face matched the left, and I had a plan to leave. I grabbed my packed bag and snuck through the house to the garage. For a full minute, I stood gawking at the empty space where I parked my car. I dropped the suitcases and checked the driveway. *What the hell?*

Sean had fallen into his usual drunken coma, his arm thrown over his face. His car keys and phone were conspicuous in their absence from their usual spot by the bed.

I tore the house apart for more than an hour before he woke up, came out to the kitchen, and dropped a kiss on the top of my head. My mouth fell open.

"Sean, where's my car?"

"Didn't I tell you? I had the guys from my garage come pick it up for servicing. They'll drop it off in a couple days. Don't worry." He pulled out a chair at the kitchenette. "Make me a cup of tea, would you?" He cocked one eyebrow. I didn't know for sure if his expression signaled a dare, but I didn't think a cup of tea merited a fist fight, so I put a kettle on to boil.

* * * *

For a while, I knew nothing but pain. I prayed every day for Simon to save me, I knew it was ridiculous and I should save myself, but my heart just wasn't in it. I'd lost Simon…lost hope…lost the will to help myself. I couldn't help but wonder if this was my punishment for the long list of sins I'd committed over the course of my life, or if it was just the product of a bad decision.

No matter why it happened, it continued. Sean piled bruise on top of bruise while keeping me a prisoner in the house. By the time Christmas came, I was broken, a shell with only Kieran to make me smile, and even his powers had begun to fade. My phone never turned up, and though Sean said he would take me to get a new one, he always ended up too busy.

On Christmas morning, I awoke to find Kieran already out of his bed, in the living room with Sean and his mother. A mountain range of gifts sat under the tree, and Kieran excitedly waited to tear into the bright colored paper.

When I walked in, Sean looked up and smiled. "Oh, honey. We've been waiting for you."

His mother stood tilting her cheek toward me. I hid a reflexive shiver by tightening my sweater around my shoulders and inhaled a big whiff of her rose scented perfume before smacking my lips into the air beside her face.

Sean moved to sit beside Kieran on the floor and handed him a big box wrapped in Ninja Turtle paper. I hadn't been allowed to buy anything, so the arrival of such a vast amount of stuff shocked me.

Kieran opened the latest technology in remote control pets. He leaped to his feet and brought it over to me. "Look, Mommy. I got a Scruffy!"

I couldn't help but smile at the enthusiasm. His happiness comforted me, and for the moment, it was enough.

An hour and a half later, after we'd repeated the routine with every gift he received, Kieran began picking up the paper strewn about the room. I stood to help him. There had to be five hundred yards of gift wrap on the floor.

Sean's mother wrapped her fingers around my arm and dug her nails in. "He needs to learn responsibility."

Seriously? The kid was barely four, but rather than risk more wrath from Sean for disobeying his mother, I sat.

Sean scooted across the floor on his knees to hand me an envelope. "This is for you."

I shook my head. "I didn't get you anything." ...because his behavior didn't exactly inspire my gift giving hormone, and I was his prisoner in our home.

"You already gave me the greatest gift in the world."

I raised my eyebrows in question.

"A family, silly girl."

He ruffled my hair, and bile made its way from my stomach to my throat. I almost gagged. Instead, I pasted a smile on my busted lips and accepted the envelope.

Tickets to fly home for New Year's. Three tickets. *Oh yay.*

Chapter 11

By the time we arrived in Storybook Lake, the worst of the bruises had faded and could be covered with foundation. My lips healed, and Sean had kept strictly hands-off since Christmas, even pretending his abuse never happened. My parents adored him, Kieran whose love had been bought and paid for at Christmas, worshiped him, and I sat quietly watching the Sean-love-fest proceed without any encouragement from me.

When we returned to the hotel, we sat up most of the night talking. He apologized, promised to be better, then made love with me so tenderly and so completely I almost went an entire night without thinking of Simon. Almost.

Then, the New Year's party happened and my world fell apart again. We walked into Hood's Hideaway and Sean's sulking began. My parents had Kieran, so we had a free night without the worry of taking care of him when we returned to the hotel. It left Sean free to drink himself into anger.

Simon arrived a few minutes after we did, and my pulse kicked into high gear. Simon in a tuxedo... The fantasy I'd indulged in on more than one lonely night was nothing compared to the reality.

"Hey, Dani." He leaned in and kissed my cheek.

For the tiniest measure of a second, I relaxed into his touch.

Oh, that smile. "Hi." I turned away. I couldn't look at Simon without wanting him, without needing him to hold me, to take me away from it all.

"You are beautiful." He ducked his head, then looked up at me with a shy smile. "How have you been?"

"Oh, you know. Just living the dream." *More like a nightmare.* I kept the thought to myself.

"It's great to see you."

One smile, one glance into those amber eyes, and my bones left me Jell-O-legged and ready to puddle onto the painted floor.

The bartender handed me Sean's drink as he stepped up and wrapped his fingers around my shoulder. "Leave it. We're going."

"But it's not midnight yet." I'd forgotten the golden rule...talking back to Sean would only earn me new bruises. He slapped me the first time in the elevator. I would have yelled, screamed for help, but I didn't want anyone to know, so I kept quiet, trying to make myself as small as I could. Luckily, he stopped with the one slap to my face. Once we returned to the hotel room, it got worse.

The next morning, he drove to my parents to pick up Kieran. He told them he'd let me sleep in, but he'd actually threatened me with death if I told anyone. At that point, I had no reason to believe he wouldn't follow through. When he returned with Kieran, he changed our flight reservations, and we flew back to California on New Year's day.

* * * *

We returned from our holiday vacation in Storybook Lake--me with two black eyes, him with a cashmere sweater and Italian loafers my mother bought him. Even though the signs were there, no one at home noticed or came to save me. Not that I'd expected much, but being there reminded me of how my life should have been. I had to get out. What was left of my life depended on it.

If I fought back or resisted, he hit harder, kicked with more precision. Because he'd turned part vampire and didn't like leaving the house while the sun was above the horizon, he *allowed* me to run his errands or buy food. He timed how long it took me to get to the grocery store and return home. If I varied by more than ten minutes, an all-out battle royal followed. I grew accustomed to losing, to hiding the abuse behind makeup and dark glasses. My only peace came in the evening when he bathed in his cologne and left for his club. This went on and on.

He finally *found* my cell when my mother, after not being able to reach me for more than a month, threatened to call the police if she didn't get to speak to me. After that, I kept it close, took it with me everywhere and slept with it at night. Time raced by me while I sat back waiting for an opportunity to get away.

The week before I finally found a way out, makeup stopped covering my bruises. He'd bought me Gucci sunglasses as a cheap cover up for an earlier punishment for something I'd done, or not done, and I'd taken to wearing them inside. My bruises scared Kieran.

Though he'd grown impressively tall and I was normally weak from the beatings, I held Kieran as often as I could, even when he slept. As I cradled him close to me, reading a romance novel I'd found in Sean's mother's basement stash, my cell chirped.

Simon: Hi, stranger.

I looked at the phone for a minute. I'd deleted his number right after I returned home on New Year's to lessen my temptation, to get him out of my system once and for all, but I'd never forgotten the digits that would let me hear his voice once more.

What could he possibly want? Our last meeting, before a couple of spoken pleasantries at New Year's, had been less than cordial, and his sister had broken my nose. She'd been angry about something I said to him, and with the full force of an enraged twin, acted quickly. I didn't blame her; I would have hit me too. Since my new marriage had become a veritable punch fest, I probably should have called to thank her for lesson number one in taking a fist to the face.

Me: Hi.

I took a deep breath and waited, hoping this wasn't some messed up fluke of technology designed to teach me yet another of life's more cruel lessons. I didn't spend long pondering the notion before he responded.

Simon: I need to ask you a question. What happened to us? Why did you break up with me?

I knew he'd lost parts of his memory because of the shooting, and I felt bad for him, but the last thing I wanted was to rehash the part of our relationship that hurt more than any beating I could take from Sean.

Me: I would never break up with you.

I would have walked through fire to keep him. The idea of it going any other way never crossed my mind. That he could think so brought a sad smile to my lips.

Simon: I miss you, Dani, and I need to know what I did to make you leave me. Please.

Simon: Simon says tell me.

The little smiley face at the end of his statement made my heart flutter.

Me: I didn't break up with you. We just drifted apart, I guess.

There was no point in correcting his version of the facts. It didn't matter who left who, or who dumped the other one on her backside. Well, it mattered less now than it did then, anyway.

Simon: I can't imagine ever letting you go.

Why couldn't he have felt that way when we were together?

Me: You wanted to go out with little Kelly Hollywood, but it's okay. We had a good run. There are no hard feelings.

If wishes were within the realm of possibilities, I would wish myself back to him, to safety, a place where only we existed with Kieran.

Simon: Huh?

But since wishes only led to heartache, I concentrated on the headline. Walking down that memory lane wouldn't help either of us.

Me: It doesn't matter, Simon. You'll find some nice girl, and you'll live happily ever after.

I swiped at a tear, then patted Kieran's back about a thousand times before he answered.

Simon: I don't want any other girl.

Chapter 12

I put the text conversation out of my mind as much as I could, but at night, I dreamed of his voice, of hearing him say he loved me.

Three days after my exchange with Simon, I woke later than usual and slipped my hand inside my pillow case feeling for my cell. I patted the pillow, turned it upside down, shook it until I had no choice but to believe the phone had disappeared. Panic vibrated through me. What if Sean went through the history? Found the texts I'd been too stupid to delete? I threw back the blanket and paced the room for a minute before I drew the blackout curtains open. The sun... It had to be at least noon. Why hadn't Kieran been in yet or cried out for me to get him?

I raced to his room. There was no sign Kieran was missing unless I counted the empty hangers in his closet. Wally, the stuffed T-Rex he never slept without, lay forgotten on the bed. But the hangers...in my panic, I dropped to my knees and looked under his bed. My heart lurched painfully, and I clutched the front of my sleep shirt.

"Oh my God." I ran through the house, calling for him, for both of them. When I stopped to listen for an answer, only an eerie creaking from the wind whipping against the house greeted me. No house with a five-year-old should have been this quiet.

As I glanced around, spinning in circles for no reason except it kept me from falling to my knees, a dark spot in the corner of the living room beckoned to me. I took a tentative step toward it, then stopped and looked over my shoulder, expecting Sean and his wayward fists to jump out at any second, to pounce on me for snooping. No one. I stepped closer to the corner. A camera?

Small and black, its lens appeared more like a blinking eye than a piece of glass shrouded in plastic. I moved to the side. It followed me, a little electronic hum whirring with the motion. "What the hell?"

I didn't really care about the camera right then. I cared about my child and where Sean could have taken him. The monitor would have to wait. After tossing all the pillows, pulling every book from the shelves onto the floor, and still not finding my phone, I logged onto the computer.

Before I'd even located a way to contact anyone, the video call icon blinked, and Sean's face popped up on the screen. I hit answer and didn't bother with a pleasant greeting. He'd decided to punish me. "Where's Kieran, Sean?"

He threw his head back and laughed. "Tell me, Dani, why did we break up?" He clucked his tongue. "I didn't break up with you."

I closed my eyes wishing I'd been smart enough to press the delete button before I hid the phone, but I hadn't wanted to let go....again... And now I was being punished in the way Sean knew would get me to comply. At least I knew the sin I'd committed. "Where is my son?"

"He's playing with his toys right over there." He flipped the camera around to show Kieran sitting on a carpet in what looked like a hotel room. "And if you ever want to see him again, you're going to do a few things for me."

Panic tinged every word as I answered. "Anything, Sean. Just bring him home to me."

"We'll see." He chuckled and pointed at the screen. "It depends on how sorry you are and how well you can follow directions."

I nodded. "What do you want me to do?"

He smiled. "Joey will be at the house in one hour. Go with him to the bank and wire me some money." He rubbed his hand over his five o'clock shadow and the speaker caught the scraping sound. "I think ten thousand should do for today. Kieran and I need a little traveling cash. When you get to the bank, tell them Joey will give them the information for the receiving bank. You walk away. He'll call me and tell me when it's done."

"You have your own money, Sean. Why do you need mine?"

He laughed. "What do you need it for?"

"I want to talk to Kieran."

"Don't call the cops or you'll never see the kid again."

He clicked off, leaving me to stare at the icons on the desktop. I hit redial and waited. He didn't answer any of the next five calls.

Joey took me to the bank, then when Sean had what he wanted, Joey brought me home and sped away as though he couldn't get out of there fast enough. It was fine with me. I didn't need one of Sean's henchmen staring over my shoulder, but something about Joey told me he was different. I didn't have time to investigate the thoughts too closely or care about their results. I had worrying to do.

Over the following three days, I lost all control. I didn't eat or sleep. Instead, I zombied my way through the house, into Kieran's room and back out to the computer to wait for a call. Sean would show me Kieran, but never let me hear his voice. He never let me talk to him. If I asked, he hung up. If I cried, it cost me more money. Joey and I made four trips to the bank in three days, sending Sean more than sixty thousand dollars from an account I couldn't believe he'd found. In the middle of the fourth night, as I stared at the computer praying for a call, bargaining with God to just let him bring my son home safe, Sean called.

"You need to talk to your kid. He won't quit crying."

"Okay." I tried to blink the tears of relief away, but as soon as Kieran came on the screen, they fell and a sob shook my shoulders. "Hi, buddy."

"Mommy, I wanna come home."

"I know you do, but you're on an adventure with Daddy. You have to be a very good boy, okay?" He cried harder and my heart broke. "Just listen to Daddy, and he'll bring you home soon, but Kieran, be good, okay?"

His body shook on Sean's lap, and Sean jerked him by the shoulder. Kieran cried out, and I bit my lip and offered a silent prayer. *Please don't let him hurt my baby.*

I blew out a breath and tried again. "Kieran, listen to Mommy." He looked up and sniffled twice before swiping his arm across his eyes. "Who's the bravest of all the dinosaurs?"

"The T-Rex." His voice lacked its usual buoyancy.

"Right. That's right. It's the T-Rex. Mommy needs you to be the T-Rex. Can you show me your growl?"

"I can't."

"Yeah, you can, Kieran. You're the biggest bravest boy Mommy knows, and you can do it. Show me." I wanted my boy home, to hold, to cuddle, to never let out of my sight again. "Please, baby, show Mommy how brave you can be."

He growled softly.

"Louder. Do it loud." I smiled when he curled his hands into claws and growled at the screen. "That's it. You're mommy's boy. Now, T-rex isn't afraid of anything. He's strong and tough, and so are you. Go to sleep now, and when you get scared or you miss me too much and you're sad, remember you're my T-rex. We'll be back together soon."

"I love you, Mommy."

"I love you too. Now, lie down so I can talk to Daddy." A second later, Sean's face filled the screen. "Are you coming home soon?"

He scrubbed his face with his hands. "I don't know, Dani. It depends on you. Tell me about your boyfriend, the one who doesn't want any other girl."

I bit back a sob. "He's out of my life, Sean. He's my past. You're my future. You're my husband. Please come home."

"Your boy is a crybaby."

Oh, God. "He's scared, Sean. He's never been without me. Come home, and we can work this out...like a family." The words burned my throat, stung my eyes, but I would have said anything to get Kieran back safely.

"You make excuses for him. I make him strong."

The blood in my veins boiled. "If you hurt him Sean..." *I just blew it.*

He laughed. "What will you do? Tell me. I really want to know."

I took a deep breath. As soon as I hung up, I was going to get a hold of Joey and force him to tell me where Sean took Kieran. "I'll kill you."

"Ooh, big talk. I can stay gone forever. You dumb bitch."

"Not without my money. If you aren't home by tomorrow, I'm going to the police."

"You'll never see the kid again."

Anger spurred me on. I'd had enough. "I think you underestimate me, Sean."

"And I think you're gonna pay for this when I get home."

"Come and get me."

The next day, Joey dropped them off in front of the house, and Kieran burst through the door, shouting my name. After a few hours of holding my breath and waiting for the big boom, I relaxed. Sean acted happy to be home with me. He played with Kieran on the floor, even helped me put him to bed. Later, he disappeared to his downstairs office, and when he returned, I'd already gone to sleep beside Kieran, grateful he'd come home.

Sean dragged me out of Kieran's bed by my hair and hauled me across the hall to our bedroom. After the first punch, everything went black.

Chapter 13

To leave I needed a plan and a bit of help. Reaching out to Joey, the only person who'd been nice to me since I arrived, I secured my golden ticket. Except it wasn't the fabled gold color of Willy Wonka and chocolate factories.... It was a dingy green with well-thumbed pages. Still, Joey slipped it to me with stealth that would have made James Bond proud, and I guarded it as if it held the combination to the safe at Fort Knox, but not before Sean turned on Kieran. I called my parents, gave them the barest details, and asked to stay with them.

As I stepped into the taxi, careful to protect my boy's wounds, I breathed deeply, hoping we could make it out of California before Sean managed to get home.

I'd taken a big chance by letting the police pick him up. It gave me the opportunity I needed, though, to steal his phone. Then, I grabbed clothes for me and Kieran and got the hell out of that house as quickly as I could. I couldn't wait to get home. On the way to pick up my car, I asked the cabbie to pull over as we neared the beach. Climbing out as calmly as I could on legs still shaking with fear, I threw the phone in the ocean. Flattening Sean's tires and destroying his credits cards had filled me with an immense satisfaction--one I hadn't experienced in years.

Driving straight through, I pulled in some thirty hours later, and nothing had ever looked as good to me as their house. I sat in the car, taking in the two stories of grandiose architecture. A thousand memories of our family roamed around inside those walls, and I needed the comfort it provided. A few years after they built the house, Daddy built a stable with its own drive and acres of flat grazing land. The horses were Daddy's pride, more so than the house, less so than my mother and us kids.

Daddy was big and strong, smarter than anyone else I'd ever met. He wore designer suits for his day job, investing money for wealthy clients around the globe, but wore cowboy boots every other moment of the day.

Because of his penchant for riding horses into town, they'd installed a hitching post in front of the coffee shop, the bank, and the hardware store. My mother, in contrast, yet complement to my father, epitomized the idea of motherhood. She cooked, baked, and drove the car pool, never lost her temper, and always dispensed *The Waltons'* style advice. Most of the time, even though she was a psychologist, she said she winged it when dealing with her own family, but I didn't buy it. She was the glue holding our picture perfect family together.

As I climbed out and came around to get Kieran out of the car, my father stood on the front porch, waiting for me. He met me, then smiled as he took Kieran from my arms. "How is he?"

"He's quiet." I whispered the words as I pushed his hair back to show my dad the stitches on his face. My baby had a rough couple days. I only hoped he would find his way through the darkness to be the little boy he'd been before Sean destroyed his innocence.

Dad hefted Kieran higher onto his shoulder and threw his other arm across my shoulders. "I'll get your stuff after we get this boy into bed." He pulled me toward the house. "Your mom has coffee for you."

Ah, coffee. The gift of the gods and my mother's go-to problem solving medicine. I resisted the urge to crumble, to let my parents pick up the pieces. Instead, I sat with my mom, pouring out the story in a flat monotone, the same voice I used to protect myself from Sean's wrath. I didn't tell them the worst parts, only the parts I'd immunized myself against.

Each word hardened a new part of my heart. It beat less rapidly as I neared the end.

The sun peeked over the horizon before I crawled into bed with Kieran. Holding on to him, I sobbed softly for all he'd seen, all he'd been through. I prayed God would replace his memory, or at least let him block it out. He didn't stir as I whispered promises of protection. If I ever saw Sean again, I would kill him for what he'd done.

Sleep eluded me. Too many worries whirled in my mind. Sean would undoubtedly find me. Because of the way small towns worked, almost the whole of Storybook Lake would close in around me, pulling me into a protective bubble, but he would never give up. He often told me I would never get away. It was part of the reason I stayed. The threat behind his words… I couldn't imagine how I would ever be safe again. After the noon sun streamed in my window, I crawled out of bed. Coffee would have to be enough to get me through the day.

"Did you sleep well?"

I smiled at the familiarity behind her words. Every morning, probably since birth, she asked the same question. I nodded, thinking a wordless action less a lie, and smothered a yawn. "Where's Kieran?"

"In the barn with your dad. He's looking at the horses." I walked to the French doors leading out to the back patio. As I turned the knob, she stood up quickly and covered my hand with hers. I'd been out to the barn a thousand times in my bathrobe. Never before had my mother stopped me. I pulled away, and she moved to stand in front of the door. "Go put clothes on, honey. Simon is out there."

"What's he doing here?" I didn't want to see him, not looking like a crash test dummy, but with the same breath, I couldn't wait.

"He's helping out with the horses. It's been a lot for your dad these days."

"Oh." I started up the stairs, but turned to face her. "Okay. I get it. Dad needs help, but why Simon, Mom? Of all people. Aren't there any kids in town itching to make some ice cream money or Friday night date cash who can shovel a stall?"

"Your dad always liked Simon, and since his...accident, people look at him differently, but not your dad. Simon respects him, and he knew your daddy needed some help, so he offered."

I smiled in spite of myself. Not that I needed more, but this highlighted one of the reasons I loved Simon. He was *that* guy. And I wanted--no, needed--to see him.

After pulling on a pair of jeans still hanging in my closet from years ago and my favorite old boots, I checked the mirror, then headed outside. Kieran and Dad were behind the gate atop a horse with long legs and a twitchy head. I jogged the rest of the way.

"Dad, he's never been on a horse before." The warning escaped my lips before I could consider my dad's feelings.

He tightened his hold on Kieran as though I planned to pull him down. "Don't worry, Dani. I've been doing this since you were a very little girl. I'm gonna take this big boy for a ride, and we're going to get to know each other. Were you planning to deny me that?"

I chuckled. "Guilt. Well played."

He grinned down at me, secured Kieran once more, then gave me a wink. Dorothy was right. There really was no place like home.

"You wait here with Simon. We'll be just fine."

I nodded and stood at the gate while Simon closed it behind my father as he took my son out to the paths he'd carved in the woods.

Leaning against the fence, I pretended to watch the tree line, but never lost sight of Simon in my peripheral vision.

"Does it hurt?" He reached out to run his finger next to my black eye. When I flinched away, he dropped his hand to his side.

"It could have been worse." In all honesty, I didn't even remember the pain of that particular punch.

"Did he do this to you?" His whisper didn't hide the hatred behind the words.

I sighed, not expecting him to understand, but... "I did it to myself, kind of. You know?"

"That's really how you look at it?" His voice went hard, judgmental.

I lifted my chin to meet his gaze. "And I don't want to talk about it, okay?" Not with him. Not ever.

He nodded. "Your boy has your chin and your lips."

I grabbed on to the fence rail for support. A moment of panic seized my heart, and I imagined it stopping cold.

Then he grinned, and the potency of it shifted my panic to desire. "He must get all those good looks from you."

If only he knew. I should have told him right then. "Oh, definitely." My white-knuckled grip relaxed. He'd always been so easy to be around and nice to look at. *Even nicer now.* He'd let his hair grow long--Brad-Pitt-*Legends-of-the-Fall* long--and he had it pulled back at the top. His eyes were a deep amber color that God only blessed to sunsets, whiskey, and Simon. Jocelyn, the hellish born twin, was the younger version of their mother--beautiful and perfect, honey brown hair with sparkling blue eyes--but Simon must have been one hundred percent his father. Seeing his smile in person rather than in my memory let me forget the horror of my life, for a moment. He stood close enough to touch, and I curled my fingers into my fist to keep from reaching out.

"How long are you staying this time?"

My heart began a mambo in my chest at the almost hopeful tone of his voice. Maybe I could wait a few days, spend some time preparing him for the big news. I had too much turmoil in my own life at the moment to consider adding more. Telling him before either of us could handle the idea would be catastrophic. That's what I told myself, anyway.

"Forever, I think." I gazed off into the pasture at the horses grazing there. It probably sounded odd coming from my lips, but I'd come to appreciate small town life--the-everyone-knows-everyone-and-would-band-together-to-protect-one-of-its-own aspect. "I want Kieran to grow up here, like I did." I shrugged. "My company headquarters is here and my family." *And you. Why can't I just say the words?* I practiced them in my mind, but couldn't convince my mouth to over-rule my apprehension.

He smiled. "A lot's changed since you've been gone."

Boy, did I have news for him, but I decided to play along. For a minute, I wanted the normal other people had. "Yeah?"

"Oh, yeah." His forehead crinkled as he compressed his lips and nodded. This was his version of serious--as solemn as he ever got. "We got a new water fountain at the high school." He looked at me from the corner of his narrowed eyes. "It made the front page of the paper."

I nodded, unable to control the upward curve of my lips or the increasing beat of my heart.

"And we got a new Dairy Queen. There's even been talk of a supercenter." He leaned back against the fence and tucked a strand of hair behind my ear.

I saw it coming and closed my eyes as his fingers grazed my cheek.

"Mrs. Rosenbury's mutt had an affair with Mr. Duncan's poodle down the street, then gave birth to seven of the ugliest pups in the history of animals." He waved a hand in the air. "Mr. Duncan went right out and got his poodle neutered." He finished with wide eyes and a few nods of his head.

"Wow, I missed all that?"

"Yeah. I'll dig up the newspaper clippings for you. You can catch up with some late night reading." He lifted one eyebrow. "Unless you have other late night activities planned."

As I stood there with the second strongest person I knew, it was easy to forget Sean and concentrate on Simon, easy to pretend like nothing had ever come between us and I wasn't a big old liar. "Same old Simon."

He shrugged. "Not exactly the same." He brought his head forward and took out the leather band holding his hair out of his face. I didn't have to guess about the changes. The scar at his hairline said it all.

"How have you been?" I asked the question to shove my shame to a dark corner in my mind.

He shrugged, his face serious, the smile faded. "It's slow going, but your mom helps." My mother had been working with him for weeks to see what of his memory remained. So far, not much survived the bullet. "At least I can cover it with hair."

My skin heated at the way I had reacted to his scar the first time I saw it, and I turned my gaze to face him completely. He'd been newly recovered, and I'd been my horrible self, saying ugly things to him about the scar, using insults to protect my breaking heart. "Simon, the day in the bakery"--I moved closer and pushed his hair off his forehead, revealing the star shaped scar--"I was upset because you were with someone else *again.* I should have held it together and not taken all my crap out on you. I'm sorry." I pressed a kiss to the scar and gasped when he pulled me against him.

"Seriously?" He leaned against the fence. "That's all I get, after all this time? You kiss my scar?" My eyebrows drew together as he continued. "I have two perfectly good lips right here and you go for my scar?"

I shook my head. "I'm married, Simon."

He nodded and dropped his arms, setting me free enough to step back if I was so inclined. Which I wasn't, no matter what I'd just said.

"I know."

"I can't do this." Even if I wanted to more than I wanted to draw another breath.

"Because you love him?"

I blew out a breath on a dry laugh. "Oh, God no. Not even for a minute." I looked out into the woods. How could I explain it? I wanted to be a better person, and better people didn't cheat. They didn't lie, either, but I was working in baby steps.

Chapter 14

Mom used words like "depression" and "overwhelming grief" to describe my *condition*. Dad's words of wisdom included "buck up" and "I'll kill that SOB." Those, incidentally, made me feel better than anything else. The plain and simple truth... I suffered from loneliness and regret from my own faulty decision-making.

I steered clear of the barn and anywhere else I might run into Simon-- town, church, the grocery store, daylight. Hiding out made sense. I wanted to see him too much and not for the right reasons. Ravaging Simon, while a very real possibility, would probably get me run out of town by a bunch of broom carrying biddies whose moral code provided the standard we were all to live by. They'd chased me off once. I wasn't giving them a second go at me. To remain in their good favor, I had to walk the straight and narrow, toe the line, become their small town cliché.

One Tuesday morning, though, fate--and my mother--stepped in. When I came down for breakfast, Simon sat across the table with a tall stack of pancakes in front of him.

I hadn't bothered with a hairbrush or changing from my pajamas, and couldn't even remember where I'd put my makeup bag. Simon, on the other hand, could have stepped out of a magazine. A vintage T-shirt with an Aerosmith logo on the front hugged his broad chest and ripped stomach. His hair was captured in the back by a ponytail and, if I hadn't known better, I would have said he had another growth spurt since I last saw him.

He whistled. "That is a stunning garment, Miss Clothing Designer."

I ignored him and poured a cup of coffee. What the hell time did these people get up? My mother's hair, sleek and straight, gleamed in the morning sun streaming through the window. I leaned over his shoulder, inhaling his bottled-by-the-gods-cologne. Early morning perfection annoyed me. His cologne did not.

"I design kids' clothes, but if I knew you were going to be here, I would have spent the night stitching sequins on my freaking robe. However"--I shot a pointed glare at my mom--"no one told me we were having breakfast guests."

"Jolly in the mornings, isn't she?" Even the sight of his grin did nothing to calm my annoyance at my mother.

"Yeah. I'm a regular Santa Claus." I sat across from him and pretended to read the newspaper for a few minutes, but ignored the printed word. Instead, I wished for a hairbrush and a prettier robe. The little hairs on my arms stood on end, and I glanced up, mouth open, ready to be flip, to ask why the hell he kept popping up, making me uncomfortable in the place where I should have been most secure. Something in his eyes made me snap my jaw shut.

After several moments of intense staring, I finally said, "Is it rude of me to ask what you're doing here?"

"Kind of." Mischief crinkled the corners of his mouth before he sobered and blew out a breath. "Your mom asked me to come."

I squinted at her. "Of course, she did." I had to find a way to convince her my relationship with Simon didn't require meddling.

"Dani, something happened." From the look on her face--tight line of her lips, drawn brow, and a wariness clouding her eyes--something very bad happened. Her lids lowered, and she wrung the fingers of one hand with the other. "I got a phone call from Sean. He asked for you, but I told him we didn't know where you were, that we hadn't heard from you."

In the semi-darkness of my first night home, the only concrete plan we'd concocted involved lying about my whereabouts.

"Obviously, he knows otherwise. This arrived last night." She handed me an envelope with a single picture of Kieran and me as we played in the yard a few days earlier. "I want you to let me and your dad take Kieran with us on a vacation."

A lump formed in my throat. I couldn't argue with the logic behind a trip, considering Sean could be sitting outside in his car waiting for me to come out. For all I knew, he could have a sniper rifle aimed at my head as I sat in the kitchen. I glanced out the patio doors fearing the worst. However, Sean was too lazy to park himself in a tree doing recognizance on the slim chance he'd be able to nab Kieran. "How long would you be gone?"

Mom considered her hands carefully. "Until you figure out how to get this mess with Sean resolved. Until Kieran is no longer in danger."

All the mistakes I'd ever made flashed through my mind--a wedding to a man I hardly knew, Keaton's face when I told him about Kieran, Kieran bloody and scared, Simon…a lot of Simon. A tear slipped down my cheek and I swiped at it. "When do you want to go?"

"Your dad made reservations for a flight this afternoon." Her no-nonsense-I'm-not-asking-I'm-telling tone left little room for negotiation. The decisions had all been made because my parents, once again, believed I'd failed. Telling me was nothing more than imparting information. She covered my hand with hers. "We want you and Kieran to be safe."

I turned to Simon, unreasonable in my anger. The rational part of me knew he hadn't forced this on me; the part in charge of my mouth blamed him for breaking up with me all those years ago. Bitterness burned my tongue as I breathed in a huffy puff of air. "So, my safety is where you come in?" The venom in my voice should have warned him away, but he grinned. A second later, at my angry huff, he sobered and used his fork to toy with food on his plate.

Instead of slinking away to hide from my wrath, he shrugged. "Depends on you, I guess."

I nodded. "And if I say I don't want your help?" Which I didn't. I wanted his gun.

He grinned. "I have a couple options I'm working on."

My eyebrows shot heavenward as I whipped my head to look into his eyes.

"Not that, dirty girl." He chuckled, then stopped when I frowned. My mother was sitting between us, and innuendo had no place in my day. Nothing about the situation amused me. "I can convince you--or try to--or I can park my car out front and watch you from the driveway. Of course, kicking me out means two of us would be watching you from the street and no one would be in here making sure you're safe."

I pulled my cell from my pocket and stabbed Sean's number into the keypad. After one split second of indecision, I hit send and drilled my fingers against the table top until he answered. "Sean, why are you doing this?" Just talking to him stole my confidence and my voice shook.

My mother's gasp almost drowned out his reply. "I want my family back."

"You didn't want us when we were your family." He'd wanted something, maybe a wife and a kid, but not what I'd given him.

"No one walks away from me."

My skin prickled while a mixture of fear and anger hammered in my chest. "I walked away from you because you hurt my boy. And we're not coming back. God, Sean." I'd found my fury, but buried it as though he could reach through the phone and hurt me.

"He's our boy." His voice rose as anger charged him.

I'd heard it happen a hundred times or more, and I could tell without seeing his face.

"And you go ahead...keep telling yourself I can't make you come home to me. I can, and I will. By the end of the week, you and *our* boy better be home."

"He's *my* boy, and I'm not scared of your threats." I could probably have been more convincing if my voice hadn't cracked, but that one weakness didn't diminish the power building my convictions. I'd almost let Sean destroy him once. I wouldn't make the same mistake twice.

"You better not be telling people what happened, at least not your warped twisted little version, or I'll kill you."

I'd been beaten, kicked, held prisoner in our house... Of course, my courage came easy at nine hundred miles away, with Simon opposite me and my Dad's gun case not fifty feet from where I sat. "I would be scared, but you'd have to stay sober to do it, and we both know that isn't your strong suit."

"I guess you'll have to wait and see, won't you?"

"You obviously know where to find me. Why wait?" My courage morphed into stupidity. I regretted the words almost before I'd finished saying them. He would come whether the welcome wagon greeted him or not.

Simon shook his head as my mother yanked the phone away from me. She hit the end button.

"Seriously, Danielle?" Her hands trembled as she shook the phone at me. "You invited a maniac to come here without so much as a single thought of that innocent baby. You take chances, and you never, ever consider those who could be hurt, or worse. He could hurt Kieran again, and what would you do then?" She stood.

"What do you want from me, Mom? I don't know what to do. I've never had anyone want to kill me before, and as far as I know, there's no handbook I can use as a guideline."

"Well, I can tell you that you don't invite them to finish the job. The scars on you, on that baby, have barely healed."

Simon jerked his gaze up to my face, his head tilted to one side.

"I can't just sit back anymore. I know you don't get it, Mom. I know, because Daddy is a good guy, but Sean isn't. He is every bad thing a person can be, and I will never be free from him as long as I'm too scared to fight back." My logic might have been flawed, but it was all I had.

"Danielle--"

I shoved the chair back. "I will die trying to protect Kieran. You can call me stupid, and you can point out all my past mistakes"--I waved a hand toward Simon--"invite them *all* over for breakfast if you want, but don't question how far I would go to protect my boy." I spoke with a control I hadn't felt in years. Quiet rage hummed through my entire body, but my voice remained calm.

I had one more card to play with Sean. My mother glared at me when I held my hand out for my phone. She put it on the table between us, probably waiting to smack my hand if I picked it up again.

"How? By getting yourself killed? Does that even come close to sounding like a resolution we would hope for?" The cell on the table shifted with vibration. Sean's face appeared on the screen. I snatched it up.

"Sean, please?" I appealed to the part of him that loved to hear me beg. "I filed for divorce. I don't want anything from you except to be left alone." I kept my tone even, measured. "All you have to do is let me go."

His evil laugh grated against my soul. "Why would I do that? We're married and we're going to stay married. I told you in the beginning, I want this to last."

I sighed. "Sean, think for a minute. I know things about you and your clients at the club, the drugs you get for them, the weird stuff your girls have to do. I think some very important people wouldn't be so happy with you if your wife goes all out CNN with their private lives."

"Are you threatening me?"

"I'm not threatening you. I'm just saying bad things could happen if you don't sign the divorce papers."

He laughed again. I tapped my forehead twice with the top corner of my phone, imagining I could choke him without actually having to be in a room with him.

"It doesn't have to be this way. You leave me and Kieran alone, and I'll keep my mouth shut." I calmed my voice to a level of quiet he responded to in the past.

"Who is going to believe you, anyway, without proof?"

I chewed the inside corner of my lip, pushing the anger down. In this case, I had ample ammunition without calling on any attitude. "Sean, I taught you how to use the computer to keep your records, remember?" From my matter-of-fact tone, I could have been talking to an old friend. "You were cussing because you couldn't figure out how to get two plus two to equal four?" He'd kicked the tower, thrown his papers, created such a ruckus I rushed in to make sure Kieran hadn't wandered into his home office. "And you know that little green notebook with all those important names with their little fetishes and the prices you charged them? The dates and times they showed up?" I plunged forward. "I have it."

"You don't have it."

"Yeah. I do."

His breath stuttered through the phone. "Impressive, Dani, all this bravery. Is your boyfriend sitting there with you? Is the half-witted former sheriff giving you all your courage? Or maybe the boy-toy you were never good enough for? The one you lived with in Arizona? Or maybe it's dear old daddy with his bum knee and his shotgun."

He could say whatever he wanted about me and I would take it all day long, but going after Simon and Dad struck a low I couldn't accept. My mean girl stepped out of the shadows. For once, it was good to see her, to give her control. "Hey. Village idiot. I also showed you how to Google, so knowing about Simon's shooting or Dad's knee isn't exactly earth shattering news." Courage replaced anger and my mind's eye played a fantasy of seeing Sean in a pool of his own blood.

"I *am* going to kill you." His voice dropped to a deadly hiss.

I nodded. "The question, Sean"--I blew out a breath--"is will it be before or after I sell all your secrets to the highest tabloid bidder?"

Again, silence floated over the phone line before a loud growl rang through.

"Sign the papers and I'll burn it. All I want is for you to leave me and Kieran alone. Please."

"I'll be in touch." He ended the connection and presumably began tearing everything he owned apart hunting for the notebook I had upstairs.

I slid the phone onto the table and walked to the steps.

"Danielle, where are you going?"

I looked over my shoulder at my mother. "To pack some things for Kieran."

Two and a half hours later, my parents, my son, and the notebook were all safely on their way to the airport. Simon, maybe sensing a need to leave for his own safety, or maybe because my father asked, sighed and walked out to care for the horses. I'd paced the living room, then the kitchen, and had just poured a glass of water when I spotted it--a bottle of well-aged scotch. It had been there so long--since my elementary school days--waiting for its chance to breathe I almost didn't notice it. After a quick twist of the cap, I took my first drink in six years. The whiskey sitting in plain view on the counter, the fact I'd let my boy down, my own weakness… I poured the first shot before I had a split second to rethink it. The second shot came as fast, and by the third, I'd forsaken the thought of a glass altogether.

Chapter 15

I stumbled outside, taking a seat on a lawn chair facing the pool. By the time Simon returned from the barn, I'd tipped the bottle back more times than once and could see the etched numbers on the bottom through the liquid left over.

"Dani." He touched my shoulder, and my head bobbled toward the sound of his soft, disappointed voice.

"Hi, you."

"I thought you quit drinking."

My laugh caught on a sob and I took another swig. "I did."

"Then what are you doing?"

"Nobody likes a quitter." He reached for the bottle, and I jerked it to the side. "Don't touch my stuff, you naughty boy." I pulled the whiskey back for another big gulp. "You would drink, too, if you knew."

"Why don't you tell me then?"

I wasn't a drunken confession kind of girl. "Because." There had to be more. I snapped one eye shut and focused on finishing the sentence. "Because we aren't friends anymore."

"When did we stop being friends?"

I nodded and puffed out my lower lip. "When you went out with Kelly, I didn't want to be your friend anymore." He used his hip to push me over on the chaise. After he settled in with an arm around my shoulders, I leaned my head against him. "You smell really good. You always did, but when you left me for Kelly…"

He chuckled. "I don't remember any of that."

I pulled a lungful of noisy air through clenched teeth. "Oh, I do. Not fun."

"Did I hurt you?"

I shrugged the shoulder brushing against him. "Not like Sean hurt me." A picture of angry Sean coming at me, fists ready, flashed through my mind. "He hit me. A lot."

"Why didn't you leave him?"

"I asked myself that so many times." I took a long drink and handed the bottle to Simon. "The truth is, I don't know. I should have. I should have taken Kieran and got the hell out of there the first time it happened, but I didn't. I didn't have anywhere to go." I shook my head. "That isn't true. I wanted someone to save me, to make it not my fault, and no one came, so I stayed. I did so many bad things before Kieran was born. I think part of me believed I deserved it." I snapped my fingers and pointed at the whiskey settled in his lap. "But I should have left before he got to Kieran."

"I would have saved you, Dani." He slid his arm around my shoulders and pulled me close to his body. "I would kill him now for you if I thought it would bring you back to me or take away what's been done to you."

"Remember when you asked me if he did this to me and I said I did it myself?" His hold tightened around me. "I know you don't understand it, but it's me, making these decisions all the time that lead me to places in my life...places where I..."

"Get hurt?"

I nodded. "But it's my decision to be there. I walk into it."

"You can't read the future. You didn't know."

Sitting up, I glanced at him, then at the concrete patio. I held up my right hand showing my naked ring finger and frowned. My thumb was on the wrong side. I considered it for a minute, turning it from palm up to palm down, before pulling it back to my lap. "He wants me dead, and I can't do anything about it. Simon, I only had one job--to protect my son from my husband--and I failed. For the rest of his life, my little boy is gonna have this awful memory of..." I couldn't say it. I couldn't speak of the horror Kieran survived at Sean's hands.

"What happened to him, Dani?"

My mind flashed on the moment I'd walked into the house, to the quiet whimper of pain coming from his dark bedroom closet. I blocked the sound ringing in my ears with another drink. "I am married, and the only guy I ever really wanted to spend my life with is staring at me right now like I let him down. I let people down. It's who I am, and you're the last person, besides my baby, I ever wanted to let down." I swayed to the side, hugging the nearly empty bottle of forgetfulness, then took another drink as his gaze softened, his disappointment faded. Swallowing a painful gulp, I cleared my throat. "They might just be excuses to you, but it's my real life. In a nutshell." I shrugged. "More like a nuthouse."

"You didn't let me down." He brushed the hair from my face and gazed at me.

My lie sat right there at the surface right alongside the number of times I had a chance to tell him and didn't. I wanted to shout my truth at him, tell him the secret he deserved to know, the one that would destroy us and any chance I could ever hope to have with him.

Instead, I turned to face away from him. "Well, you better get away now, because I will."

"You didn't know Sean was like this."

I craned my neck to look at the always-forgiving Simon. "I married someone I didn't know, and I stayed with him. I might not have known in the very beginning, but I think after my first broken rib, I should have gotten a clue he isn't Prince Charming. Although I'm kind of slow, so maybe I can forgive myself." I looked away, running my fingers through my bangs a few times before putting the bottle back to my lips to stop the babbling.

"Some people aren't meant to be parents. Like me. I just do things and hope I can deal with the consequences. I never realized how hard it is to put someone else first." I looked at Simon, imagined him parenting Kieran. He would always be the only choice I ever had. No one else would ever measure up. "But you grew up doing that. You always put Joss first, and Keaton, and your mom. You're gonna be a great dad, somebody a kid can look up to. But not me. What kind of mom who cares about her kid marries a stranger?"

"I've been meaning to ask why you got married." He said it quietly, as though he believed living together would have been a better option.

"He was my replacement." I shrugged, then brushed a hand down his cheek. "And you were my Simon." Ah. What the hell. "You broke my heart, pal. You left me for Kelly Devlin. I know. She's pretty and so-o-o sweet bees ask her for honey, but it was supposed to be us--you and me--in every dream I had, and every fantasy I could think up. Always us, together. Then one day--poof--you're with Kelly." I threw my arms into the air almost smacking his pretty face with the bottle.

"I got out of here as fast as I could and who did I meet? Sean. Good old Sean. One-night-stand-in-a-limousine-Sean." I looked down at the almost empty bottle and frowned. "When I ran into him again after you got shot, I thought fate must have stepped in. If fate had a plan...and if I couldn't have you, then why not Sean? Maybe I earned a consolation prize or a... I don't know. But he sold it like a used car--the happy family all tied up with a little silver bow." This time I raised the correct hand holding up my Tiffany's wedding ring about two sizes too small to come off my finger. With the other, I drained the rest of the amber-colored liquid, then hugged the bottle to me like an old comforting friend. "I wanted something I couldn't have, so I grabbed the closest thing I could get."

"You know after I got shot"--his voice warmed me and I leaned into the sound--"I woke up thinking about you. I've dreamt of you every night since then. Almost three years of dreaming of you. Waking up without you every morning..." He raked his fingers through his hair.

The accident had left him without memories past the very first time he asked me out. We'd had some good times over the years and another layer of sadness piled on top of the rest of my troubles.

"You should talk to my mom. She's probably got some secret shrink magic to make men not think about me. I figured she used it on you already."

"There's nothing she could do to make me stop thinking of you."

"Hang in there. She'll think of something. Probably patent it."

He smiled. "Always so clever."

I shrugged and wished I had some sort of magic power to refill my magic whiskey bottle.

"I remember the day you and Keaton broke up. I asked him if he would mind if I asked you out." He'd wandered down some sort of memory lane, and I had no inclination to take that journey with him. I tried to sit up, but he pulled me back to him.

"You did ask me out. Then you blew me off for him and your sister." He'd made up for it later...many, many times. My body warmed and I ran a finger down his arm.

"I remember being with you, loving you, holding you, thinking I would never be able to live without you. I don't have many true memories left, but I remember you." As if to emphasize his point, he lowered his lids to a sexy half-mast-just-woke-up-gaze. "The first time you kissed me, at my mom's Christmas party, you had on a white dress with fur at the collar. Do *you* remember?"

I nodded. "You brought me upstairs to play video games. And you let me win."

He chuckled. "I didn't let you win. I couldn't concentrate on the game. All I could think about"--he ran his thumb over my lips--"was this mouth and how perfect it fit with mine."

If only he knew...later the same night, I'd fallen into bed with Keaton and ended up dating him. "It was a long time ago, Simon."

"Not for me, Dani. For me, that's the moment I knew loving you wasn't my choice. It's my destiny, and I'll do it for the rest of my life, no matter what happens between us. I will always wait for you."

"Yeah. You waited for me with Kelly. God, I wanted to hurt you so bad. I couldn't think of anything else." Our relationship did not need any more of my drunken admissions, but the words poured out. "I really did go to help Keaton. He was so broken. But boy did I want you to know where I was at. I wanted you all to think I'd made him my love slave."

I shook my head and tried to suck the last drops of whiskey from the bottom of the bottle. Nothing. "Still, no matter what I did, he would *not* give it up. I tried for a while. But he loved her so much. I watched him die a little bit every day. So, I did what any good friend would do. I talked him into trying to win her back. Somehow, he turned it all around and convinced me to come home to see you. I hauled my butt across two countries to find you playing kissy face with Lizette, the Amazon baker." An admission like that deserved another drink. I pushed him off the chair and swayed to a half stance, holding onto the arm for support. When the world stopped spinning, I staggered to the door. I turned to face him and bumped into his chest. "I mean, logistically, how did it work? Isn't she like seven foot tall?"

He wrapped his arms around me and pulled me back to the chair. "Six, and I'm still taller." He used his thumb and forefinger to indicate the fraction of an inch he had on her.

"Oh. Are you sure?"

He had such a great laugh. "Yeah."

I leaned into him and closed my eyes. "You were the guy I always wanted, Simon."

Chapter 16

For the next week, Simon, as my big protector, watched me drink every stashed and locked-up drop of alcohol I could get. Every night, he put me to bed, and when I awoke, we started the cycle all over again.

"Why are you still here?"

"I hate to miss a good pity party." He shrugged his shoulders.

"Well, gear up, big fella, because you're in for a treat today. I found the key to my dad's wine cellar, and I am holding a bottle of Chardonnay *dying* to be opened." It took me three tries before I got the screw into the bottle's neck, but finally, with a few quick twists and a determined pull, the cork hissed free with a quiet pop. The fine aroma of Italian grapes delighted my nasal passages.

"I have a surprise for you."

"Oh, good. I love surprises. Can't get enough of those." I rolled my eyes and swayed backward.

His body, close enough my back rubbed against his chest, prevented my fall. "I know. And I went all out for this one." With a hand on each shoulder, he propelled me away from the counter.

"Well, spectacular planning, then." Over my shoulder, I toasted him with the bottle as he steered me through the kitchen. He opened the door and pushed me through. My mouth hanging open had a direct correlation to the rest of my appendages becoming useless and immobile. I blinked a couple of times, unsure of the message my eyes were sending my brain.

"Hey, Dani."

Keaton. Had I really sank so low Simon felt he should bring Keaton in on this whole debacle? Of course, I had.

He reached out a hand I ignored as I brushed past both of them. With a look at Simon, he shook his head. "I'm probably going to end up divorced over this."

"No, you won't. I'll handle Jocelyn. You handle this one."

Keaton nodded, then turned his entire body to face me. "Wow. You look frightening."

"Who asked you?" I weaved my way to a chair at the table and sat heavily as I flipped him off. "Keep your 'pinions to yourself, Keats. I'm not drunk enough to not care what you think about me." I took a big gulp and grinned. "Hang in there, though. It won't be long."

"Have you been feeding her?" He ignored me and looked over at Simon.

"She won't eat. Just drinks herself to sleep."

"Obviously not a big fan of hair brushing, either." His dry tone should have inspired some sort of reaction, yet I couldn't produce more than a pointed finger in his direction. I looked down at my bottle and focused on the flavor of the wine as I swished it in my mouth. He put a hand on my shoulder. "Wanna talk about it?"

"Nope." I turned my body halfway, his stomach at my eye level. After a moment of searching, I found his face. "Why don't you hate me, Keaton?" It was a question I had been dying to ask him since I returned home.

He stroked the top of my head. "You saved my life." He crouched down beside my chair, cupped my cheek in his hand. "And now it is time for me to return the favor. Give me the wine."

"No."

"Come on."

"Get your own, Keaton." I pulled the bottle to my side, thinking I could keep it from him.

With a smile, he wrestled it away and emptied the wine out on the cool concrete, then pulled a chair up next to mine as Simon stood back, arms crossed, and watched. "You wanna tell me about it?"

"Yes, you moron. It was a three hundred dollar bottle of wine--semi-sweet with an oaky finish and just a hint of buttery tones.... And I really wanna smack you for pouring it out."

"Yeah. I remember that feeling." He took my hand for a gentle squeeze. "I seem to recall you pouring three bottles of Jack Daniels down the drain."

I glared at him for a moment before a sob I didn't expect bubbled up and out of my mouth. "I am not a good person. I'm a terrible friend, an awful mom. I didn't protect my baby and now my parents had to take him away, because even here, in the fortress of solitude, I can't keep Sean away from him."

He pulled my chair closer to his and threw an arm around my shoulders. "Dani, you got him out of there. You *did* protect him. You saved him from whatever worse things that bastard could have done to him."

"I don't know if he's ever going to smile again, or laugh. God, what have I done? He can't ever be carefree again. He'll always have *that* look from *that* memory of what Sean did." Tears streamed down my face. "Of what I did."

Keaton brushed his palm along my cheek, then raked his fingers into my hair. "You didn't do it, but you're the only one who can *un*do it." He petted me as though I belonged to the feline community rather than the human one. "You made him strong, Dani. You made him brave, and he'll get through this."

My shoulders slumped. I couldn't imagine a time where I'd ever believe his words.

"Hey." He tilted my chin up. "There is something magical about you. You slayed the dragon and he knows it." He grinned and brushed away a stray tear from my cheek with his thumb. "You're the super hero in his story. We should get you a cape, and some tights. Maybe a hair brush."

I half smiled, then frowned again. "I let him get hurt. A mother, a *good* mother, doesn't do that." I spun away from Keaton and came face to face with Simon. Walking toward the house seemed like a good idea. There was a whole cellar full of wine in there.

"Well, you can't help him like this, and you can't beat Sean if you're going to spend all your time too drunk to stand. Do you really want Kieran to grow up with a drunk for a mom?"

When I caught a glimpse of myself in the glass, I let go of the doorknob and lifted a hand to smooth my hair, but my fingers became tangled in a knot hours of conditioning wouldn't remove. "Wow. I look bad."

"You look like you gave up." Keaton came to stand beside me, arms crossed, head down. "You know, you have a lot of people here who will help you if you let them." At my nod, he chuckled. "Now, go get cleaned up so the argument I'm going to have to suffer through with my wife isn't all for nothing." He grinned. "Besides, if I don't quit pawing you, your boyfriend over there"--he nodded toward Simon--"is probably going to push me in the pool."

"I doubt that."

Keaton shook his head and moved closer. "You're such a dumb girl." He bumped his shoulder into mine, then reached out to prevent me from face planting into the concrete. "He couldn't leave you, Dani." He leaned closer. "You told me once you wanted someone to love you the way I love Joss. All you have to do is let him."

My smile caught on a sob.

"And maybe take a shower."

Melissa Shirley

"Shut up, Keaton."

He hugged me one more time. "You good?"

I nodded.

"No more drinking, okay? Promise?"

"I promise."

"Good. Now, get cleaned up and give him a reason to stay."

After I showered, combed my hair, and brushed the stale wine taste from my mouth, I curled my hair, and picked out clean clothes. I'd lost a bit of weight, and they hung looser than they had a week earlier. *Shit.* Oh well. I could buy new clothes, but I could never replace Simon. And God knew I'd tried.

I trudged slowly downstairs unsure how he would react to last week's events, but I could almost stand up straight and not bob or weave into the walls. Maybe that would be enough.

He stood in front of the stove with a spoon in one hand and a spatula in the other. Plates and bowls along with silverware gleamed under the lights over the counter. The flames from two tapered candles in crystal holders danced in the middle.

"You look pretty." He brought my hand to his lips before leading me to a stool.

"You're easy to please." *Thank God.*

His eyes crinkled at the corners as he snapped my mother's linen napkin through the air before placing it in my lap. "I made grilled cheese and French fries."

My stomach flopped and I shook my head.

He cocked his head to the side. "It's good drunk food."

"Oh." I followed him to the stove, slipped my arms around his waist, and laid my cheek against his back as he flipped the sandwich. "Thank you."

"It's just grilled cheese." He laid a hand over mine as I squeezed him.

"No. It's you." I loosened my grip so he could turn. On my tiptoes, I tried to press a kiss against his upturned lips, but I only reached his chin. "I don't remember you being this tall."

He leaned over and kissed the tip of my nose. "I don't remember much of anything."

Being with Simon made me more whole than I'd been since I first left Storybook Lake, and more vulnerable than the last time he'd dumped me. I stared up at him for a few seconds, pondering how I'd ever be able to keep him. I'd messed up everything in my life so badly; I wouldn't have blamed him if he walked away right then…. But he wouldn't. Sean or not, I wouldn't let him.

The reasons he'd left me before no longer existed. I'd changed from the semi-spoiled, more-evil-than-I-cared-to-admit-girl who used my body for her own wicked pleasures. Not that the new version of myself had turned out much better, but the old reasons--my mean girl, don't-give-a-crap-life decisions--had been dispensed with. Warm realization spread through me. With Simon, I had a chance for the happiness Sean promised and never delivered. It might have been a chance I didn't particularly deserve, but if I didn't grab onto it with both hands and hang on as long as I could, it would be my own fault if he left me. I had to tell him.

As I opened my mouth to bust out my secret, he brushed his soft lips across mine and I held on, deepening the kiss, need pooling in my stomach. With one hand on my hip and the other tangled in my hair, he walked me backward until I leaned against the counter. He lifted me so I sat on the cool granite and we were eye to eye. Everything I needed to say was forgotten. Only Simon existed in that moment. Only he mattered.

"Dani."

The whisper spurred me on as I left a trail of kisses down his neck. Something about this man captivated me, and I couldn't let go, even as the smoke alarm shrilled.

"I think your sandwich is finished."

"I don't care."

Chapter 17

We didn't fall into bed that night. And the decision to walk away tested my willpower in ways I'd never known. After some serious making out in the kitchen, we chit chatted over lunch. More than once I thought of telling him about Kieran, but I wanted to say it the right way. Or maybe, I was selfish and wanted more time with him before I dared risk losing him over a secret I never meant to keep. Maybe I just wanted him to see me in this version of myself.

It didn't escape me that the longer I remained quiet about it, the worse the fallout would be. I imagined a nuclear war reality more than once. That was the dystopian feeling I always experienced when I thought of losing Simon. It should have been enough to get me to talk to him, but no. Instead, I sat beside him with his arm around my shoulders. I grinned like a hopeless fool. We watched a couple movies, ate dinner, then watched more TV. Sometime close to dawn, I went up to bed. Alone.

I spent a long time thinking of Simon while he slept downstairs on the sofa. Everything about him seemed effortless. His smiles were easy-- never had to be coaxed or pulled. His wit came quick, his courage without a second thought. Even his recovery from a bullet tearing though his brain had progressed with a speed doctors took dubious credit for.

The problem in our relationship hadn't been with him. I'd been exactly the person Jocelyn believed, worse even, and no matter how hard I wished to be better, I hadn't changed. He deserved more.

I hadn't planned to split up Joss and Keaton, not consciously, anyway. Maybe it had been my subconscious kissing him. Or maybe, I was so damaged I couldn't help but to let my need for vengeance take over. Or there was always the lead paint excuse I'd used as a kid. Either way, Simon deserved better. I wanted to believe I'd grown into something more than an evil teenager, hell-bent on her own destruction, as well as everyone else within striking distance. But considering the lies I clung to like a rope while I hung off a mountain, I couldn't be sure.

I threw the blanket back, thoughts of Simon heating my room in ways that had nothing to do with the ambient temperature. After a little while of sweating through my memories, I stood and started pacing. I wanted to earn the right to be with him and the thoughts racing inside my head-- Simon, sleeping steps away, the fun ways I could wake him, the way his body fit with mine--did nothing to help me calm down.

Finally, I flung the door open and tiptoed to the living room. This was the moment. I was going to tell him. No more hiding the truth. No more. Period. I couldn't have Simon with this lie standing between us, mocking me. If he left, I earned it. If he stayed, I would know it was the right thing. I stood at the bottom of the steps watching his chest rise and fall with each breath. After a moment, I started forward, walking until my knees brushed the blanket half covering his stomach and legs.

Reaching out a shaky hand, I ran my fingers through his hair. A slow smile spread across his lips. "If this is a dream, I don't want to wake up." He slid his fingers up my arm and laced them through mine in his hair, then brought my hand down for a kiss. "Lay by me?"

Oh, the temptation. I wanted so badly to be worthy of him, to build this relationship on more than sex and my need for protection. On the other hand, I wanted Simon. I wanted to feel his skin pressed against mine, to run my hands over his etched stomach muscles.... I shook it off. That particular train of thought would lead me down the wrong track....

I squeezed his hand and gave him a good tug. "Can we talk?"

He closed his eyes for a second, then sat up. After taking a moment to stare at me, he patted the spot next to him.

I swallowed hard and pointed over my shoulder to the recliner. "I should probably maintain a safe distance."

"If you don't want me, Dani, I'm not going to force you."

"Not wanting you isn't the issue. Trust me." I sat beside him and turned my body so my knee pressed into his hip. The blanket slipped to his lap, leaving his chest bare for a long, mouth-watering perusal. I curled my fingers into my palm to keep from reaching out. "Seriously, not the issue."

We sat quietly for a long time, staring out into the muted light of a sunrise hidden behind a rainstorm, before he chuckled. "Great talk, babe. I think we got a lot ironed out here, don't you?"

I took a big, loud breath, trying to organize my thoughts. Instead of calmly telling him, I blurted, "I want you."

He grinned, tangled his fingers in my hair, and laid a kiss on me that had me ready to throw all my good intentions into the wind. His lips brushed across mine, then struck with an intensity I was too Simon-weak to fight. I slipped a hand over his heart, the wild beat beneath my palm as exciting as his tongue caressing mine. His fingertips massaged the back of my scalp and I fell away. Earth and gravity no longer held me. My entire universe narrowed until only he mattered--the perfect, lovable, and infinitely strong Simon.

I gathered the mental will I had left and pulled away. "I don't want to just fall into bed with you."

His lips on my neck stilled. "It's a couch."

"You know what I mean."

He brought his head from beneath the veil of my hair, closed his eyes, and reclined against the armrest. His chest puffed with a deep breath followed by another, then a third. When he'd used an unfair proportion of oxygen, he sat up and clasped his hands in front of him. "What's up, Dani?"

Before I could think to stop it, my eyes ventured to his lap. I bit my lip as he pulled the blanket into a bunch, covering the evidence of how much he wanted me.

"Don't stare. You'll make me self-conscious."

I lifted my gaze to find his smile. He'd never been a man affected by a single second of shyness. "Sorry." Heat crawled up my cheeks.

After a moment, a grin spread over his face. "Okay. So, you didn't come down here for sex. Is there a discussion in there somewhere we need to have?"

I nodded, trying to keep my eyes on his, on anything above his waist. "Yes."

He waited a few seconds. "Should I start?"

With Simon, I could never tell where the conversation would end up if he started it, but I nodded.

He cupped my cheek with his palm. "I know you've been hurt, Dani, but I never dreamed"--he rolled his eyes and wobbled his head from one side to the other--"okay, I did dream of having you back here with me. I have spent most of the last few years remembering being in love with you, and I don't want to do anything to run you off like I did before."

"You didn't--"

"It's not your turn." He put a finger over my lips. "We don't have to sleep together. I will be happy holding you or looking at you from across the room as long as I know you're not thinking of leaving or being with anyone else." He grinned. "I might walk a little funny for a while. I still have this horny teenager thing going on."

I fell a little more in love with him with every word he spoke. "I don't want our relationship to be tainted by this Sean thing. I have been buried under him and all his crap for such a long time. I want this"--my hand waved between us--"to be more than just…" I didn't want to diminish all the things I felt for him by labeling it as something tawdry, but I couldn't find a way to get the words out. "There are some things you don't know."

He nodded. "They don't matter to me. You are the only thing I care about. Nothing is going to tear us apart again."

The devil on my shoulder won this one. If we were together, anyway, maybe it didn't matter. He would be a part of Kieran's life. How important was it to make it official?

"We could lay here and listen to the rain."

In a tangle of arms and legs, we cuddled until long after the rain quit, holding on to the perfection of the moment, the peaceful quiet of the house; the thing we'd lost so many times before.

Chapter 18

A month or so after my parents and Kieran returned home, I hadn't heard any more from Sean. So, with a false sense of safety guiding me, I decided to buy my own place. I had the money thanks to my "little clothes business" and nothing to spend it on, so I found a cute little Snow White cottage in the fairy tale section of town--a half mile from my parents. It wasn't because I didn't love or appreciate all they'd done for me. This was the new start I wanted for Kieran, one to dispel the bad memories with new ones in our own house. I wanted a place of my own, privacy, a place where Simon and I could be together without my mother busting in on us with fake offerings of cookies or beverages.

For all of ten minutes, life rolled on without any of the big speed bumps usually contorting my every day. Before I waved the truck into the driveway, a process server met me at the sidewalk and handed me a blue-backed set of papers. Sean had initiated a custody suit.

Grace, my high school best friend and the only lawyer I knew not in California, said not to worry about it. No court in the world would ever give Sean custody, or even a minute of visitation if she could help it, but the prospect of such a monster coming near my son caused panic attacks, horror-filled nightmares, and an almost constant hand tremor.

It took three intense therapy sessions with my mother before we figured out the trembling stemmed from Sean knowing where I lived. He'd known enough to send the process server to my brand new address.

Yet, life went on. Once people discovered I'd come back to town--another newsletter announced my home purchase--invitations poured in for social engagements I never dreamed I'd be invited to. Having Simon as my bodyguard went a long way to smoothing everything with the town.

A few days after I moved in, Gatlin Reid's birthday party invite, addressed to me and Simon, arrived. I'd said I would go, but standing in my living room the night of the party, I changed my mind, and doubts negated the fact I'd spent more than an hour on my hair and makeup.

"I don't want to go to a party where I have to see your sister and Keaton, Simon." How could he even suggest such a thing? I'd almost single-handedly destroyed their relationship--mostly out of pure spite. While Keaton had forgiven me, from past experience, I knew Jocelyn could hold a grudge. The chances of a party brawl were all too real. It didn't inspire me to want to go to a place where we would be shoved together in a room while a member of their circle celebrated his party-boy pants off.

Simon and I squared off in my living room, arguing over whether or not we would be going. Kelly, Simon's ex (another reason to say home) had phoned earlier in the day, before my butterflies came calling, to ask if we'd be there. I hadn't done her or Gatlin wrong and she promised, even though the guest list included Keaton and Jocelyn, it would be fine. With a clearer knowledge of our past and a slightly crooked nose thanks to Joss's fist, I didn't buy it for a second. However, even before she moved away and came back, I believed Kelly saw the world through the rosiest pair of glasses ever invented. She probably honestly thought Jocelyn could let bygones be bygones as long as I made Simon happy.

"I talked to Joss." He grabbed my coat off the wall tree by the front door and held it out like a matador's cape in front of a charging bull.

"And how many times did the word *bitch* come up in the conversation?"

He grinned. "Only once or twice. It was really tame by Jocelyn standards."

I turned and started for the bedroom to throw on a pair of old sweats, but he propelled me back to him with a hand on my elbow. He licked his bottom lip and I smiled. "Come on. If it's too uncomfortable, we'll leave." He waved the jacket again.

I shook my head and crossed my arms. Okay. I'd sent Kieran to my parents' and spent the afternoon ignoring work in favor of getting dressed. My intricate up-do elongated my disproportionately short neck. Black patent stilettos added a good four inches to my height. Yet, with no reason other than fear not to attend, I stood my ground.

Right up to the moment he blinked his beautiful amber eyes at me and my heart melted. His eyes did me in every time, made my hands tremble, my heart quiver, and my stomach tighten in delightful anticipation. "Okay. We can go, but if it gets ugly, I'll probably never forgive you."

He wiggled his eyebrows and pulled me against him, wrapping his arms around my waist. "I have ways of making you surrender to my will."

I had one hand in his hair and one on the hard lines etched beneath the tuxedo shirt, and my breathing quickened. Yeah. He had methods--crazy, exciting methods of holding out on me.

He drove toward the Munie building, holding my hand and chattering over things I ignored as I crushed my bag in my other hand. I hadn't seen these people since I moved back to town with the exception of Keaton and Simon. The butterflies in my stomach flapped like bats on speed.

As we walked in, a dozen pair of eyes zeroed in on my face. The bruises had faded long ago, and I looked the same as always, but people stared as though I'd forgotten my clothes. I clutched his arm until he leaned over beside me. "Hey, Simon, it's kind of uncomfortable."

He squeezed my hand. "They can't believe how beautiful you are. Come on. Let's get a drink." He tugged me farther into the room. "You'll see. It'll be fine."

We stood in front of the bar holding daiquiris with little umbrellas and a distinct lack of rum as Gatlin captured me in a hug from behind. "Just the drama girl my party needs." His whisper tickled my ear. "I heard you were in town. Come to make an honest man out of our boy?"

I glanced over at Simon who had his eyebrows raised, also apparently awaiting my answer. "I heard you went straight." I turned to face Gatlin. Dressed in a dapper black tuxedo, his normally iridescent hair had been dyed a magical brown that brought out the glow in his olive- toned skin. For years, he'd pretended to be gay as a marketing ploy for his beauty shop. He never had been, and I had the insider information to prove it. More insider than I cared to remember, and nothing I wanted to come to light.

He laughed a real laugh. "You've been gone way too long, sweetness. I roared back into the closet and, now, I'm on the prowl for a lovely single lady to blow out my birthday candle."

I made a face at him. "I hope that isn't your pick-up line."

He shook his head. "Oh, baby, I do not need lines. And if I did, I only use those on the single girls." He waved a finger in front of my face and nodded to Simon, who was talking to the bartender. "And clearly, you are not single."

"You never know. I've always found your particular brand of masculine very attractive."

"You never noticed me. I wasn't even a blip on your radar. You were all wrapped up in the pretty boys. Never had time for me." He pretended to pout.

"Fishing for compliments. I expected better."

"And I'm waiting for my compliment."

I over-exaggerated my sigh and rolled my eyes. "Fine. I don't think there's anyone in this town who could ignore how pretty you truly are. It sparkles from the inside. Men and women alike imagine not only spending the night with you, but being you. You are--"

"Enough already. You're making me blush." He bowed slightly, then pulled a strand of hair away from my head, inspecting the curl. "And might I just say, I've never seen Simon happier than when you showed up in town."

Behind us, Simon laughed at a joke someone else told.

"I don't know. He seems a little depressed these days."

Someone called out to Gatlin, and he leaned in to kiss my cheek. "I must mingle. Save me a dance."

"Happy birthday."

Simon handed me another alcohol-free drink and smiled. "See? Gatlin's happy you're here." He led me away from the bar as I opened my mouth to tell him I wanted to leave. "Did I tell you how beautiful you look?"

I'd designed a simple dress made of the softest crushed velvet with wide shoulder straps and a diamond studded belt at the empire waist. He was wearing a black three-piece tuxedo with a black silk tie over a crisp black shirt. Black was definitely his color.

Instead of voicing my desire to run home and hide, I smiled and ran a finger down his chest. "Well, it's tough to keep up with you."

"I should have let you convince me to stay in tonight." He clasped his hands at the small of my back and leaned in for a kiss. Lost in the moment, it took a second after he pulled away for my vision to clear and notice Kelly standing beside us.

"Hey, Kell." He stood at my side again, his arm still cradling my waist, and his thumb drawing a lazy back and forth trail on my ribcage.

Kelly leaned in. "Your sister is here, and she doesn't look too happy with you."

He shrugged as though he couldn't have cared less. "She'll get over it." But he lowered his eyes and downed his drink. Hmm. For all his big talk, he had a nervous tic to one eye as the always radiant Jocelyn stopped to talk to Gatlin.

"She's making her way over here." I resisted the urge to hide behind his broad shoulders.

Simon lifted his chin a notch higher, poked a finger between his collar and his throat, then tilted his head to the side as Kelly spoke to me. "Don't worry. She's all bark."

I nodded as Keaton and Jocelyn approached.

"Joss, you look really pretty tonight." Simon ignored her glare by turning to shake hands with Keaton. "How's it going?"

Keaton chuckled. "I guess we'll see in a minute."

Jocelyn aimed her displeasure at him a second before pointing it at me. "How long are you staying this time?"

"I bought a house." What more did I need to say? People who purchased real estate didn't usually up and leave.

"And there goes the neighborhood." Her mouth turned downward, and she rolled her eyes.

"Jocelyn." Simon shot her the one-eyebrow-cocked-scowl. She mirrored the look, and the tension in his fingers cut off my circulation. I pried his hand away, then flexed mine a few times before shaking the blood back into it.

"Joss and Keaton just bought a gorgeous place on Mother Goose Drive." Leave it to Kelly to try to give us a common ground to stand on.

"Oh, what a pretty neighborhood." I faked a smile, but I reached around and pinched Simon. At this point, he'd be lucky if he got a good night kiss ever again.

Keaton grinned. "This is going well. Don't you think, Joss?"

"Dandy." Clearly, Keaton wouldn't be getting any that night, either.

"Simon"--Keaton's boy band grin was still firmly in place--"let's go check out the food. All this woman drama stresses me out, and you know, when I'm stressed, I eat." And when he was happy…and sad…and tired…and wired, he ate.

Simon silently asked permission with his eyes. I nodded and received a kiss on the cheek for my trouble before he followed his best friend to a banquet table across the room. Jocelyn regarded me with the wariest gaze I'd ever seen as she took three steps away.

"Joss, wait." I held my breath as she faced me. Kelly sucked in a loud breath. "I know, okay? I wouldn't forgive me, either, but we both live here and neither one of us is looking to move away."

"And your point is?"

"My point is…" I swallowed hard. "I'm sorry." I'd never apologized to her before and figured it couldn't hurt the situation to try un-burning our bridge.

"It takes more than words, Danielle." The crunched gravel of her voice ground out past her clenched teeth, but it didn't deter my hope that someday, probably not soon, she would soften toward me.

Kelly stepped around us to the bartender. "Three shots of tequila." Obviously, Kelly was either unaware or didn't care I'd jumped on the path to reformation. Standing with Jocelyn's anger in my face, I didn't care too much for reformation myself.

"Great plan, Kell. Tequila is just what two angry chicks who hate each other need." Jocelyn had one hand on her hip. The other accepted the drink.

"Yeah, Kelly. Pure genius." I didn't necessarily want to agree with Jocelyn, but my mind flashed with pictures of us engaged in one of those drunken girl-fights so popular on the Internet.

The flaw in Kelly's reasoning didn't stop us from accepting the next three rounds after the first. We walked outside together for some fresh air.

"How did all of this start between you two?" Kelly swayed as she held the door open for us, and Jocelyn reached out and grasped her around the waist. They took two tilted steps together.

I plopped down on the stairs outside the front double doors. Kelly sat between Jocelyn and me.

"She pushed me in a puddle in kindergarten, then she told everyone I pooped in my pants." Jocelyn frowned, puffed out her lower lip. "They called me poopy butt until fifth grade."

"That is *not* what happened." *How dare she blame this on me?* Our feud started months before the mud puddle incident. I leaned around Kelly to give Jocelyn my best version of the stink eye. "Yes, it is."

When satisfied we had both achieved a modicum of stability, I looked at Jocelyn. "No. No. It is not. We need to correct your warped little memory, right now."

"There is nothing warped about my memory. Trust me. Poopy-butt is not a name a girl forgets."

"I'm not saying I didn't push you. It was one of the highlights of first grade for me. I'm saying it all started long before your ass ever got wet. Don't you remember? You had your stupid slumber party, and I sat home and cried my heart out because my bestest friend didn't like me anymore." My own speech slurred, but I continued undaunted by my inability to be coherent. "You had these really cute Strawberry Shortcake invitations. And you gave them to everybody but me." As though it had happened only a week earlier, hurt surged through me, and I sniffed as I blinked back tears threatening to ruin my mascara.

Kelly looked from one of us to the other. "This can't-be-in-the-same-time-zone thing started over a mud puddle and a Strawberry Shortcake slumber party?" She shook her head. "Un-freaking-believable."

I shrugged, but Jocelyn stood, staggered a step, then popped her hands on her hips. "I am not going to sit here and pretend like we're friends. You slept with my husband."

She had her facts wrong, again. "No. Joss. I didn't. I tried everything, but your man is in love with you, and he always has been. I couldn't budge the lock he put on his zipper. Nobody is ever getting in there but you."

She shook her head and stared out at the sprinklers watering the lawn in front of us. "Bullshit, Dani."

I held up a hand. "I swear. I couldn't get him drunk enough to forget about you. I tried."

"I'm sure you did." But something in her tone--hope, maybe--said otherwise.

I shrugged one shoulder. "Whatever. It's true."

Kelly hiccupped, then looked up at Jocelyn. "I always thought you were taller." She shook her head and stood. "He wasn't your husband whether she slept with him or"--her gaze slid from Jocelyn across to me--"not. You weren't with him and you forgave him, Joss. You should forgive her too." Her words fell on Jocelyn's back as she stalked to the door. Although, she held it open so we could enter behind her. She'd probably hoped only Kelly would follow, but she didn't slam it shut when I came through. I took it as a peace offering.

We wobbled inside in heels far too high for tequila shooters to have been a good idea. Simon and Keaton still stood in front of the banquet tables gazing open-mouthed at the giant ice sculpture rendering of Gatlin's anatomically correct, naked body dripping into a large silver pool. All the quitting, drinking, then drinking, then quitting, drinking, and drinking again played hell with my system, and I swayed unsteadily. Keaton shot me a look I shrugged off. Jocelyn took her place by her husband, who planted a sweet kiss on the edge of her upturned nose. Gatlin joined the group, then whisked me away to the far end of the dance floor. As he pulled me close, I put one hand on his shoulder and he laced our fingers together.

"I wondered when all that Simon love would bring you back to town."

"Here I am," I slurred, leaning heavily into him.

"Jocelyn looks happy to see you."

"Pfft. I haven't ever seen her when she didn't look like was training for the Suck-A-Lemon Olympics. Tell me you don't need more proof than her puss-puss face?"

"The air in the room changed when she got her first look of you. It's good for her. Sometimes, we need reminded we aren't universally loved." He grinned. "Except me."

"Of course."

As we danced, he filled me in on the trials and tribulations of living in small town America as though I hadn't grown up here. He moved from subject to subject until he got to Kelly. Then, his stance grew more rigid, his face colored with a dreamy she-is-too-good-for-me-look only guys who experience unrequited love in the movies get, and the tone in his voice dropped from happy to wistful. Apparently, Gatlin itched to evolve his way out of best-friend-zone with Kelly.

"You okay there, pal?"

He craned his neck and popped his eyes wide. "Of course. Why would you dare ask?"

I grinned. "You love Kelly?" I said the words in tune to a sing-song nursery rhyme. And I repeated them twice more.

"Of course I do. She's my best friend."

Ah, but his cheeks colored and the irrepressible Gatlin Reid couldn't meet my gaze. "Gatlin?"

He wobbled his head from side to side. "Maybe I could see us together in a way that's more hearts and flowers than basketball games and girl talk, but I need to know some stuff before I can even entertain a thought of being with her."

"You've been entertaining thoughts all night, haven't you?"

His warm breath tickled my ear as he whispered, "I never told anyone about that night."

I patted his cheek. "Thanks, buddy."

"But I have a calculator and a science book. Before I can move on with Kelly, I need to know."

My mouth dropped open. It flat amazed me how many men were willing to step up and take responsibility for a child who might not have been theirs.

"Gatlin--"

Rather than ask me the question I assumed he wanted the answer to, he grinned. "Does he look like me?"

A chuckle bubbled through my lips. "Not even a little bit."

He blew out in a loud whoosh. "Oh, thank God. I am not dad material." He took a hanky from his pocket and wiped a few droplets of sweat from his brow. "Seriously, what a relief."

I smiled and we turned a few more times, sloshing the alcohol in my stomach. He stopped mid-step. "I told you. You're so taken." He stepped aside as Simon pulled me close.

I ran a hand over his upper arm to his shoulder and around to wind a loose strand of his hair around my finger.

His chest rose as he breathed in deeply and fell as he released the air.

I rested my ear against his chest. "Did you sniff my hair?" I looked up at him.

"Of course not." Then he smiled down at me. "Maybe a little."

I laughed and he spun us. Jocelyn eyed us from her spot at the table. "Did you and Jocelyn finally get everything worked out?"

Being in his arms made me not care and I shrugged. "I doubt we'll ever get everything worked out, but we might be able to live in the same town without becoming an episode of *Cops.*"

He pulled a hand from my waist and caressed my cheek with his thumb. After an intense moment of gazing into my eyes, he lowered his head to deliver a toe-curling kiss.

Whether the alcohol, the kiss, or his arms holding me so gently affected my perceptions, I floated on a cologne-scented cloud of Simon and nothing, not his sister, or my big secrets, or my husband, could drag me back to the surface.

When he pulled away, he leaned his forehead against mine. "How could I have ever chosen anyone else over you?"

I smiled, caught up in the what-could-have-been of the moment. "I was a different person then." My face heated as much with shame as embarrassment. "I've changed a lot since I had Kieran."

"I wish I remembered more."

I snuggled closer, my hands creeping inside the tux with him. "I'm glad you don't."

Chapter 19

Our little chat outside turned out to be a big fat waste of time. Jocelyn didn't warm toward me at all. She and Keaton stayed on one side of the room while Simon and I hung out on the other. Our men took turns having Gatlin race between us all, trying to keep everyone happy. Between the two groups, he probably walked ten miles at his own party.

I ended up having a lot more fun than I expected, between dancing and the giant ice sculpture falling onto its back halfway through the night. The last month had been peaceful, and I got complacent, forgot someone out there had been waiting for me to relax. I stopped watching over my shoulder.

It took one phone call to remind me of the far-reaching effects of my life with Sean. It came as I walked, heart pounding, from Simon's car to my front porch. Across the front of my stone house, in reflective orange paint, someone had written the word "whore." I read the poorly designed graffiti while my phone chirped inside my bag.

After yanking the purse open, I barked my answer without so much as a consulting glance at the screen. "Hello."

"Honey, I redecorated." Sean's drunken purr fed the flames seething inside me. "Do you like it?"

If I'd checked the caller ID, I would have answered quite differently. "You painted my house? What the hell, Sean?" The fury lacing every syllable almost replaced my fear until I realized if he'd done it, he was close. I spun from facing the ugly word to run down the sidewalk, looking up and down the street for an odd car or the telltale glow of a cell phone screen. Finding nothing off about the quiet in front of me, I focused on his words.

"Don't be a silly goose." Another of Sean's personalities came out for show and tell. "I don't paint. And I damned sure as hell wouldn't paint your house." He said it with the disdain of a man who thought any form of manual labor to be beneath him. "But I had it done just for you."

This had turned into a fun little game for him, a way to abuse me from across the country.

"Why are you doing this?"

His other personality--the angry one--made its appearance. "You stood before God and said we would be a family."

Had I not been choked by anguish, I may have actually laughed aloud at the irony of his words. "I stood before Elvis. And you hurt my son." Every time I said the words, my heart shifted in my chest and my stomach clenched. Hearing Sean, though, having him laugh at me the way he did when we fought, before he hit me, had my knees trembling as I walked to the house.

"He's my son too."

"No, no he's not, and if you think I would ever let you near him again, you're crazier than I thought." And that would have been a tough achievement.

He huffed out a drunken puff-puff through the phone speaker.

I pictured his face contorted in anger, his eyes bulging, the veins of his neck straining against his skin.

"You talk really big, like I won't get to you. Do you really think your little boyfriend can stop me? Do you really think I couldn't kill you if I wanted you dead? Stupid bitch." He blew another breath out in my ear. "This is your last chance to come home. I will go a lot easier on you if you do it on your own than if I have to come and get you."

"I'm not coming back there, Sean." As a footnote to the sentence, I lowered my voice. "Ever."

"Well, then I guess I'll see you soon." His hiss chilled me from the inside out. He hung up.

I glared at the phone and unlocked my front door. Simon tried to stop me from going into the house with a hand around my wrist. I shook him off, stalked to the kitchen, and flung open the door to the cabinet, housing my newly acquired cleaning supplies.

"Dani, someone could be in here." I glared over my shoulder and he disappeared, presumably to check for an intruder who would be long gone by now. By the sound of things, he opened every cabinet, closet door, and curtain in his search for the mystery vandal. The lack of scuffle assured me he'd found no one.

"You okay?" His voice fell in soft curved tones, and his hand caressed my back as I stared into my cabinet.

"Do you know why I'm still here when he knows exactly where I am?" I slammed a mop bucket onto the counter and a bottle of pine cleaner. Next, I extracted a sponge and scrub brush, then smacked them on the counter.

"My charm? My amazing good looks? The idea that if you play your cards right, I will willingly lie down and be your love slave?"

I flung the door shut, ready to pounce on the way he made light of my very real danger, but when I looked up at him, the anger faded away. His smile was powerful enough to melt the panties off of a ninety five-year-old blind woman. The honesty in his eyes dispelled all other thoughts. "Love slave, huh?" I leaned against the granite counter top and crossed my arms.

He nodded and wiggled his eyebrows. As he took a step closer, he held out his hand and used it to pull me against him. Death could literally come knocking at my door, but I snuggled closer, drinking in the feel of the contours of his chest and the sound of the beat of his heart. He released the clip holding my hair, then ran his fingers through it, releasing the curls to flow over his arm. When he finished, he rested his hand at the nape of my neck and gently pressured my face to his. Our lips touched and the world stopped. Sound, light, danger, nothing existed but me, Simon, and one long rush of feeling.

Our mouths fused together as though welded by fire. After a few minutes, he drew away. "Why don't you let me clean the mess off the front of your house, then we can finish this?"

My senses always came to me at the worst times for my hormones. Further kissing, or touching, or being in the same room together could potentially get him killed. He'd been through enough, and I couldn't be the one who risked his life.

"Simon, I can clean it up myself. You should go home."

He cocked his head to one side and regarded me with eyes as full of promise as question. My resolve weakened. Sean hadn't left California as far as I knew. I hung on to the thought for a full minute before I decided hormones had no place making decisions in this situation. This being responsible business caused an ache in my chest no one ever warned me about, but I'd never survive if something happened to him because of the mess I'd gotten myself into. "Look, you already checked the house. I'm safe. Go home now."

"Danielle--"

"Please, Simon?"

"I can't just leave you here." He shook his head and crossed his arms. "I won't."

"Because what I want doesn't matter?" Didn't he get it? I couldn't stand to lose him again, especially if it turned out to be my fault.

"Because what you want is dangerous."

"I know what's best for me, and right now, it isn't having you here."

Hurt flashed through his eyes. "Fine." He stalked to the front door, flung it open, and slammed it shut behind him.

I ran hot water into the bucket, and in my evening gown, carried the cleaners and the bucket to the porch. The front of my house had been covered in a light stone in various sizes and textures. As the bright pumpkin-colored paint sliced through the different textures, the water did nothing to fade the color, only spread it into a blob.

This time, I went with a mixture of Tide and bleach. I scrubbed and scrubbed, until my arms ached and the detergent bleach mixture splotched my dress with an irregular polka dot pattern. Still, the stain remained. Three and a half hours later, I dropped the scrub brush into the bucket and gave up.

I left my supplies and went up to bed. Sleep came slowly in bursts of bad dreams. By the time the sun rose, every bone and muscle in my body screamed with each move I made, but I managed a shower and a cup of coffee before my phone rang. I checked the caller ID and threw the phone into the sink, not owning the kind of energy required to deal with Sean. Unfortunately, he had other ideas, and seven consecutive calls later, I snapped into the phone. "What do you want?"

"Rough night, Dani?" Sober, drunk, or stoned, his voice still inspired a round of shivers.

"Actually, I had a pretty nice night. I went to a birthday party. Had a little to drink, a few kisses in the moonlight." I summoned a bit of courage, and the bite to my tone softened by the real memories of my night.

"Slut."

I hung up.

He called back.

I put the phone in the drain and turned the water on. *Another new phone. Another new number.* I walked out to the front porch and leaned against the porch rail to stare at the ugliness of the neon colored brick while sipping my coffee. It wasn't hard to imagine glee on Sean's face as he thought of me and his plans for destruction.

I'd been standing for about twenty minutes when Kelly, Gatlin, and Simon arrived dressed in all manner of cleaning attire. A bandana matching the neon green of her T-shirt and spandex shorts held Kelly's hair away from her makeup free face. Gatlin's overalls, polo shirt, and straw hat gave him the appearance of a preppy farmer. Behind Kelly and Gatlin walked a musculature extravaganza--Simon in a pair of basketball shorts and a tank top, his arms bulked by years in the gym.

He shuffled from one foot to the other, and I wondered if he could possibly be as happy to see me as I was to see him. My stomach did a funky little dance when his tongue slipped across his bottom lip.

Without any fanfare or discussion, they attacked the front of my house with spray bottles, scrub brushes, and sheer determination. I helped as best I could, but my overnight exertions left me weak. Every lift of my arms higher than chest level caused a groan.

Kelly frowned, her fingers brushing against my shoulder. "Come on. Show me your house. I need a bathroom break and a beer."

I nodded and led her through the front door.

Before we'd made it three steps inside, she put a hand on my shoulder. "You okay?"

"Just a little sore." I rubbed my shoulder, wishing for a deep muscle massage, or a steaming hot bubble bath, or a tall glass of whiskey.

"Simon said you were out there until three-thirty in the morning."

How the hell did he know how long I'd been outside?

She smiled. "He has it bad, Dani. He isn't going to leave you alone here until he knows you're okay. He sat outside in his car last night to make sure no one bothered you." She plopped down at the counter. "Simon is afraid someone is going to get to you, and he won't be able to save you in time from across town."

For a guy who was supposed to be in love with me, Simon shared an awful lot with her. I squashed down a bubble of jealousy. "Oh." I didn't know what else to say.

"He wigged out when your phone went straight to voice mail this morning."

"I gave it a bath so it quit working." When her eyebrow cocked, I finished with, "Sean is a psycho caller." I shook my head, digesting what she'd said. "Simon sat out in his car staring at my house all night?"

"If you were outside, he was going to be there too, sleep or not." She smiled the slow Kelly Devlin smile that made men drop at her feet. "Plus, he has a thing now, since his accident. He doesn't sleep like the rest of us."

I couldn't keep Simon without putting him through more than he'd been through already. Pulling beers from the fridge, I wondered how many second chances God handed out. He'd already given one to Simon. What if God meant for him to only have the one? What if Sean got to him? What if…

When they finished, only a blob of smeared light orange (rather than bright orange) remained. We piled inside to drink another six-pack.

"So what are you going to do about this guy?" Gatlin had his hat splayed across his chest. He held his beer against his forehead.

Since I had no clue, I shrugged. "Isn't Jocelyn going to kick you all out of the club for talking to me?" I'd tried to smooth our rocky relationship somewhat. Joss refused, her grudge bigger than my apology.

Kelly chuckled. "Keaton's working on it as we speak. He's at home working on her honey-do list so he can talk her into coming out with all of us tonight." Her wide-circle arm wave included me, but I had no illusions left of my safety. Unpredictable as he'd always been, Sean could show up at any moment. Their safety would be compromised by being near me.

"I can't go out tonight." I stood to clear the empty bottles.

Kelly, a whirlwind of courage and energy, scoffed. "Oh, come on. Take Kieran to your Momma's--you know he'll be safe there--and come along." When I ignored her, she continued. "Do you have any idea how many single girls in this town are rubbing their grubby little mitts together, waiting for the first indication Simon is a free man? It's shameful really, the way they keep throwing themselves at him." She kicked Gatlin.

"Yeah. Pretty boy has a Facebook following that puts Brad Pitt to shame. Chicks love the scar."

Another bout of jealousy in my stomach warred with the idea of keeping him out of the line of Sean's long-armed fire. "Yeah, well, getting him killed is not my idea of showing my love for him." I shrunk a couple inches under the well-meaning gazes directed my way. "We have to be realistic here. I have so much baggage even my carry-on screams psychopath. He's better off with someone else."

Simon tilted his head to one side. "Maybe I should have some say in all this. I know exactly what I want." Softer he added, "What I've always wanted."

I'd made up my mind. "Simon, I'm not going out tonight or any night until this thing is cleaned up with Sean. He's got friends who're apparently here. Being with me is dangerous. Someone could get hurt." The zip in my tone should have warned him off. "*You* could get hurt." I sounded more like a mother warning a toddler away from the street than a girl who cared about someone she loved being killed.

"He already knows about me, already thinks I'm your boyfriend, so what difference does it make?"

Logic didn't help my turmoil. It added to it. "I don't want to have this conversation with you. I appreciate what you all did with the front of the house, but it's too dangerous for you to be here. Go." I hadn't meant for it to sound so harsh, but he sat back as though my words had given him a good hard chest shove.

"I'm not leaving. You can make me go outside if you want, but I'll still be here." He pointed beyond the front window. "Right out there."

My body warmed at the sight of Simon digging in his heels. Oh my. I had it bad. Unfortunately, one of us had to be the voice of reason.

Gatlin raised a tentative hand. "As enjoyably uncomfortable as it is to watch your little lovers' quarrel, I think I'm going to go sit in the peaceful quiet of a bubble bath." He patted me on the head as he passed. "Good luck, Simon."

"Thanks, G."

Kelly followed before he got his first foot out the door.

Simon and I stared at one another, neither willing to back down. Finally, I looked away. "Simon, do you have any idea what it would do to me if he hurt you?"

"Dani." He took my hand between his, brought it to his lips, and kissed my knuckles. "Do you have any idea what it would do to me if he hurt you?"

"I just think it would be better if we stayed away from each other until this is all over." My chest burned as the words hung in the air.

He gave me his best come-hither smile. I couldn't do anything but watch him--breathing seemed beyond my capabilities.

"I don't care for that idea." His lips brushed against my ear.

"I suppose you have a better plan?"

"Naturally." He pushed an errant strand of bottled blond off my forehead. "I believe we should spend all of our time together. Eat together. Sleep together. Hell, even the shower can be a very dangerous place, so we'll have to shower together."

I crossed my arms between us.

"The point is I can protect you." He grinned. "In return, you can entertain me." Mischief glinted in the adorable grin he used to get his way.

"What do I look like? A magician?" He wrapped me in his arms, then aimed his whiskey colored eyes into mine. Forgetting everything but him came easily. When his lips hovered within even a few feet of me, I didn't find it at all necessary to continue thinking.

"There is definitely something magical about you."

Ten minutes later, we were still wrapped around each other when my mother rang the bell, then poked her head in the door. We sprung apart like two teenagers caught at third base. Kieran burst inside chattering at lightning speed. "Grandpa said I can be a hobbit this weekend for the story festival. He said you can make my costume, and I can ride a pony in the parade. Will you make my costume? A hobbit with long, hairy feet?"

Finally, I saw a trace of the little boy he used to be. "Of course."

Chapter 20

I hadn't heard from Sean since the house painting incident, and Kieran and I settled into a routine. We played together every morning. He went to Mom's in the afternoon so I could work. In the evening, if Simon worked or was called out of town to investigate a fire, we ate alone. If Simon had a free night, he joined us. For a while, I believed Sean had given up. I got complacent again. Not that I didn't still lock the doors at night. I'd also nailed the windows shut, which drove my firefighter boyfriend into a tame rant at least once a week. But mostly, I didn't think about Sean or the danger of his ever coming to Storybook Lake.

It took exactly six months and eleven days for the last shreds of my peace of mind to be ripped away. I'd gone to bed early. It felt as though I'd just dropped off to sleep when I woke up panting and sweating, a scream dying on my lips, the smell of cigar smoke and sweat as prevalent as it had been in my dream. I wiped the salty moisture from my forehead with a trembling hand as I flopped back against my pillow. The digital clock read 3:07AM, but I reached for my bathrobe. Simon offered to sleep on the couch when he'd called earlier, but I declined. *Complacent.*

Aside from my no-fear outlook on life, I refused because the temptation to touch him, to tear his clothes off, itched through me whenever he so much as glanced my way. And since Sean hadn't signed the divorce papers, we were still in PG-13 land.

Maybe because the dream seemed so real, or because the lack of moon made the night so dark, or even because I had all but given up on sleep lately, I wished I'd taken him up on his offer. In the dark, the street lights cast eerie shadows on my walls.

I checked on Kieran, then walked into the kitchen, staring at the screen ID on my cell. *Un-freaking-believable.* Sean had to have some kind of magical power. I'd changed my number so many times since I returned to Storybook Lake, I almost applied for a job in the store. Somehow, he had it again.

I flipped on the light as I popped a pod into my coffee machine. When I had a fresh cup in front of me, I punched the envelope. A picture of me in the very pajamas I wore that night sleeping in my own bed filled my screen. I ran down the hall, dropping the phone on the way. Scooping my son into my arms, I took off almost before I had a good grip on his limp, sleeping little body. I drove like a pack of hungry wolves followed me, and I had a T-bone strapped to my back.

Finally, after what felt like hours of banging, the lights came on, and Dad stood in front of me in his bathrobe, rubbing his eyes and yawning in my face. In a burst of words, I told them what happened. Daddy forced me to let him take Kieran upstairs, even though I'd rather have died than let him out of my sight. When Dad returned, we sat in the kitchen deciding what to do next. Mom dropped her hand on my shoulder in comfort while Dad sat across from me in the same bathrobe he'd had since I got it for him in fifth grade. They took turns making suggestions--private security, a safe-house until the divorce became final, a trip abroad. In my family, decisions like this were made as a group rather than as an individual. Besides, I'd come running to them, drawn them into the center of the drama. It seemed only fair to let them have their say.

"Obviously," Dad said, "if you won't go out of town, you're going to stay here. We have a security system. Tomorrow, I'll ask Fred to keep an eye out." Fred Martin, our neighbor, had been feeble for as long as I could remember, but the man could shoot the wings off a fly at eighty paces. Dad considered Mom through his most apologetic eyes. "Honey, we need to cancel our trip to see Mary."

"No. Don't cancel. You guys should go. Take Kieran with you." Tears streaked down my cheeks. "I don't know what's going to happen, but I need to know he's safe so I can think straight without worrying about him."

"Of course, we'll take him. Don't you worry about Kieran. I'll protect him just the same as I will you." He pulled me into the best fatherly hug ever. When a sob jerked through my body, he squeezed me tighter. "But, honey, I think we should all go."

More than anything, I wanted to hop on the plane and fly to Aunt Mary's cottage in England and maybe never return, but hiding from Sean would only intensify his efforts. If he didn't find me, it would be like I won. And if there were Olympic Games for poor sports, Sean would gold medal in every event. No. I couldn't leave.

Staying and fighting made sense to me, even if it did not to my parents or Simon. This cat and mouse game had gone on long enough. "I'll be okay, Daddy. I just want Kieran out of here...you know, in case." He released me.

"Then I'll stay with you. I can't leave my girl out here on her own."

There were days these people had me rethinking my renewed no drinking stance. Today was not one of those days. "No, Daddy. I would rather you help mom with Kieran." He opened his mouth. "Please, Dad."

While Mom called the police and told them about my house and my phone, I called the club to see if Joey had seen Sean. I wanted some assurance that my husband hadn't yet booked a flight to kill me. Joey, the man who'd given me the little green book to use as leverage, told me Sean occupied his usual corner table at the bar. I breathed a sigh of relief for my short-term safety as I checked the peephole in the window. I couldn't take the chance that Sean would take our lives from a Springer episode to *Law & Order*.

After Luke Mabry, town sheriff, went over to investigate at my house, he came to Mom's to share what he had, and mostly what he hadn't, found.

Mom offered him a "nice hot cup of coffee." In our house, she didn't use her PhD to shrink us or analyze our problems. She offered us internationally flavored coffee. From her spot by the coffee maker, she gave him his choice of the dilemma-solving flavors for the night--hazelnut or a light butterscotch caramel. Luke, manly man, sheriff in his brown uniform and shiny gold badge, chose a cup of hazelnut cream. then went on for a good five minutes about the delicious "aroma."

By the time he finished, I'd practically tapped a hole through the table with my fingers. I'd lost the last of my patience after his third "Mmm. This is good!"

"Luke, I'm sure the coffee is delicious, but maybe we can focus on *my problem* for a minute before you start buying stock in the company?"

He pushed his mug away. "Sorry, Dani. There were no broken windows, no forced entry, nothing to indicate anyone's been in your house but you."

"But you saw the picture, right?" Oh, Lord. He had to believe me.

He nodded as he handed his cup to my mother for yet another refill. "And we know what is going on with you and your husband. Don't worry. No one is going to get you in this town." He chuckled. "Well, except maybe Joss."

I pantomimed a laugh. "Funny."

He handed me my phone. "If I were you, I'd get the number changed. He won't be able to call you then."

I nodded, biting my tongue. "Good idea. I don't know why I didn't think of that."

He either missed the sarcasm or ignored it. Instead, he accepted his mug and took another big drink.

Mom grabbed me by the shoulders to steer me out into the living room away from where Luke and my father sat discussing the personal security measures I should take. After a few moments of cursing my bad luck, my personal security measures arrived.

Simon gathered me into his arms. "I told you I should have spent the night."

His hair hung in damp ringlets from a shower. I stood there inhaling his fresh clean scent as he held me.

He rested his cheek on top of my head. "Dani. Dani. Dani."

Minutes after Luke left, my parents climbed the stairs to their bedroom. Simon and I sat on the couch in the family room, the TV tuned to some too-cute-to-be-real nineteen-nineties sitcom. In moments like these, I wished Simon had wanted me enough the first time to keep me. "What's that face about?" He tipped my chin up and gazed into my eyes.

"What face?"

"This frown." He reached out and ran his finger over my lips.

I focused on the TV, trying to will any forlorn or wistful looks from my face. "It's been a rough night."

"I'm here now." He brought my hand to his lips. "Let me protect you."

"If something happens to you, Simon…"

He kissed the rest of my sentence into oblivion. "It won't."

"You don't know what he's capable of." And I couldn't bring myself to share the gory details.

"I was sheriff here once, you know."

"Okay, but you're not now."

"I still have the gun."

"Really? Where is it?" Because I hadn't seen it in ages.

"In my car. Don't worry. If I need it, I have it on speed dial."

"I don't think this is a time for your humor, funny man." I scooted away, fluffing a pillow for behind my head. Simon watched me, an amused smile playing with his lips as I worked to get comfortable, flopping like a fish from side to side until finally I found a semi-comfortable position.

"Do you remember the fifth grade?"

He wanted to take a jaunt down our middle school memory lane? The inner workings of his mind amazed me. I smiled in spite of myself. "Most of it." I remembered Simon in fifth grade--adorable even then. He'd always had a sweet face. His playful nature was a bonus.

"Did you know you're the first girl I ever kissed?"

"Oh, whatever." I tossed my pillow at him. "You were always holding hands with Leslie Anderson. I know you guys were making out whenever Sister Irene wasn't watching. And you're changing the subject right now because you know I'm right."

"No way. You were the first." He tilted his head. "You know, people go their whole lives thinking they'll never feel the magic of that first kiss ever again. They search for that little tingle of thrill. They always wonder why it can't ever be so perfect again. Most of them don't ever feel it after that first one, but"--I raised my legs to let him move closer--"I feel it every time I kiss you."

My heart thrashed around in my chest as though it were trying to escape. "Are you saying I kiss like a fifth grader?" My voice rasped as I tried to make light of his revelation.

He chuckled softly. "We need to work on our communication." He pulled my hand until I sat up, then kissed the tip of my nose. "I'm saying how much I like kissing you."

"Well, in that case..." I leaned into him at the same moment he moved forward. We ended up bumping heads. "I think we may have been better at it in the fifth grade." I rubbed the spot between my eyes for a second before we tried again.

He pulled me close, my ear resting against his heart. "I don't know. I think we're pretty good at it now."

"I think you're too good to be true, Simon Hunter."

Chapter 21

My parents left two days later, taking Kieran on an adventure to "where dragons lived," and my boy couldn't have smiled wider. I hadn't been out of the house at all since I arrived, and spending so much alone time with Simon, who always seemed to be touching me in one way or another, wore on my resolve to hang on to the innocence of our relationship. The simple fact remained…. I couldn't sleep with him until he had all the facts.

"Hey." He couldn't have been more tempting if he wrapped himself in chocolate. My heart thumped harder as I stepped behind him, inhaling the scent of his cologne. With a tingle shooting from my chest down each leg, long ignored areas of my body vibrated to life.

"Hey." With a final quick sniff, I levered away from him. I went in search of the coffeemaker.

"Kelly can't afford her apartment anymore, and she's moving in with Gatlin today. I thought maybe you'd like to go along to help?"

Visions of the dream I'd had the night before danced through my head, and I curled my fingers into my palm to keep from grabbing him. While moving furniture didn't constitute my idea of a party, I would be with Simon. "Sure."

He leaned in for a kiss that had me rethinking my whole position on temptation and good behavior. I couldn't take another minute of staring without jumping on him. His smoldering gaze said he'd been equally affected.

"You ready?" His voice had climbed an octave higher than normal. I smiled and he led me out to his car, which presented a whole other problem. Not only were we more confined with no room to flee and no distractions, but his car smelled like him and the scent intoxicated me more than any alcohol that ever passed my lips. During the five minute ride, his thumb rubbed small circles on the back of my hand as he drove.

By the time he parked behind her building, I panted as though I'd run a marathon. A sheen of sweat glistened on his upper lip and, for one second, I smiled, secure in the knowledge our suffering equaled out.

With a lusty gaze up and down my body, he took my hand again. I willed my jelly legs to reform as solids before I climbed out of the car. Hand-in-hand, we walked through the garden courtyard into Kelly's home sweet home. The front of the building looked like every other apartment building in town--blooming flower beds, a brick front, ornate moldings, and a door stolen from some far off fairytale castle.

Her apartment, however, demonstrated exactly how much color could be stuffed into a single room. The couch, a bright shade of turquoise blended nicely with throw pillows in the same sunny shade as the walls. The dinette set, sitting off on a neon orange rug, had been stained a blond color, and the chairs held cushions that matched the couch precisely. Bright orange lamps cast a triangular glow on the hardwood floor, and the sofa shared space with banana colored chairs that winged each end. The focal point of the room--a movie screen sized TV--hung over an ornate fireplace in a muted, but still quite bright turquoise.

"Wow."

Kelly strolled up. "My mom liked things very bright."

I didn't comment on her use of the past tense. As far as I knew her mother had gone away, not died.

Gatlin handed her a cold beer and a warm slice of pizza. I declined the food, but chugged Keaton's bottle of water as he stared at his now empty hand. "Gatlin has been working in my closet. I thought we could use my car and Simon's to transport my clothes while the boys move the furniture."

Simon laughed. "Sure, Kelly. Bail on us when it's time to lift the ten-ton couch."

Kelly smiled at him. "You sound like a big baby in front of your girlfriend." She pinched his cheeks as he continued to grumble, then raised her hands in surrender. "But, hey, whatever." Pulling me by the wrist, she tugged me into her room and pushed the door shut. Gatlin popped his head out of the closet.

"Okay, we need details." She stood with her hands on her hips, a curious glimmer twinkling in her eyes.

"Details?" My innocence wasn't hard to fake, since I had no clue what she was talking about.

"Yeah. We have a little bet going on."

"Bet?" I could hardly manage a single word with the scent of Simon's cologne still fogging my brain.

"Have you and Simon…?" Her head bobbed from side to side.

"Sealed the deal?" Gatlin supplied.

My mouth dropped open.

"Hey, sister," he continued. "You wanna be in the group, you dish. It's our rule. We even have a call tree." He drew imaginary branches in the air. "And if you haven't, Kelly wins dinner at Hood tonight. If you have, I win something to be determined at a later date."

I raised my eyebrows at Kelly.

"I get three vetoes plus final say over his prize."

Who the hell were these people? We didn't have a kiss and tell kind of friendship. Thankfully, or Kelly would know a lot more about a drunken mistake I'd made with Gatlin.

I shot him a glare, and he flopped on his stomach onto the bed with his hands tented under his chin.

"Aren't you supposed to be moving furniture with Simon and Keaton?"

He shrugged and buffed his nails on his shirt.

"So, I tell you, you tell Jocelyn. Who shares with the rest of the town?"

They didn't need details of my love life, besides there were none to give.

"I do. It's the bonus of owning the gossip hub of Storybook Lake." Gatlin fluffed imaginary hair like an old movie diva.

"Thought you went straight."

He sighed and threw an arm around Kelly. "Old habits." As a single unit, they looked up at me and waited. "So? Have you?"

In the absence of my best high school friend who'd run off to Texas and only took my calls periodically, I had no one to discuss my romantic issues with. They were all I had, and I needed to talk for a while. I shook my head.

Kelly gasped in shock. "Why the hell not?"

"I'm still married."

"Not dead." Gatlin clucked his tongue. "Listen, girl, he is Simon Hunter, hero of all men, fantasy of all women, and he might be content hanging in there for now while he plays the hero to your damsel, but if you don't give it up soon, he will either A: explode or B: find someone else." He twisted his shoulder in another diva move. "Seen it happen."

"There's too much going on right now for it to be a good idea." I cocked my head to one side, picturing his hands, those lips, his eyes, the thousand wonders hidden by his clothes.

Before I could expand, a knock sounded at the door, and Gatlin winked at me as Simon walked in. "I just got called into work." He frowned and tucked a piece of hair behind my ear. "Maybe you could stay with Kelly and Gatlin tonight. I have to go up to Chicago. I don't know how long I'll be gone."

"I'll be fine at Mom and Dad's."

"I have a date tonight, but Gatlin could stay with you."

Gatlin frowned. "A date?"

She rolled her eyes. "For the article."

I considered the last time I spent the night with him. It wasn't that I didn't trust him or myself, but people in this town talked. A lot. I didn't need more drama in my life. I'd once waded into Gatlin infested water. Coming out unscathed had been lucky, but I didn't see a reason to take another chance if I didn't have to. "Don't worry. We'll figure something out."

Simon took my hand in his and pulled me close to plant a kiss on my lips. What he surely meant to be a quick good-bye kiss, morphed into a prelude to porn. "I'll try to see you tonight." His whisper warmed me from the inside out at the moment I'd finally resumed regular temperature from the earlier car ride.

"Okay." My voice squeaked out of my throat.

It took a full minute for my heart to slow and my breathing to resume a semi-normal rate.

When Kelly and her thousands of belongings were shoved into Gatlin's rooftop apartment, he packed a bag to stay at my mom and dad's with me. Packing actually meant grousing over her evening's plans while he shoved enough clothes for a week's trip into a bag. For ten solid minutes, he wondered aloud when she'd made these mystery plans and what had tripped her switch about this guy so much she would skirt out on spending time girl chatting with us. He must have missed the part where she'd said this date was for work, but I had no intention on interrupting his rant to inform him. Someone needed to tell her how he felt--and soon--before Gatlin expired from her lack of attention. Since Kelly and I weren't close, I filed the idea away to share with Simon when he returned.

After a two minute ride and another fifteen minute pout, Gatlin trimmed my hair and touched up my roots. Then we settled in with pizza delivery and an action flick, sating his appetite for action and my penchant for hot actors.

After the movie, and almost twenty minutes of listening to Gatlin snore on the sofa, I climbed the stairs to bed. Around three-thirty, I got my first hang-up call. Another occurred at four-ten, and the last one before I shut off my phone came a few minutes later. How the hell did this maniac keep getting my number and bypassing the block I'd had the phone company put on my account?

Forgetting my guest on the sofa, I stomped down the stairs to fling cabinet doors open in search of my favorite coffee mug. I screamed as though the scary guy from *Hellraiser* tapped me on the shoulder instead of Gatlin.

"Good morning to you too."

"Sorry. You scared me." My heart danced the-Simon in my chest.

"What are you doing up at this God forsaken hour?"

I jerked my phone out of my bathrobe pocket and waved it around in the air, glancing at the butcher knife in the block on the counter. "My stupid husband keeps calling me and hanging up."

He shoved the knives out of reach. "Whoa, girl. No carving the cell." We waited side by side as the coffee brewed in Mom's antiquated coffee maker. "Wanna go horseback riding today, or does fun violate one of Simon's rules for safety?"

I chuckled. "Yeah. We can take the horses out." Rules, shmules.

"I'll go get changed." He raced out of the kitchen and I smiled. I would have to break it to him we needed to wait for daylight, but his excitement had him bouncing up the steps before I ever managed a syllable. Not a full ten minutes later, he bounded downstairs and proceeded to huff, puff, and pout when I said we needed to eat breakfast first. Spending time with Gatlin reminded me of hanging out with a little kid who'd eaten a few too many sugar cubes with his energy drink.

"Don't forget your mace." He slammed out the door as soon as the sun peeked over the horizon.

I saddled the horses while Gatlin released the others into the pasture. We rode for about four hours until he started complaining his "man parts" were suffering to the point of never being usable again. When he claimed women of the world would be cheated of knowing what a caring lover he'd become, we turned back.

Brown uniformed personnel huddled in the driveway as we rode up unnoticed. Police lights swirled atop the vehicles behind them. Simon walked onto the patio with Luke. He kicked at the concrete with a booted foot as Luke patted his shoulder. I took off at a full gallop and stopped at the fence line. After I tethered her reins to a post, I climbed over the wooden slats to meet Simon and Luke.

Luke turned to his assembled troops as I tapped Simon on the shoulder.

"I thought you were missing." Simon squeezed most of the air from my lungs, then kissed the rest of it away.

Gatlin arrived a moment later and chuckled. "Good Lord. They're away from each other one night and they celebrate like Christmas morning the next day."

I smirked over my shoulder. "He thought we were missing."

"I tried to call you this morning. Your phone went straight to voice mail." He hadn't stopped shaking since he first pulled me against him.

Gatlin, however, laughed until tears streamed down his cheeks. "You called the entire police force out here because we went horseback riding?" He gasped for breath, holding his stomach.

It took more than an hour for the police and emergency personnel to leave, and another hour to get Gatlin to go, but finally, we were alone. As ridiculous as I found some of Simon's safety precautions, it occurred to me how wide open Gatlin and I had been all morning. What if the person taking my pictures for Sean decided to shoot me with something other than a camera? Or worse, what if Gatlin got hurt because of all this mess? *How would I live with the guilt?*

As Simon showered the smoke smell off his body and hair, I paced the perimeter of the living room, trying to figure out what to do. I couldn't stay. It put everyone at risk. He came back into the room at the same moment I plopped in my mother's favorite chair, tears streaking down my cheeks.

He squatted in front of me and put a hand on each of my knees. "Hey. Wanna talk about it?"

I wiped my eyes and looked up at him. I'd loved Simon and been loved by Simon for a lot of my adult life. Now that it almost worked out for us to be together, I had no choice but to leave him. "Not really." I couldn't let him go until I told him the truth about Kieran and as soon as I told him how I'd lied, we would be nothing more than two people who fought over custody or support.

He watched me for a minute as I took a few deep breaths to pull myself together. "Are you trying to leave me?"

I couldn't speak as he pulled me close.

"Don't go, Dani." He tilted my face up. "I'm not going to let anything happen to you."

I couldn't stop the tears, and he kissed me gently.

"I would die first."

"You don't know everything." I needed to tell him and he'd just given me the perfect opportunity.

"There is only one thing I need to know." He kissed me again. "I love you." In the next second, our kissing turned into frantic unbuttoning, desperate touching, and frenzied unzipping. I couldn't wait any longer. Being a better person would have to wait until later. Much later.

After A few intense moments, he turned out of the kiss. "Dani, I don't want our first time to be like this."

It took a second before his words sank in. "It isn't our first time." I yanked him toward me and reclaimed his lips.

He turned away again. "It is for me."

I took a deep breath and blew it out before stepping away from him and clapping my hands together. "I have to talk to you first."

"No. No more words, Dani. No more talking about leaving or reasons we shouldn't be together. We are meant to be, and nothing is going to change that. Not now, not ever. There are no words as important as this minute." He tilted his head and held out a hand. "Let me love you."

Gulp.

"Let me explore all the places I have been dreaming about touching."

Every cell in my body caught fire.

He crooked his finger. "Come here."

Hunger and need laced his words, but his eyes, vulnerable and wanting, asked me in the sweetest way. I closed the distance, and he rewarded me with a soft, almost chaste kiss.

His lips grazed over mine, then honed in for a more thorough examination. As the kiss deepened, our tongues involved in an intricate dance, my bones melted. Short gasps of air choked from my lungs as I struggled for control of my body. Nothing existed for me more than his touch, than his body pressed against mine.

I tightened my hold. The pure pleasure, the anticipation, the longing and desperation surging through me, inspired a gasp. My back arched and our gazes met, primal and hot.

He smiled and lowered his head, taking a hardened nipple between his teeth through my shirt. A whimper escaped along with all control as he lavished one, then turned his head to devour the other. His stubbled cheek created a perfect friction against my sensitized skin where my shirt gaped open. I clasped my fingers in his hair. Need thundered in my heart, intense, heightening every sensation.

"Simon."

He swung me into his arms, carried me to my room, and deposited me gently on the mattress, his eyes trailing up my body burning the skin, trapping me in a wave of desire. As he stretched out next to me, he ran the back of his hand over the throbbing center of my desire through my shorts. Damn the clothes. I sat up, yanked them off, then tossed them to the side. There could be nothing slow. Not now.

As I reached for him, he moved away. "No, no, no." I slid a hand down his boxers, this time persistent, wanting to feel the weight of him, needing to know his level of excitement matched mine.

"Oh, so you want"--he inhaled sharply--"to play?"

I nodded. "Please, Simon." Kissing anywhere I could reach, I bent toward his hand, to his fingers sliding in and out, craving more in, less out. Fever burned through me as I rocked more insistently, the flames inside causing an ache, a desperation for more.

His thumb circled slow. I cried out, whimpering, begging for the release I needed with every fiber of my being. My pleasure spiked, building into a crescendo of feeling, out of control. I pushed against his fingers, every touch as devastating as perfect.

"Dani, you're so..."

We had so much to talk about, so much to get straightened out. Insecurities didn't come close to summing up my sudden turmoil. Sheer terror overtook the pleasure, and my entire body stiffened under his touch. "I can't, Simon, this is... I just can't."

He stopped. "Don't shut me out, Dani. If you're not ready for this, it's okay, but you have to tell me what you want." He ran a finger down my stomach, but his gaze never left mine.

I blinked against an onslaught of tears threatening to spill over.

"We can stop. I'll hold you. It's enough for me."

"I have waited so long for this moment. I don't want to let it go."

"I don't know what to do here. I'll do anything you ask, but I need you to tell me."

This was Simon. My protector. The boy I'd loved since I'd been old enough to love. I kissed him then, hard, demanding, desperate. He opened his mouth, swirled his tongue with mine. All the doubts, the fears, every uncertainty I owned disappeared with one blazing touch. Fire raged across my skin. I gave thoughts over to feelings, to the sensation of his body, his hands, the wonders of his mouth.

"Anything?" I brought my lips a breath away from his.

"Yes." His whisper echoed more powerful than any scream.

"Make love with me."

"I wanted to go slow, to savor every second, but I can't."

Close to the edge, I wanted to take him with me, to bring him the same pleasure he'd given me.

"Simon, please." I could do nothing more than beg for his body, for his touch. He kissed the hollow of my throat as he shoved his boxers away, then pulled me on top of him.

The sheer ecstasy of feeling him inside me, the weeks of waiting, denying ourselves this moment, sent shockwaves through me. I shuddered above him, the moves coming faster, more frantic.

My body convulsed, squeezing him, holding him inside until he let go. He threw his head back and a growl of enthusiasm rang out in the quiet of the room. His body bucked with its release. With a final moan of pure pleasure, he grinned. "We should do this more often. Once, twice, ten times a day."

He kissed the spot where my neck and shoulder met, then turned us so we lay facing one another.

I couldn't stop smiling even as he kissed me. "That was amazing."

"I think we're gifted." He pulled the side of the blanket up, wrapping us in a cocoon of cotton.

I snuggled closer. "I love you, Simon."

"You're not supposed to say you love the other person during sex."

"It's not during. It's after." I ran a finger down his spine.

"We could compromise and say it's before."

* * * *

As soon as the sun came up, my stomach started begging for food. The begging turned into wailing, and I decided to surprise Simon with breakfast in bed. Unfortunately, since Mom had been gone so long, the refrigerator stood cold, empty, and lonely. After a quick shower, I grabbed his keys, needing to make a trip to the grocery store. I left a note on the counter.

I'd just pushed the shifter into park when I saw him.

Sean.

In Storybook Lake.

Walking out of the bakery.

I ducked down in the seat, pulled my hat lower to shield my face, and waited. He stopped in front of his car, tapped the screen of his phone, then climbed in. After a few revs of the engine, he zoomed away toward the resort. *Shit.*

My heart pounded as though trying to break free from its spot.

Sean.

In Storybook Lake.

The words circled my mind like a skipping CD. I had to get out of town. Or hide. Or something. The last thing I expected to do was swing the car onto the road behind him, all the while slouched in the seat, keeping my focus on him in the space where the steering wheel rounded over the dashboard.

He passed the road to the resort, but turned into the motel by the interstate and angled his rental into a spot not far from the front door. After reaching over the seat for his bag, he climbed from his car. I'd left the house with a twenty and Simon's car. Everything I could use to save myself--my phone, my little can of mace, my bad ass former sheriff boyfriend--was all waiting for me at home.

Thinking of nothing but what Sean being in Storybook Lake meant, I watched the door. I counted every beat of my heart, every breath, but time meant nothing. He came out around noon, when his bar manager, Joey arrived. They stood outside yelling at each other--I could hear their voices, but couldn't make out the words--before Sean stormed back inside. With the slam of the door, Joey left.

And still I sat. Until I couldn't sit anymore.

Chapter 22

I missed most of Keaton's direct testimony. I'd already heard the explanation of how he found the body after receiving a volunteer responder call to the hotel. I hadn't cared the first time I heard it and couldn't summon an inkling of interest now, either. As I floated back to earth, Grace stood for her turn.

"Hey, Keats." She smiled and walked to stand directly in front of the witness box.

"Hi, Grace. How you been?" I could have sworn I heard a sigh as he flashed his golden boy smile at her.

"Pretty good." She nodded, then looked him up and down.

His too-sexy-for-his-shirt act and the smug little grin producing dimples in his cheeks had juror number two flushing deep scarlet as he glanced at Grace.

Grace nodded. "Keaton, when did Danielle tell you Kieran was yours?"

"I don't think she did."

"Ever?"

He cocked his head to the side. "No."

I shrugged one shoulder and he grinned.

"I'm certain. She never did. I guess I just assumed."

"I want to be very clear about this, Keaton, because the prosecutor is making a pretty big deal of Danielle lying to you. You're sure she never said anything like 'Hey Keats, you're gonna be a daddy' or 'we made a baby'?"

Who knew lawyers were such good actors? Grace's wide-eyed shock at his revelation almost had me fooled. We'd gone over this a couple hundred times, but never clued Keaton in. She wanted him to realize it on the stand. She'd said the shock value would be priceless.

"No. She said she was pregnant." He considered me over her shoulder with his eyes squinted and his mouth in a twisted line. "I believed it because we lived together. I figured we slept together at least once. I mean, we have history, and she's Dani." He lowered his head. "In my defense I drank a lot." He lifted his chin. "She made me clean up my act, though. She kept me sane." *Praise. Much better.*

"Big job, huh?"

"Aw, Grace. You know me. I don't do anything halfway. I do it completely, or I don't do it." His aw shucks, down-home country boy talk had juror number two all but drooling down her shirt as cartoon hearts formed in her eyes.

"But you don't drink now?"

"No."

Her posture, her stance, the way she smiled at him, indicated her comfort. I assumed it came from making out with him the first week he showed up in Storybook Lake in eighth grade, or maybe from our years of friendship. I didn't care, but to me, in this setting, it seemed important.

"Now, back to when you were married to Jocelyn Shaw the first time. You said she thought you were having an affair. Did she believe you'd slept with Dani?"

"Yes."

I'd done everything I could to reinforce the notions she had about me and her husband. My chest pinged with guilt and I chewed my thumbnail. Keaton shot me the stop-it-I've-raised-my-eyebrows-at-your-behavior look, and I jerked my hand back to my side. "Were you having an affair with Dani?"

"No."

"But you lived with her in Arizona while you were still married to Jocelyn?"

Their exchange resembled a promenade. She stepped left; he followed. She spun; he whirled along.

I almost resisted the urge to look over my shoulder at Simon, but at the last second, turned halfway in my chair. Instead of meeting his eyes, I met Jocelyn's and she half smiled, half grimaced back. I spun to face the front.

"Yes, but by the time she got to Arizona and we got together, Joss and I had already been to court and signed the papers. I'd been gone a month or so when Dani came out west. We only went back for a court hearing at the end." A quick image of Jocelyn's face as I shoved my tongue down Keaton's throat at their final hearing floated through my mind. Heat crept up my cheeks.

"When you both came back to Storybook Lake, Danielle left again. Do you know where she went?" Grace made this all sound like a conversation she'd invited the jury to eavesdrop on rather than an examination of facts and details.

"To Arizona, I think." He looked down at his hands. "She ran into Sean at the Grand Canyon, anyway."

"Before his death, did you ever meet Mr. Turner?"

"Yes. They were here for New Year's the year they got married. We were all at Hood's Hideaway for the big countdown celebration."

"And at the party, did you witness an altercation between Mr. and Mrs. Turner?" She turned, rolled her eyes, and half chuckled. "I mean Dani and Sean?"

Calvin objected to her mention of our argument. When the judge sustained, Grace asked the same question without referring to the fight, but Keaton knew what she wanted for an answer. "She was standing at the bar talking to a friend of ours when Sean came out of the bathroom. He grabbed her by the arm and shoved her out the door."

"Did you run into Mrs. Turner after New Year's, before they left town?" All this Mrs. Turner business made my stomach clench.

"No. Her mom said he took her back to California the next day."

"Now, with regard to the day you discovered Mr. Turner's remains, you're not a police officer, correct?"

"No."

"A crime scene investigator?"

"No."

"Did you actually see the body?"

"Yes. He'd been beaten and shot."

"Nothing further."

Chapter 23

Keaton stepped down, then Cal called Luke Mabry, Storybook Lake's sheriff, to the witness box.

I ignored the testimony for a while, not needing a play-by-play of what they found. I'd seen it firsthand, walked in and found Sean. I left without calling the police or anyone else. Instead, I rushed home. When I pulled it together enough to get out of the car and face Simon, I acted as though I knew nothing. He'd been furious at my "lack of respect" for the danger Sean posed, and we argued. He'd spent the afternoon looking for me--tearing around town with Luke, growing more panicked with every stop. It hadn't occurred to me to worry about what he was going through until that moment.

"Simon, Sean's dead." I poured the rest of the story out in broken sentences, and he called in an anonymous tip, never once questioning my tale of events. Even to me, they sounded flimsy.

Near the end of Luke's direct testimony, I pushed the memories inspired by his words away to focus on the heated interaction between Luke and Cal.

"During your investigation, what did you discover in regards to Mrs. Turner's whereabouts at the approximate time of Sean's death?"

Luke's eyes flipped over to meet mine, his apology written in the cool blue depths. "I tried to verify an alibi, but I couldn't." His lips formed a tight line.

"How many days after finding Mr. Turner's body did you speak with Mrs. Turner?"

"It was the next day."

"Did you conduct the interview at the police station?"

"No. We talked in her mother's living room."

"Did you record the interview?" Cal's voice held just a note of reproach.

Luke frowned. "No. I didn't have a recorder." Each word came with its own full stop.

"Why not?"

"I didn't see a reason. I didn't consider her a suspect at the time." The sentence bit from between clenched teeth.

"Isn't it customary to treat the estranged spouse as an automatic suspect?"

"Not when you grow up with them. I know her as well as I know my own sister."

Cal rolled his eyes and shook his head at me. "So, being friends with the defendant affected the way you handled this case. Are you saying you ignored procedure out of friendship?"

Fire blazed behind the cool blue of Luke's eyes. "No more than I ignore it when you run the stop sign on the corner of Dr. Seuss and Mark Twain, *counselor*. As soon as it looked like Dani might have known more than she said, I treated her like I would any suspect or person of interest."

Cal stomped three steps away from Luke, then turned back. "During this unrecorded interview, did Mrs. Turner tell you she had been involved in an altercation of any kind with Mr. Turner?"

"No."

Luke's answer obviously surprised Calvin. Red splotches bloomed on his face as he reached a finger between his collar and his neck before he turned back to Luke. "Sheriff, did you feel Mrs. Turner's reaction to Mr. Turner's death to be genuine?"

"Yes, but considering everything I knew about their relationship, and the bruises, I couldn't imagine why. But even Julia Roberts couldn't fake that kind of surprise and emotion." Luke may as well have been a defense witness for all the bite in his tone.

"Fine." Cal's word spat from between his clenched teeth. "When did you next interview Mrs. Turner?"

"A couple of weeks after we found the body."

By then, makeup completely hid the evidence of a run-in with Sean.

"And you recorded this one?"

"Yes."

"And, at any time, did she mention seeing Sean Turner the night of his death?"

"No."

"In fact," Calvin's voice rose to chipmunk pitch. "Didn't she specifically tell you she hadn't seen Mr. Turner and didn't even know he'd come to town?"

"That's correct."

Cal strode angrily back to his table and extracted a stack of papers along with a CD. He handed it to Luke. "Is this the conversation you just mentioned?"

Luke perused the papers, nodded, then handed them back to a waiting Calvin who delivered the papers to Grace. Without objection from my attorney, the court reporter marked the CD into evidence. Cal popped it into a video player.

I chewed my thumbnail. This was bad.

Chapter 24

Court ended for the day with Luke explaining the procedure for evidence collection. In a longwinded monologue, he detailed the importance of each piece of evidence Cal handed him--sections of wall and carpet, numerous photos which showed blood spatter and pools, and a diagram of the hotel room. The next day, he would face Grace's examination, then the Medical Examiner would be called to the stand.

After my arrest, my parents posted my bond in exchange for the majority share in my company. I had an ankle bracelet with an alarm in case I tried to stray too far from the confines of my parents' yard and house. If I took one step too many from my little blinking box, Luke assured me a swarm of cops would come banging down the door to haul me to jail.

Grace dropped me off, and I walked up the steps to the house. Kieran threw himself into my arms, and I smothered his face with kisses as Mom came into the foyer, drying her hand on a dishtowel. I loosened my hold on Kieran when she reached in to kiss my cheek. "How did today go?"

I begged my parents not to come to court because I couldn't stand the thought of them thinking worse of me than they already did. A lot of things were going to come out, and I couldn't bear for my mom to know how bad I'd become. I also needed someone to keep an eye on Kieran, so not having a lot of close friends had finally worked to my favor.

While I knew they could stream it live online or watch it on TV, they wouldn't. They would respect that I wanted to keep my secrets private, if only from them. "Okay, I think."

"And Grace?" My mother had never liked any of the Wade girls, but she especially hated Grace. "With all the drinking she did, it's a wonder they even let her practice law anymore."

I smiled. "Did you know Grace has never lost a case?" I'd heard that once and decided to impart the pearl of wisdom to my mother.

"Of course not, when she makes a production out of sleeping with the prosecutor."

Mom hung on to gossip like a lifeline. Grace's liaison with the prosecutor had nothing to do with my case. In her defense, it only happened one time when she worked in Texas with her college roommate after opening a law practice. For her indiscretion, she almost lost the guy she loved more than anything in the world--her perfect match. Instead, she came home, hauling him right behind her. "Mom, she made mistakes, but so did I, and she's my best friend. I can't think of anyone I would rather have defending me."

"Well, I'm just saying…."

She had been saying it since this whole damned mess began. I sucked in my anger, replacing it with a peaceful smile. "I know, just try not to say it to me."

Mom wrung the dishtowel through her hands and huffed out a breath.

"Honestly, wouldn't you rather someone who loves me be my lawyer, rather than a hack who only sees dollar signs and TV cameras?"

She sighed. "Are you seeing Simon tonight?"

I never knew when Simon would be free, since he'd become an arson investigator and the dry weather made him all the busier. "Maybe. I don't know." I shrugged. "I'm taking Kieran out back."

"Your dad and I have a dinner tonight with one of the associates at his firm." She checked her watch. "As a matter of fact, I better get ready. Your supper's in the oven." After bending down to ruffle Kieran's hair, she kissed my cheek, then walked away.

We ate dinner, then I played outside with Kieran until dark. At his first yawn, I gave him a bath, read him a story, and settled him with the dinosaur blanket I'd brought him home in from the hospital . As he hugged me, I wondered how many more bedtime hugs were in my future. A dull ache worked its way from my heart to the left side of my face and settled in behind my eye.

Ten trips to the bathroom later, he dropped off to sleep. I wandered around downstairs for a while, then opened the door and plopped into a lounger on the patio. With my eyes closed, I took a few deep breaths, willing the pain away. I concentrated on the soothing sounds of the night. Wind chimes tinkled above my head. Leaves on the branches smacked into one another as the wind whipped them back and forth, brewing up a summer storm. A not so distant rumble of thunder said rain loomed in the near future.

"Hey, beautiful."

If there existed a single thing with the power to make me feel better, his voice held the magic.

"Are you sleeping?"

Without opening my eyes, I murmured, "No, just listening."

"To what?"

"Silence."

He leaned down and touched his lips to mine. "How was your day?"

I didn't want to talk about it so I shrugged.

He scooted me over with his hip to sit facing me, and pulled my hand into his. "Lizette called me."

The ex. "Yeah?" A little ball of jealousy crept into the pit of my stomach, starting a war with the pot roast I'd eaten for dinner.

"She wanted to get together and talk." He took a long pause, probably waiting for my tantrum. "So, we met for coffee at the bakery."

The battle in my belly intensified. If he wanted to flounce around town with her, I had nothing to say about it. Yet, the world narrowed.

"Cal is calling her to testify."

Nothing about her being a part of my trial made any sense. I barely knew her. "Why?"

"Apparently, Sean stopped at the bakery the morning he died, which explains why he was walking out when you saw him. He told her some things about you and him."

I couldn't have ventured a guess, but blood pounded in my ears and my breath came in short shallow gasps. "Did she mention what he said?" My voice squeaked out as though I'd inhaled a tank of helium, but I had to ask.

"Not really. She only said it had something to do with Kieran and Keaton. She said he was pissed, and he told her he might lose Kieran because of it."

I loved Simon because he never pried, never asked me for details, and still acted like I was some sort of goddess. Even as the world came crashing down around me, I held on to his hand and pretended nothing could ever come between us.

Chapter 25

I lay cuddled with my pillow, snuggled deep into my blanket, when Grace came bounding into my room on Saturday morning. She yanked on my arm, almost pulling me out of bed. "Wake the hell up!"

I angled my head to look at her and pulled the pillow from beneath me to cover my eyes from the morning sun. "Go away, Grace."

She snatched the pillow and held it by the corners as though she intended to deliver a wallop. "Get up so I can kick your ass!"

"What's your problem?" I couldn't summon the energy to yell back so I stayed in bed and watched her.

"Did you know I hate looking stupid? And I went to school for a really long time so there would be no mistaking I'm pretty damn smart?" She paced as she continued holding my pillow.

Uh-oh. Having a lawyer who rose with the sun spelled trouble, especially one who had no compunction about kicking my ass.

"Did you know all that?"

"Yes, Grace, you were queen of the A-plus papers. Did you come over to brag or is there a point to all this?" Under her bright-eyed glare, I sat up straight, ready to duck and cover, or tuck and roll, whichever need presented itself.

She leaned across the bed, bracing her body on her fists as she glared at me with the angriest eyes I'd ever seen. With her face inches from mine, heat radiated from her body. "My point is you and your lies made me look stupid in front of the prosecutor. And now I'm going to kick your ass for it." She advanced across the bed, ready to strike

"Wait!" I scooted backward, only to fall off the other side of the mattress. "What are you talking about?" In case she'd found something else--anything else--I needed an explanation before I stepped in an even bigger pile of crap.

"Lizette Lightener, I'm talking about Lizette freaking Lightener."

"Oh. I didn't lie to you, Grace." I shrugged, but swallowed hard. "I just didn't tell you."

"Which leads me to wonder why the hell you wouldn't tell me. I'm your lawyer, and supposedly, your friend." She threw her hands up in the air and slammed them back to her thighs. "I like to think growing up together, and sharing secrets for thirty or so years, would mean we're friends. Maybe I'm wrong. In which case, I should never have told you about Blane and Jamie. Why the hell would you keep something like this to yourself?"

I stood and sighed. "Because, Grace. I never told Keaton he was Kieran's daddy, and I never told Sean he was, either. I can't just blurt out to Simon that he's got a kid." Well, that was one way to tell her. "Not now, after all this time. He'll think I kept it from him because of his injury, or because I didn't want him to see Kieran, or because I'm going to jail and I need him. I don't *need* him. I want him, but I'm not telling." I paused as her glare burned through my forehead. "Period."

She rolled her eyes and sighed in a loud whoosh of breath. "You're so stupid. The longer you wait, the more hurt he's going to be. You'll lose him no matter what."

"Then let me have this time with him, even if it's only a few days or hours. If I tell him, it'll be on my time, not yours or Cal's or that stupid baker bitch's."

"Well, is jail okay with you, moron? Cal has you caught in a lie. Another lie." She poked a finger at me. "And you don't think it matters? The jury is going to hear that you lied again, and they're going to be sitting in those chairs wondering why they should believe a *liar* who seems to think her child doesn't deserve to know about his own father. A *liar* who doesn't seem capable of speaking the truth. *Period*." Her head flounced to one side, and her hands fisted on her hips as she mocked my choice of words.

"Well, Grace, you're supposed to be the best damned lawyer in the history of damned lawyers. So, *you* figure it out. Make it not matter. Isn't that what you do?" Telling him now would only ruin everything.

Chapter 26

As though Grace's raging anger wasn't enough, Mom cornered me in the kitchen as her coffeemaker released one drip of coffee into the pot every three seconds. I tapped my foot waiting…and waiting for a full cup. "That woman said he came into the bakery and told her the baby doesn't belong to him, either." Mom sniffed in a big breath and blew it out, waiting for a reply I didn't have.

She'd obviously caught up on all the latest gossip during her morning trip to Gatlin's salon. "Yeah. I heard."

Kieran was outside with Dad, so I went to the sofa quite intent on watching a movie. She spoke more words, more of the story she considered pertinent. When I continued to focus on the screen, she snatched the remote off the table and clicked the TV into silence.

"Do you really plan to keep ignoring me?"

"Well, it's half naked Matthew McConhaughey, for goodness sake." And her earth shattering headline stopped being big news to me the minute Grace burst into my room that morning.

Unconcerned that one of *People Magazine*'s sexiest men alive stood shaking his moneymaker on the screen, my mother held the remote out of my reach and plopped down on the arm of the couch. "Your dad and I are worried about you, honey."

I sat up and pulled my knees to my chest, hugging them, curling into my own fears. "Mom, no matter how this turns out, I'm going to be fine." The words choked out of me, broken by an untimely breath.

"And what about Kieran? Have you thought about him?" She licked her lips and tears sprung to her eyes. "He needs you. If you know who killed Sean, then you'd better tell someone. You can't leave Kieran without a momma when you won't tell anyone who his daddy is."

This wasn't a new bandwagon she'd hopped on. She drove the damned thing and probably took reservations for others to join her.

If the jury came back with a guilty verdict, I intended to tell Simon he had responsibilities to our child, but not one minute before twelve of my judicially charged peers forced my hand.

"Don't you think I know, Mom? It's all I think about. I'd rather die than leave him." I sighed, content to repeat my story once again while I hoped for a reaction of belief this time. "Sean was dead when I went in there, and I didn't see anyone leaving or hanging out waiting to be identified." I suspected who'd killed Sean, but I couldn't let someone who'd gone out of their way to protect me go to jail. I just couldn't.

"Dani"--her voice softened, and she put a hand on my shoulder--"you know your dad and I will do everything we can to help you and to keep Kieran safe, but we're getting older and he needs--"

"Mom!" She'd picked the absolute last thing I needed to hear. "Stop. I'm not going to jail. Grace is going to make sure." I cleared my throat and repeated those words in a more forceful tone.

She scoffed before leaving me alone so she could finish dinner. With a grim set of her lips, her usual huff and a big bowl of pasta in her hands, she continued the badgering from the other room until I finally flounced out in a cloud of rebellious attitude.

"Dad." He turned his gaze away from the pasture and looked down at me. "It's time to eat."

"I'll be in a little later." A piece of my heart broke for the anguish I'd put in his eyes.

"Dad." I touched his shoulder. "I know you don't understand my decisions about everything, but please know I'm trying to do what I think is best for Kieran."

"I know."

I leaned against his chest. His heart thumped a reassuring rhythm under my ear. "I wish I could get along with Mom as easily as I do you."

He chuckled. "She's a worrier. Don't get me wrong, I'm worried, too, but she does hers with a little more volume than I do." He pressed a kiss to the top of my temple. "Want me to talk to her?"

"Would you?"

"Of course, but if I end up sleeping on the couch tonight, you're making me breakfast in the morning."

"Deal."

As we walked across the wooden deck, he stopped, my elbow in his palm. "I would never let anything hurt you or Kieran. You know that, right?"

I nodded and reached up to kiss his cheek. "Of course I know. It's why we're here, Daddy. You're my hero." A girl couldn't go wrong with the daddy hero figure.

When we made it inside, Dad took Mom into the pantry, claiming he needed help with something. After their return, she quieted, instead using body language to silently perform her interrogation. Her perfectly shaped eyebrows raised more than once in question as we ate in uncomfortable silence.

When Dad walked Kieran down to the stables to feed his new pony, I washed the dinner dishes. I whipped my head around at the sound of the back door opening. Gatlin stood with one foot and most of his head inside the back door.

I smiled broadly at him as soon as I noticed the antique doctor bag he used to carry his house call hair supplies. "Not that I'm complaining"--I beamed my best cover girl smile up at him--"but what are you doing here?" We'd never been the kind of friends to drop in on the other.

He clucked his tongue. "I saw you on television Friday and you looked a little brassy." He set the heavy bag on the table and extracted the magical bottles--dyes, gels, mousses, wax, conditioner, Heavenly Gate shampoo-- that would have me back to glowing in no time--well, in about two and a half hours, anyway. "And, in my book, brass is a hair emergency."

After the kind of hug I saved for special occasions--weddings, births, visits from a master colorist with scissors--the processing began. He stood to the side, chewing a thumbnail, considering me from every angle as he tilted his head. He'd trimmed, colored, conditioned, spritzed, gelled, and sprayed my hair into a flattering style without chopping off a lot of length.

I checked out my new do in a hand mirror. "You are a hair genius."

"Everybody has to be good at something."

By the sly little grin turning his lips heavenward, I knew he had more to add.

"I happen to be good at everything." He wiggled his brows and dropped down in the chair. "I have been after your boyfriend"--he rolled his eyes--"for weeks to let me get a hold of that mop on his head to put some fresh color in it."

Visualizing Simon sitting still for thirty minutes with enough foil in his hair to pick up Spanish television produced a smirk. *Challenge accepted.*

He cocked his hip, balling his fist and punching it into the bone. "What? You think I can't convince him?"

"I could convince him, but you? Not so much." I looked him up and down. He'd toned down his previously eccentric wardrobe choices and wore jeans and a T-shirt advertising his salon. He was a little too masculine, but not masculine enough to have any kind of power over Simon.

"Whatever. Our little golden god has changed since his accident. I think you might find he's not so easily swayed by your pitiful powers of persuasion." He narrowed his eyes and grimaced as though my persuasive attributes were in need of some surgical enhancement.

"Are you challenging me, diva boy?"

"My diva days are over. I will simply force him to sit in the chair while I work my magic."

I laughed and he put his hands to his cheeks and made a perfect circle with his lips. "I suppose you have a better plan?"

"What do I get if I win?" I didn't care about Simon's highlights or the prize at the end, but it had been a while since anyone joked with me. I missed it.

"Oh, no, little sister. When *I* win, and it will be me, you have to cook my dinners for a solid month. And no hamburger helper. I want full meals like your momma makes--steak and potatoes, fresh picked corn, garden green beans, and I'm thinking some mac and cheese that melts on your tongue."

"Again, if I win?"

He sighed. "If you win--not to be repetitive, but I find it highly unlikely--but *if* you win, what do you want?" He huffed his bangs out of his face and drilled his fingers on the counter, while I contemplated a suitably nasty punishment.

"You have to clean the stable for a week." I could have pressed for longer, but he'd never have survived more than a seven day span of shoveling manure. I'd probably end up in court for that one too.

"Deal." We shook on it, and then Gatlin looked up at me with narrowed eyes. "And no using that body of yours to entice him, either."

I dropped my mouth open. "No way. I get to use all my weapons the same way you'll use yours."

"I have no weapons. I plan to use sheer force."

I couldn't help but laugh. The idea of someone built like Gatlin--tall, lanky, his muscle-tone mostly in his brain--producing enough force to badger someone like Simon into bending to his will, didn't seem likely. Before I could respond, Simon strolled in. He dropped a quick kiss on my lips as Gatlin clucked his tongue. "That's cheating, girlfriend."

I pulled back.

"What's cheating?" Simon tugged me in close to his side.

I didn't resist when he tilted my chin up and gave me the toe-curler. When we parted, I waved a hand toward Gatlin. "Ignore the diva. He just came over to do my hair, and he's afraid you're going to mess it up."

Simon chuckled and Gatlin shot me a narrow-lidded glare. He turned to shove his bottles and emollients into his bag. After a few seconds, he whirled and stared at Simon. "Let me put highlights in your hair." His demand burst out loud and strong.

Simon looked from me to Gatlin. "No." His almost quiet reply lacked enough force to bring an end to the subject.

Gatlin slammed his fists onto the counter. "Come on." He spoke the words through clenched, pearly white teeth. If he thought pestering Simon into compliance would work, he'd forgotten how to win a bet with me.

"No way."

"Come on."

"What the hell is wrong with you?" Simon narrowed his eyes but smiled. He ran a hand down my back to tuck a finger into my belt loop, pulling me even closer. He moved past Gatlin to fold his body into a chair at the table.

I glided over to him--yes, glided--then straddled his lap. My chest rubbed against his as my hips shimmied a bit more than necessary. I plunged my fingers into his long semi-blond locks. "It would be kind of sexy."

His gaze honed in on my tongue as it ran along my lower lip. "You think?" His nose scrunched, but I had him.

A surge of victory sweetened the words out of my mouth. "Oh, yeah." I nodded, staring into his amber colored eyes. "Girls appreciate guys who put in that kind of time to look good." I gave him the coyest look in my arsenal of sweat-inspiring gazes. "At least, I do, and when I appreciate something, I am very"--I leaned in close to glide my tongue along the shell of his ear before I whispered--"very grateful."

"Okay." His voice squeaked out an octave or so higher than normal. He cleared his throat. "I mean, you know." He found his natural tone once again as he relaxed his arms and slouched a bit under my weight. "I guess a couple of highlights would be okay."

"Sweet." Gatlin pulled me aside as I climbed off Simon. He leaned down. "You cheated, you hussy. I'm not cleaning stalls."

"Welcher."

"Cheater."

We hissed insults back and forth before he started mixing color.

Chapter 27

The next night, my parents loaded up and took Kieran to Midland for dinner and a movie, leaving me home with nothing but the TV to keep me company. I crawled into bed early and had just fallen asleep when a clink-clink of rocks against my window woke me. After throwing the covers off, I pushed up the sash with one hand, wiping the sleep from my eyes with the other.

Simon stood on the front lawn, smiling up at me. "Come out and play with me?"

I could think of worse ways to be roused from a half-worried sleep. "I have to get dressed."

"It's clothing optional." He yanked his shirt over his head.

I giggled like a schoolgirl--high pitched with a tinkle of giddy attached. "You're crazy."

"Crazy about you." He swirled his hips and flicked open the button to his jeans.

"You getting naked out on my front lawn. What will Mrs. Hopewell think?" I propped my elbows on the window frame and my chin on my fists. If he wanted to get down and dirty, I'd never forgive myself if I missed a single hip gyration. "Ah, screw her. Take it all off, baby."

He laughed and took three running steps toward the porch. Using my mother's heavy marble planter, he vaulted high enough to reach the guttering on the porch that ran parallel to my room. Using either momentum or his vast upper body strength, he made it to the gap between the roof and my side of the house. His muscles bunched and relaxed as he wind-milled his arms, preparing for the next jump. At least ten feet of nothing but air remained between him and my window. "I'm coming in." He backed up to take a run.

"Don't! You're going to fall, Simon. Just climb down and use the front door."

"Now, where's your sense of adventure?"

I covered my face, peeking through my fingers as he leaped through the air. His hands connected with my windowsill and he shimmied his way inside.

"You scare the crap out of me." My heart pounded in my ears as he wrapped himself around me, rolling me on top of him

Instead of answering with words, he brushed the hair from my face, staring at me through half-lidded eyes burning with desire.

"What are you doing here?"

"Sneaking into your room." He rolled us again until his body rested almost on top of me. Then he leaned down and kissed the corner of my mouth. He moved to the other side as my fingers skimmed over his shoulder.

His gaze held mine while he toyed with the exposed skin of my stomach.

My breath caught. "You're not very good at sneaking. You probably woke half the neighborhood."

"I wanted a good night kiss."

Even if I had a good reason, I wouldn't have said no. Trembling with need, I yearned to feel his body pressed against mine, to let each of my senses absorb every Simon-detail I could. He kissed with his whole body, caressed with every piece of himself, and because of it, he swallowed the soft whimper that escaped my throat.

When he pulled away, I savored the taste of him as he laid his head on my shoulder. "What am I going to do with you, Dani?"

I slipped my hand on top of his, sliding both up my stomach. "I have an idea."

He lifted his head and smiled. "You dirty girl." He nibbled on my earlobe. "I love you. It's always been you."

A lump formed in my throat. I had to say something, tell him all the things I felt and the ones he needed to know, but I couldn't make a sound. I couldn't form a syllable. He kissed his way down my neck to my shoulder, took the strap of my tank top between his teeth, peeling it down my arm. With stealthy moves I could never have managed, he moved back up to my neck and across my collarbone as a thousand sensations vibrated over my body.

I wouldn't have stopped, wouldn't have moved or breathed or done anything to break the spell around us had a loud bang not shattered the sensual haze around me. "What the hell?"

Shoving him away, I stood as though my body hadn't been reduced to a puddle of liquid passion. He pulled me behind him, grabbed my hair dryer, then tiptoed to the door.

"What are you going to do, blow dry them to death?"

He put a finger over his lips. Without a sound, he mouthed, "Stay here."

No way. I couldn't stay in my room while he faced whatever danger lie ahead armed with only a blow drier and his own rousing sense of courage. I leaned in close, popping my arm through the strap of my shirt. "Do you see anything?"

He turned and put his finger to his lips. "Shh."

As we made it to the landing at the top of the steps, the click of metal stopped me in my tracks. He smacked the intruder in the skull with the blow drier. Shards of plastic ruptured from the side of my very necessary piece of hair equipment.

Luke grabbed the side of his head. "What the hell, Simon?"

"You what the hell, Luke. What are you doing here?"

"Mrs. Hopewell called. She said she saw someone climbing in the window." He rubbed a spot on his scalp and extracted a tiny piece of plastic. "I'm the hero, here, Einstein. You're the prowler."

I chuckled at the absurdity my life had become. "Hero?" I pointed a finger at Luke, then shifted it in Simon's direction. "Prowler? What does that make me? Should I be clutching my chest and swooning?"

Luke pointed toward the hallway. "Go to bed, Mae West." He holstered his gun and looked up at Simon. "Next time, use the front door."

Simon shrugged as though Luke wasn't staring at the half-naked version of us. "I was going for romance points. Thanks for screwing with my mojo."

Luke turned and walked down the stairs. "Every once in a while, I forget you have some stuff wrong with your brain. Then you go and pull shit like this to remind me. You're lucky you didn't get shot. Again."

Simon held out his arms and completed a full circle turn. "Haven't you heard? I'm invincible."

"Yeah, tell her dad when he sees the front door."

Chapter 28

Monday morning brought with it a few thousand rays of sunlight and another day away from court. Cal had witnesses who were testifying in another case, so the judge postponed the trial for another day.

My mother, who'd made arrangements for Kieran to join a playgroup, stood by, waiting for me to get him ready. When the house phone rang, Mom turned her attention from us to the jingle across the room. She spoke in angry hushed tones as I battled Kieran's shoes. With a bear-like growl, she slammed the receiver down. "Hey, Big K." She turned to Kieran with her brightest, toothiest, most fake smile. "Why don't you go help Grandpa water the flowers while I talk to Mommy?"

He looked at me, his eyes wide. "Did you do something wrong?"

I shrugged. "I never really know, buddy."

"Well, if you get into trouble, I'll stand in the corner with you, okay, Mommy?"

I kissed his cheek. "I don't think I'm in trouble, pal, but thanks."

He ran out the back door to chat with my dad about flowers and bees.

I turned to my mother. "What's up, Mom?"

"The women in this town!" One hand white-knuckled the side of a dining room chair as she stared down at me. She made the word "women" into a swear word. "Those--those--*women* think Kieran should wait to join the play group until your trial is over. They're afraid he might talk about you killing his daddy." She glared once more at the phone as though the caller could feel her anger. "It would open up some uncomfortable questions for them."

My blood pounded in my ears. Tears blurred my vision. I stood up all in one motion and nodded slowly. "Really?" These women had been my friends once--the girls I grew up cheering next to, went to college with, and stood up for at weddings too tacky for words. "So they're too good for my innocent son to play with their kids? I mean, whether I killed

Sean or not, Kieran didn't do a damn thing. He's a victim no matter how you look at it."

Mom nodded.

"You know, I kept their secrets. I lied for them. I helped them out of messes too ugly for this town to believe their golden girls could make." And to prove my point…"Did you know Misty Cannell cheated on David last summer. She called me in California to brag about what a good lover her pool boy is. And Erica McDonald watched that Julia Roberts movie. Then she turned around and fed her husband poison last summer because he stepped out with Cassie Morgan's nanny. And Cassie had a check-bouncing thing a few months ago. I lent her a thousand dollars to clear it up."

"How do you know all of that?" She stared at me openmouthed. "Never mind. We should run down to the beauty parlor and spill the dirt."

"Beans."

"What?"

"It's spill the beans, Mom, and don't get all *Harper Valley PTA* on me, okay? There has to be a better way to deal with my friends." Damn. I'd grown more than a little tired of turning the other cheek.

She glared at nothing in particular and everything all at the same time.

"Some friends I have." For a minute, I envied the relationships Simon enjoyed with Keaton, Gatlin, and their whole crew.

"I'm going to take Kieran to the toy store over in Midland. I think he needs a new toy." She tapped her finger against her chin. "Collection."

I smiled at her.

Finally, with a tilt of her perfectly coiffed head, she nodded. "When Simon gets here, I trust you can entertain him." At my raised brows, she rolled her eyes. "Tell him I'll call to reschedule his appointment."

"Sure." I swallowed a lump in my throat, waiting until they were out of the driveway before I broke down. Collapsing onto the sofa, I hugged a pillow to my chest. This had been my childhood home, where I grew up happy and popular. Not that I could blame those women completely. My presumed guilt drew attention from an editor's column, a front page photo spread featuring my high school glory-day photos and daily social media stories. The town divided. Some waved and smiled, others turned to walk the other way when they crossed my path.

Simon arrived ten minutes later. Without question, he wrapped me in an embrace that comforted every part of my aching soul. "Wanna talk about it?"

I shook my head and buried my face in his shirt. His aftershave tingled my nose with the sweet and spicy smell of heaven, and I breathed deeply.

"Okay. Wanna make out then?"

I glanced up and smiled through my tears. "If I said I wasn't really in the mood, would you understand?"

He chuckled. "Of course."

"Well"--I grinned and tinkered with the buttons of his shirt--"I'm not saying it, at all." I pulled his head down for a soft kiss.

After some intense groping on the couch, he pulled away and ran his hand through his long hair. "You tempt me, woman." He took a deep breath, then released it slowly in a loud whistle of air through his lips. "I didn't come here for this, you know. I have an appointment with your mother."

Flustered from the kissing, I couldn't follow his whole train of thought. "I'm sorry." I tried for contrite, but ended up sounding smug and arrogant.

"I'll bet."

"And you don't have an appointment with my mother." I spilled the entire story in a rush of run-on sentences. "So, she took him to the toy store to make up for an entire town blaming him for his bad luck in the maternal gene pool."

"Wow. Those bitches." He licked his bottom lip. With him this close and still holding me, my troubles didn't seem so big. "They were so jealous of you in high school. That's what this is about." He spoke with force.

This time they had a way better reason than jealousy to hate me. "No, Simon, this is because they think I killed my husband so I could be with you."

"Hey, the only real memories I have are of high school. I remember them standing in front of my locker junior year telling Joss how you didn't deserve Keaton. They were so jealous of you--especially Jocelyn, and these were her friends too." He tucked me into his chest.

It turned out evilness hid behind popularity. "This sucks, Simon. There should be a limit to the amount of hurt I can inflict on this kid because I married Sean. I deserve what I deserve, but he's innocent."

With a curled finger under my chin, he lifted my face to meet his gaze. "Those girls aren't worth your time. Even if you killed Sean, even if you did it in coldblooded anger, I will love you every minute until I die."

I shook my head. "I didn't kill Sean."

"Yeah. That was my point." But his face lit up, eyes sparkling, cheeks dimpled.

Chapter 29

So many questions zoomed through my mind as I watched Simon and Kieran swim together and play with Kieran's trucks on the patio.

My mother, the eternal hostess, served lemonade and homemade chocolate croissants before whisking Kieran off to a nap he fought like a trooper. Finally, he settled on letting Simon tuck him in, and was sound asleep before Simon made the third step.

When he returned, he sat across from me, his hand outstretched, palm up. I slipped mine over top, and with his other hand he traced the veins leading from my fingers to my wrist. It took a while before he spoke. "I saw the scar on his back."

I nodded. "The doctor said it would fade with time."

"Do you want to tell me about it?"

I pulled away and folded my fingers in front of my mouth. "Not really." But didn't he have a right to know? If we were going to really be together, shouldn't he know it all? "Before that day, he never hit Kieran. He yelled at him, but he didn't hit him." I wished I could erase the pictures of that day from my mind, but I couldn't. They haunted me even now with Sean dead and buried. I shuddered at the thought of all Kieran had been through. "It was so hard there. I never knew what would set him off or how he would punish me, but he never touched Kieran; I promise that."

Simon nodded and scooted his chair closer.

"I wanted to leave so many times. I saw what the tension and the bruises on me were doing to Kieran, but I just stayed there like…" Like a fool? "I just stayed. Kieran was so quiet. He never talked anymore… barely said five words in a day if Sean was home, sometimes even if he wasn't." I'd thought I'd hardened my heart to the words, but my eyes burned and my throat closed as I wrestled with how to continue. "The day… The day it happened, I had a meeting with a department store. They'd offered me this huge contract a little earlier, but they lost a page or something. I didn't want to bring my kid along to re-sign, you know, but I couldn't leave him with Sean because he'd already run off with him once. I didn't trust him. I took Kieran to a girl who lived down the hill from us." I concentrated on the mundane details to avoid the ones I couldn't stand to relive.

"She hurt him?"

"I would have killed her." There was no doubt. If she would have touched Kieran, I would probably have ended up in jail way sooner. "Since things got so bad between me and Sean, Kieran saw things he shouldn't have seen, heard stuff I can never erase from his memory. Because of it, he started wetting his pants. A lot. And I was in such a big hurry to leave that morning, I forgot his bag, but I thought since he was with her, he would be more comfortable. I didn't think he would have an accident. I was wrong. She didn't know Sean was home, and she took Kieran to the house for more clothes. When she got there, Sean knew I lied. He knew I didn't take Kieran with me, so he kept Kieran."

This was the part... My heart lurched and my stomach rolled in agony. A trail of tears washed down my cheek.

"Baby, you don't have to do this."

I sniffed and nodded. "But I do." I flicked a tear away and stared through the sunset as though all I saw was darkness. "I haven't told anyone what happened. Not even Grace." I cleared my throat. "I have a lot to tell you."

"Okay."

After a few deep breaths, my eyes dried, my stomach settled, and my voice came in its solid form. "When I got back, I went to pick him up, and he wasn't with her anymore. She told me Sean had him. I ran up the hill into the house. It was quiet, too quiet. I called them both, and when no one answered, I started screaming for Kieran. Sean's car was there. His wallet was on the table. I knew he didn't go far." My mind retraced my footsteps as I raced through the house that day. "I found Sean passed out in the bedroom. When I shook him, he started screaming at me to shut up and leave him alone, but I needed to know Kieran was okay, so I just kept badgering him. He had locked him in the closet in the dark after he beat him with the belt."

Simon stared at me, his face blank.

"The scar on his back came from the belt, the one on his face came from the buckle, I think. When I found him, he was all bloody and scared. Sean came storming in there. He told me to put him back in the closet because Kieran was being punished." In my mind, my fury blinded me to Sean's. "I fought back once and he didn't take that very well, but this time, I went after him. My boy, my baby, was standing behind me bleeding, scared to death. I had to do something. He made me promise not to tell the cops what happened when I took Kieran to the hospital."

"But you told."

"Yeah. First thing I did. This really nice cop came to talk to me, and he helped me get out of there. He stayed with me while they sewed up Kieran, and he helped me plan how to get out. He even let me use his phone to call for help." I'd only known one California number by heart. My fingers had shaken as I dialed, hoping the vibe I'd always gotten hadn't been wrong. "While it was clearly the worst night of my life, it was the best, too, because I got away, made Kieran safe again."

"I'm glad that son of bitch is dead."

I couldn't lie. Although, I hadn't wished it out loud, I'd felt it almost since our wedding day. "Me too."

"I'll never hurt you."

"I've always known that, Simon."

"I love you."

And for that night, it was enough.

Chapter 30

Tuesday morning, court started with a full-out battle in chambers between Grace and Cal. The judge and I each stared at them as they volleyed back and forth, their arguments enraged. Cal wanted Lizette's testimony to proceed uncensored or clarified by a direction from the judge. Grace argued the testimony would do nothing but make me look bad. While certainly Cal's intent, Grace argued my rights took precedence.

"She's going to testify to hearsay evidence." Grace stood, bent at the waist, her face inches from Cal's. "She has no proof of anything he said or if it's true."

"Your Honor, the jury deserves to hear all the evidence. They deserve to hear Sean Hunter believed the child belonged to someone else, and he'd just found out. He was only in town to verify the truth of it." Cal spoke the words without ever tearing his gaze from my attorney's. "He's being painted as a vicious stalker when he had every right to use whatever means necessary to learn the truth."

"He painted the word 'whore' across the front of her house. He stalked her, terrorized her and, if you ask me, the kid is lucky he doesn't belong to that psychopath."

"Oh, speaking ill of the dead, Miss Wade, the person your client killed. That's gonna earn you a few extra minutes in hell."

Grace rolled her eyes and probably would have thumped him in the head had the judge not intervened.

"Let's try to keep our comments confined to the legal issues before us." The judge spoke quietly from behind a massive desk with a picture of former president Clinton behind it. "Miss Wade."

Grace remained standing nose to nose with Cal. When the judge repeated her words, Grace straightened her skirt, fluffed her hair, and took her seat.

"Mr. Cooper, she cannot testify to the truth of his words. She may only testify the conversation happened. You may not imply, infer, suggest, or in any way lead the jury to believe the words he spoke to Miss Lightener are the truth."

Fire flew from Grace's eyes. "Just because he told her whatever he told her does not make it fact."

With a wave of her hands, we were dismissed to return to the courtroom. After the initial commotion of the jury being led in and the gallery dwellers bustling for seats, Cal called Lizette Lightener to the stand.

"Don't look down, and don't look away from her" had been Grace's pearls of wisdom. *"Let her see your face or she won't show mercy."*

I kept my eyes pointed at her, wiped the hostility away with the thought of my boy being left alone with my parents. Lizette, in her ivory linen pant suit straight off the rack at Sears, strolled up to the witness box, raised her right hand, and swore to tell the truth while I bit the inside of my cheek to keep my face impassive. She took her seat and my gaze never managed to break free of hers.

From the grin on his face, Cal had started springing mental cartwheels in anticipation. I remained staring at Lightener. Her glare spoke volumes and I smiled, testing the waters. She squinted hard.

"Good morning, Ms. Lightener."

Grace clenched her pencil as Cal spoke.

"Good morning."

"On June fourth of last year, where did you work?"

"In the bakery I owned with Jocelyn Shaw."

The ridiculous cartoon voice and her oversized man body were at complete odds with one another, and I hid an inappropriate giggle behind my hand.

I prayed Cal stayed with the boring, mundane questions rather than jumping to the gasp-inspiring scandal version she probably couldn't wait to deliver.

"At the time, I owned half of the business and I worked the counter, made donuts, and handled business transactions."

"On June fourth, did you speak with Sean Turner?"

She nodded. Her coal black hair, cut short around her face, caught the light of the overhead fluorescents, making it seem almost Elvis Blue. "He came in looking for Jocelyn. She was gone so I asked if I could help him. He asked if I knew Danielle."

"And did you?"

"I'd only met her once before, but I'd heard a lot about her." Her frown dug deep into the lines around her lips.

"Did Mr. Turner share with you the reason he wanted to speak with Jocelyn?"

"About her brother, Simon, and his new relationship with *her*."

Wow.

She pointed a finger in my direction.

"And what about their relationship?" His smirk, as he turned to face me, said Cal loved this a little too much.

I hated him for it.

"He said she had some big secret. He said he would see her in hell before he let her have his son." Yeah. She flipped me a mental bird with that one.

Cal nodded. "Did Mr. Turner give you anything to give to Mrs. Shaw?"

Lizette nodded and licked her lips. I clenched my fist but remained seated as I waited for the answer. She paused and looked around Cal at me. "Yes, he did."

"Did you give it to her?"

Lizette feigned shame. "No. I'm friends with Simon and I wanted to see him happy. I didn't want to ruin their relationship." Her voice climbed an octave higher than it had been a moment earlier.

Pfft.

Cal strode to his desk--a man on a mission--and extracted a piece of paper from an envelope.

Shit. Damn. Shit. I looked away as he handed the paper to Lizette.

"Is this what he gave you?"

More teeth than I'd ever seen before enveloped her face as she smiled. "Yes."

Cal reclaimed the paper, then handed it to Grace. She stood and without ceremony approached the bench.

Oh, shit. Oh, shit. Oh, shit.

Grace returned to the table, paper in hand. "Your honor, we ask for an immediate recess so my office can verify the validity of this report."

The judge cast a weary glance at Cal. He shrugged as though he hadn't a care in the world. I sighed and she granted a recess until Thursday at one PM.

Grace grimaced at me. "I guess it's time I earn your money."

"Please, I can't have it come out this way, Grace. Not now."

She dropped me at home and promised to call me later. Fear stuttered my steps as I walked out to where Simon and Kieran lounged on the chaise, both dripping water all over the concrete.

"Are you gonna marry my mom?" Kieran looked over at Simon and I stepped behind a column holding up the awning over the patio. Anticipation pooled in my stomach. I wanted to hear his answer before I made my presence known.

"Would it be okay? If I asked your mom to be my wife?"

"I guess." Kieran pulled his towel tighter. "My dad hit my mom." Simon stayed quiet and Kieran added, "He hit me once." His finger touched the spot where a two-inch white scar remained. He turned away from Simon and stared out at the floating ring on the surface of the pool.

"I would never hit your mom, or you."

I had known him all my life. Simon solved life's problems with words and love, not fists and anger. Gentility rolled off him in waves. Believing him was easy.

Kieran turned to Simon. "Promise?"

Simon nodded. "I promise."

I stepped from behind the column and up to the chair they shared. "Hi."

Kieran looked up. He used Simon's leg as a springboard to launch himself into my arms. I stumbled backward, but caught my balance as I landed against another pillar. "I missed you today, buddy!" I pressed a kiss against his scar, then his cheek.

"I missed you too. I went swimming with Simon, and he said later we're going to muck a stall." He said it fast, as though all one word.

I laughed. "Do you know what mucking a stall means?"

"Nope."

Simon beamed a grin over the top of Kieran's head, and I, once again, thanked God for all I had and all I no longer had to worry about. I had one detail gnawing at me, the one I'd hid so long--too long.

"Simon, I need to talk to you." My voice trembled and I clutched my son tighter. The time had come for the big reveal.

Concern furrowed his brows as he regarded me with what I could only call wary eyes. "Do you have another husband stuck away somewhere?"

I smiled. "No." I watched him pull on his T-shirt, and for once, I hated all things cotton. As soon as I said the words, everything between me and Simon, everything in my entire world would change, and before it happened, I selfishly wanted one more perfect afternoon with him. "But we can talk later. I'm going to go put on a suit and get some sun before it all disappears."

"I'll wait here and take my let's-have-a-talk shirt off." He grinned, and yanked his T-shirt over his head.

We spent the afternoon with Kieran, splashing and playing in the last of the summer sunshine.

"Mom, don't you think I should have a nap?" He had a fisted hand on each hip, a wide stance, and a tight line for a mouth.

"I suppose so." I chuckled. "Let's go."

He ran upstairs, changed his clothes, and hopped into his bed before I made it to the landing. I kissed his cheek and pulled the blanket up to his chin. "If you need me, just call out."

But his eyes were already closed in sleep.

I took a deep breath and walked outside to sit by Simon.

Finally, he pressed his lips to mine. "Why were you home so early?"

"Recess so Grace could take care of something--an evidence thing." I'd never been vague with him about my case before--never had a real reason--but, if he noticed, he didn't react. His smile remained in place, and his gaze raked over my body.

Taking in every detail of his face, I slowly memorized as much as I could. I didn't know how the next few moments were going to go, but if it went badly, I wanted to be able to recall everything about him later. The summer sun lightened his blond hair even more, reacting with the highlights Gatlin begged to put in. His eyes glowed the color of warmed brandy. He needed to shave, but the look on him inspired a desire to run my hands over his cheeks. His body glistened, smooth and rippled, as though it had been chiseled from stone, and I slid a hand over his abs.

The only flaw, if it could be called such a thing, was the small sunburst at his hairline that showed his courage, his willingness to die to protect others. Unless he pulled his hair straight back, the scar hid behind long strands. He'd always been beautiful and perfect, and I had about six seconds left before I lost him. My body trembled at the thought.

He sat quietly as I continued my inventory of all the things that made him the Simon I loved. After a few minutes, he tipped my chin up with his finger. "Whatever it is, Dani, you can tell me."

I swallowed hard. For the first time in my life, I didn't have words ready. I put my head on his chest, listening to the steady thrum of his heartbeat.

"This is us. You can tell me anything."

"I don't want to lose you."

His thumb caressed my cheek. "Dani, don't you know?" He pulled me close and touched his lips to mine in a kiss so gentle I sighed when he pulled back. "I don't remember my life after I turned seventeen, but you are familiar to me. As soon as I saw you in the bakery that day, I felt a connection to you. It's why Lizette and I didn't work out. I needed you before we ever touched again." His forehead rested against mine. "Nothing you can say will drive me away. I'm here because I *can't* be without you. And as weak as it makes me, I don't want to be without you."

As I opened my mouth to say the words, my phone rang. I looked at the screen. Grace. "I have to take this, okay?" He dropped his hands as I answered. "Well?" We'd dispensed with hello as a greeting long ago.

"There's nothing I can do to stop it. You are going to have to testify, and it better be good."

I closed my eyes.

"Dani? Are you there?"

"Yeah." Taking a deep breath, I blew it out into the speaker of the phone, trying to disguise my turmoil from the waiting Simon.

"You'd better tell him and soon. Today might not be soon enough."

"Okay." My voice shrunk into a squeak. "Grace, am I going to jail?"

She took a long pause, then came back in a whisper. "I don't know, Dani. I hope not." She ended the call without a good-bye, and I stared at the phone in my hand.

"Simon, Sean isn't Kieran's dad, and I have to tell the person who is." I blurted the words in a quick breath before my courage escaped.

"I know."

My eyes, previously downcast, searched his face.

"And it's going to come out in court on Thursday."

"It's okay." He didn't understand. In fairness, he didn't have all the information yet.

I ran my hands through my hair and took two steps away, needing the distance. "Before I left Storybook Lake to"--to what? Be with Keaton? Sleep with Sean?--"to go to Arizona the first time, I had a little fling. The timing's why Keaton thought…why I let Keaton think… Kieran belonged to him. I was pregnant when I got there."

"And Sean?"

I sounded like a big slut, but I continued with my tawdry tale. "I met him a couple days after I got there. He also assumed because of the timing and how old Kieran was when we ran into each other the second time." Why couldn't I just say the words? I took a deep breath as his hands came up to rest on my shoulders and his body warmed mine. "Anyway, before I left, I slept with someone."

"So you said."

"Two someones actually." A little love drained from his eyes and the gap between our bodies widened.

"Two?" He dropped his hands. "Who?"

"It was a few days apart." I didn't want to give him names. I couldn't bear to consider what he would think about me and closed my eyes. "There was no reason to tell. I did everything I could, I mean, I still do, to make it not matter to Kieran."

"And you think that's fair?" He backed off five or six more steps. "You think *he* doesn't have a right to know? What are you going to tell him when he asks?"

"I don't know." His eyes darkened and his hands clenched at his side. I moved closer, needing to touch him, if only this one last time. "There were so many reasons I thought I couldn't tell." And every single one sounded stupid. "I made a mistake."

"Then why?" He shook his head and crossed his arms. "Why the hell would you not tell a man he has a son as soon as you know you're pregnant?"

I reached for him and he moved farther away. "Does he not deserve to know? You're not being fair to Kieran or...his father." He ran his hands though his hair, capturing it at the crown of his skull before he let it fall around his face. "Don't you think he needs a dad? Someone to teach him right from wrong? Someone to scare the monsters out from under his bed?"

A fight with Simon wouldn't help the situation, but my blood turned cold. "I scare the monsters away." It didn't matter. I had to tell him. "I have to get this out, Simon."

He ran his fingers through his hair and turned away. "Oh, man."

"There's a reason I never told anyone about Kieran."

"Oh, I'd love to hear how you justify that." The sarcasm fell from between clenched teeth.

"Would you stop being this way?" Not that I could blame him, but my newfound courage waned in the face of his anger. "I'm trying to tell you something."

"I don't want to know, Dani." His voice turned to steel, and the pain of his words slammed into me the same as if he'd slapped me in the face.

"You don't get a choice. I'm sorry. This isn't the way I wanted to handle it, but I don't have a choice now. There's a very real possibility I'm going to jail. I have to tell the truth."

"Isn't it a little late for that?"

"Seriously."

"I can't deal with this right now."

He turned to walk away, and I gave a three step chase to grab him by the arm and step around him. "Why do you get to choose what you deal with when the rest of us have to buck up and handle things we don't want to? What makes you so special that you get to pick?" My voice rose parallel to my anger.

"Because I haven't spent my life lying to everyone who loves me."

"I didn't lie." I shook my head and crossed my arms. "All I have ever done is take care of Kieran. I hold him when he cries. I teach him right from wrong, and I protect him from the big bad wolf." My heart shattered with every word I spoke. "I'm the one he cries for. I'm the home he knows. Once, I thought I would tell, but so many things happened and I couldn't. He wouldn't have been able to deal with it, or maybe he wouldn't have believed me, but I didn't lie." My eyes blazed a path up his body.

"Bullshit. And it isn't about protecting Kieran. It's about you. Always about you." He moved closer, towering over me.

I shoved against his chest. "You go to hell, Simon. Everything I do is for Kieran." I knew he would be angry and upset. I expected it and tried to brace myself to handle it like an adult. I failed. "And what about the things you kept from him? From me?"

"Fuck. You."

He looked over my shoulder at the door to the house where Kieran stood, tears dripping down his cheeks. "Shit."

I went to Kieran, pulled him into my arms, then turned to Simon. "Go, Simon. Just go."

"I'm so sorry. I would never hurt you or Kieran." His chin hung against his chest, and his voice turned soft as he reached out a hand. "Please, Dani."

"Go." I shook my head, then walked into the house cradling my son in my arms, and never looked back.

Chapter 31

I woke up sadder and lonelier than I'd ever been before, mourning the loss of yet another man in my life. The worst part? This one had been right about everything. I'd been selfish, but not in the way he thought. When I'd first figured out who Kieran belonged to, I wanted nothing more than to tell, but I couldn't. He needed to decide on his own. Just once, I wanted someone to pick me, not by default or because of obligation, but because *he* really wanted *me*. Because of my selfishness, I hadn't taken Kieran into consideration. Who would take my boy on his first camping trip? Or be the Boy Scout troop leader? Coach his soccer games?

I hadn't concentrated on the trial at all during the morning session, and the afternoon wasn't looking promising, either. Snippets of Grace's conversation with the detective broke through my grief, but for the most part, I wallowed my way through the day.

After the judge called the daily recess, I stood next to Grace. "I think today went our way. They can't prove the gun was Simon's, and they handled so many things incorrectly."

I nodded, but couldn't summon a reaction to wipe the wide-eyed look from her face.

"What the hell is wrong with you?" She jerked me to a halt by the arm as I walked ahead of her to the car. "I'm telling you what a great day we had today and it's like you don't care. This is your life, Dani. You think you might want to participate in it a little?"

"What do you want, Grace? A cartwheel? A 'you go girl?' I'm paying you a lot of money, so I figured by the decrease in my checking account, I was absolved from being your damned cheerleader."

Instead of drawing back a fist and punching me in the face, she dropped her hand, laughing. "Wow. You and Simon aren't playing nice anymore, I guess?"

"What? No. We're fine."

"For doing it so often, you're a shitty liar." She fell into step beside me. "He wasn't in court today."

"Thank you for pointing it out." I sighed and stomped a few steps away before I turned to find she'd stopped. "I wanted to tell him about Kieran last night, but we got into an argument." I leaned against a minivan, lamenting the horrible choices I'd made.

She patted my shoulder. "Not that I don't hope you and Simon have a happily ever after fit for a fairy tale, but don't you think you should be concentrating on this case and your testimony tomorrow?" She nudged me in the ribs. "If you go to jail, things with Simon are over anyway, right?"

I nodded and sighed. "Right."

"Let's go get you prepped for testimony."

We drove back to my parent's house to do a run through of the things safe to talk about and the things I needed to stay away from.

"Remember, I know all the details, okay? But the jury doesn't. So share. Be wordy. We want you on the stand so they get to know you, to feel everything you felt, but choose those words carefully. Even if they think you're guilty, we need them to know you had a reason bigger than the law. If by some chance you're found guilty, it'll make all the difference in sentencing. Be careful, though. Whatever we bring up, Cal can grill you about on cross."

We spent the evening working on what clothes I'd wear, how my hair should be fixed, and what questions she'd be asking. A little after midnight, she climbed into her car, and I went to bed. I checked my phone repeatedly all night, but no call from Simon ever came.

Chapter 32

Along with the sun came the butterflies and anxiety of having to testify in front of not only a jury, but the gallery, along with a television and Internet audience. For court, I wore a very feminine white dress with cap sleeves and a sweetheart neckline. My shoes were low heeled and closed toe. Grace had turned me into a puritan for what she called the performance of my lifetime. My hair fell free over my shoulders in soft wavy curls. Finally, after a thousand deep breaths and a few reassuring nods from Grace, she moved to stand behind the podium in front of me. Reporters and sketch artists sitting alongside high school classmates and acquaintances crowded into the gallery. Simon was still nowhere to be seen. I focused on Grace.

"Danielle, there are probably two big questions everyone wants the answer to. Did you kill Sean Turner?"

"No."

She paused and I knew she wanted more.

"I should have… I wanted to, but I didn't."

Her eyes popped wide open, and she cleared her throat as she nodded and flipped pages in her notes back and forth. "How long have you lived in Storybook Lake?" A safer subject.

"Most of my life. I was born here and I went to school here. After I went north for college, I came home. I've gone away a couple of times but somehow, I always end up in Storybook Lake."

"And you went with Keaton Shaw?"

"Yes."

I told the story with enough bits and pieces to be true, but no one needed to know about my impure motives, so, at Grace's previous urging, I kept them to myself.

She led me through the years I lived with Keaton, meeting Sean, the abuse, and the agony of his behavior.

"Why didn't you leave?" In a move more inspired by friendship than her job description, she moved around the podium and took my hand in hers. "Why didn't you come home then?"

"I was ashamed, embarrassed. After everything I'd done, I thought I deserved it."

I filled the time with story after story of abuse, and with every tale I finished, she asked why I didn't just come home. The excuses ranged from desperation, to no way to get there, to nowhere to go. No one seemed to care beyond the first couple. We'd spent too long making me pathetic.

Before Grace had the chance to fix it, the judge took the opportunity to call a twenty minute recess.

* * * *

After the break, we went through the day I left California. I detailed what Sean did to Kieran, and Grace held up pictures I'd seen too many times.

"He let you take Kieran to get help?"

"Yes. I drove to the hospital and told the doctor everything, then the social worker and the cops. They arrested Sean. While they kept him at the police station, I got as much stuff for me and Kieran as I could, called a cab, flattened his tires, and threw his phone in the ocean. I cut up his credit cards and hid his money in the dishwasher. Then, I walked out the door, got in the cab, and that was it."

"You didn't take his money?" Grace turned from me to Cal as she asked.

"No. I had my own money. I'd signed a really big contract, and anyway, I put all the money into our relationship even before that. His club and the drugs cost him more than he brought in. The house, the cars, the furniture, all of it was mine."

"How long were you back in Storybook Lake before Sean got in touch with you?"

"He contacted my mom a little while after I came home." I took a big drink of water. "I called him and asked him to sign the divorce papers, and he told me he would kill me before he signed anything. After that, he would text and leave voice mails at random times, threatening me."

"Did you tell anyone?"

"I told everybody. I let them listen to the voice mails. My dad called a security company to upgrade our system. Then, for a while Sean left me alone, stopped harassing me, so I thought he gave up and I moved out."

"Did it stop when you moved out?"

"No. He amped up his level of crazy." I related all the details of the harassment I'd gone through in Storybook Lake. Every gaze in the room stuck to me. I'd never been the object of such rapt attention, and my heart raced under the intense scrutiny.

Grace slid her hands into her pockets and leaned her butt against Cal's table. He slid back and moved his chair to the side as though he wanted to watch me while I spoke. "What happened when you went to Sean's hotel?"

"I sat in the car for a long time, watching, waiting for something to happen. Then, Joey, one of the guys who worked for Sean, showed up and they argued. I couldn't hear but it looked bad. Afterward, Joey walked away and Sean went inside."

"What did you do then?"

"I knocked on the door. He just stood there and looked at me like he couldn't believe I'd been brave enough to come. To be honest, courage had nothing to do with it. I think at that point, a bit of mania had seeped in. I had Simon's gun in my pocket and Sean in my face."

"How did you get Simon's gun?"

"I took his car that morning. He kept it in his glove box."

"So did you point the gun at Sean?"

"Yes. I held it out like to shoot him, but I didn't know about the safety on the gun and I couldn't get it to fire. I tried. He took it and hit me in the face with the handle. I went down, and I think he expected me to stay there, but I didn't. Not this time. When he raised the gun--I guess to shoot me--I kicked him. The gun fell and while he laid down there, holding himself, I kicked him again and again. Then, I just stopped. I got in Simon's car, locked the doors, and left. A few blocks later, I pulled over and cried." As I sat there, reflecting on the feeling I'd experienced, I lost my breath for a second. I sucked in a shallow puff of air and blew out a long one. "I know I should have called the police, but I didn't."

"But the police here are your friends."

"And yet"--I didn't hide a grimace--"I'm on trial."

"I'm going to ask you again. Did you kill Sean Turner?" This wasn't her lawyer voice. This was her best friend, please-tell-me-the-truth-I-think-you're-lying voice. In fairness, all those years of alcohol abuse may have blurred her ability to reason.

"No. If I did, I would be claiming self-defense right now."

She sighed. "What happened next?"

"I wanted to finish it, you know? So, I went back, and I would have let him kill me. I just wanted it to end that bad. I knew Mom and Dad would take care of Kieran." I rubbed my hand over my face and looked out at the gallery. All my old friends sat in the rows in front of reporters and media crews recording my every word.

"What happened when you went back to the hotel?"

"The door wasn't shut all the way and I pushed it open." My arm swung in a sideways arc as my mind and my body worked together to recreate the act for the jury. "I didn't see Sean. I checked the bathroom, the closet."

Her eyes shifted, above me, around me, beside me, everywhere but at me. "What did you see, Dani?"

Another batch of tears formed and spilled over onto my cheeks. "Grace, you believe me, right?"

She looked down at her hands. "I don't know, Dani. Why didn't you call the police? They were looking for him to question him. It would have gotten him off the streets, taken the heat off of you so you could figure out what to do. You know the cops here. They're your friends."

"Again, friends who arrested me."

"Not until later." She brushed her hands down her skirt, still not looking at me. "What did you see when you walked into the hotel room, Danielle?"

"The windows were open, and I came out of the bathroom, facing the bed. I saw his foot. Someone had trashed the whole place, maybe Sean did it himself, I don't know, but someone had thrown the clothes and bed sheets on top of him." I had never talked with my hands before, but now waved them like a flag on a windy day. I clasped them in my lap, afraid I looked silly. "It didn't feel like he'd gotten drunk or stoned, then collapsed in a messy room. He was too still." My mind's eye replayed the scene in digital clarity. "He had a line of blood on his face, right here." I trailed a finger down my cheek below my left eye. "And a few blood stains on his shirt, but I didn't get any closer to look. And he had all his clothes on except his shoes." I shuddered at the thought of what he'd been through. "Someone shot him in the head. And I saw Simon's gun next to him on the floor."

"Did you take Simon's gun?" Her voice hadn't yet recovered the confidence in her stance, and her words quivered as she spoke.

"No. I didn't. I just stood there and stared at him."

She cleared her throat and I smiled at her. She had to pull it together. Quick. "Did you touch Sean?"

"I touched his hand and I moved some clothes off his leg." I might have kicked him.

"Why didn't you call the police?"

"I brought the gun there. I wanted to shoot him, and my fingerprints were on the gun." At the time, I'd assumed the gun would be found. "There was no way anyone would believe I didn't do it."

Grace's face tightened, and she had her going-to-kick-my-butt-face on.

"We had a bad relationship and everybody knew it. So, in terms of suspects, I would have been a really good one. I obviously didn't have an alibi. I'd been sitting outside his room for hours. I mean, I've told most of this story a hundred times and here I am."

"Do you have any idea how Sean's blood got into your house?"

"I assume I brought it back with me. I changed my clothes in the mudroom and threw them in the washer."

"Was Simon there when you got back?"

"He came later. He'd been out looking for me."

"Was anyone home?"

"No. I was alone."

Chapter 33

When I left the courthouse, Jocelyn stood on the steps waiting. I shifted my neck from one side to the other and looked down at her. "Are you waiting for me?"

She nodded and fell into step beside me and Grace. "I didn't know about your husband or what you went through."

"It's not something I'm proud of."

"Simon explained a lot of what happened in your life, and today, hearing all of that from you… I wanted to say… I'm sorry, Danielle."

I wasn't sure if she was sorry for our entire relationship or just for the moments that inspired the pity reflected in her eyes, but at the moment, I didn't care. It was an apology and it was good enough for me. We could resume our battle another day. For now, I needed all the friends I could get. "Me too."

She nodded, turned, and walked a few steps before stopping to look at me again. "Good luck."

"Thanks. I think I might need it." As Joss made her way down the sidewalk, Grace led me to her car.

"Luck? I'm kicking ass in there." Grace drove for a few minutes before she pulled into a parking lot. "If you didn't kill Sean, who did?"

"I don't know." I had a couple guesses, each one with as much merit as the other, but none I would use as a get out of jail free card.

"Maybe it was somebody in the notebook."

"No. Sean wasn't the big time. He was just some penny ante drug dealer who owned a strip club."

"But the book was more. It had fetishes and real names. Important names. What if he was blackmailing someone and they took him down?"

"And they would come all the way here and do it? I doubt it. Sean was a flea compared to those names." I'd read them, memorized them. Captains of industry, finance, and politics had quite the sexual preferences and used Sean to sate their perverted appetites.

"Then who, Danielle?"

"I don't know."

"Okay then. What happened after you got back that day? Didn't Simon want to know where you were?"

"I already told you. He wasn't there when I got back." I took a moment to consider the notebook. *Could she be right?* I doubted it. It had to be someone here who took justice into their own hands…someone I probably owed my life to…someone who loved me. Where had Simon gone that night?

"I still want to check the notebook and see if anyone associated with some of those names has turned up here."

"I need to see Simon." Maybe I wasn't the only one who had a few secrets in the metaphorical back pocket.

"I thought he was mad at you."

"Well, he's gonna have to get over it." I blew out a breath. "We have some things we need to discuss." So many things, I couldn't even formulate an entire list without losing track.

Instead of speaking, she pulled the car back onto the road and, before I knew it, we'd arrived at my house. I rushed up the walk and burst through the front door to silence. Mom must have taken Kieran out for the day.

I walked into the kitchen, dialing my cell. A moment later, I dropped the cell onto the floor and watched the battery slide across the tile. "Joey?"

He held up both hands.

"How did you get in here?" I looked around for a weapon, anything I could use if Joey turned out not to be the person I'd believed.

"We need to talk." His voice was the gentle, but no-nonsense one he'd used when he gave me the notebook and told me to only use it if an absolute need presented itself and my life was in danger. "Sit down." His black hair gleamed under the light at the counter. He stared at me, then motioned to the chair at the table.

I crossed to the coffee maker, close to the knife set in the butcher block. "How about a drink, Joe?"

"Sure." He stood and leaned against my mother's counter, for all the world looking comfortable and happy in his chosen profession as break-and-enterer with his legs crossed at the ankles. He braced his hands at his sides on the cool granite. "Danielle."

His voice caused me to flinch, and I inched a hand closer to the blades.

"I'm not here to hurt you."

I spun around and moved a step to the left. If I needed to grab a weapon, I wanted to have an easy reach. "Then why are you here?"

"I'm not who you think I am."

I rolled my eyes, somewhat tired of being wrong about people. "Join the club. No one is ever who I think they are."

He reached into the pocket of his jacket, and I yanked a knife forward. "If that's a gun, I swear to God, Joey…" I had nothing to swear. I wasn't Superman and I had no way to beat a speeding bullet.

"How did you manage to keep yourself alive all this time?" He shook his head and smiled. "It's a badge." Wow--shiny gold, FBI, alongside a picture ID. "Now, can we talk or are you planning to carve a turkey?" He nodded toward my left hand.

I put the knife in the sink and stepped close enough to snatch his credentials out of his hand. "How do I know it's real? How do I know you didn't get it at a hobby store or something to trick me?" It looked real, was heavy in my hand, and laminated in all the right places. I glanced from Joey to the picture and back again.

"For what? What purpose would I have to trick you?"

"I don't know. What *purpose* do you have for being in my house?" What did the FBI want with a girl from Storybook Lake, Illinois with an ankle bracelet as her only jewelry, who'd at worst only ever gotten a single speeding ticket? Not counting this murder thing.

"I'm here to help you stay out of jail."

"I have a lawyer for that."

"Well, the way I see it, you're about five witnesses from kissing your freedom good-bye." He shrugged and took his little black wallet back. "Your lawyer's probably one of the best I've ever seen, but the prosecutor is about to get a forensic report that puts your prints on the gun."

"What?"

He reached down and picked up my cell, took his time reassembling it and powering it on while I stood gaping at him.

"Dani, some very powerful people need to make sure you go to jail for Sean's murder. I can't explain it all, but the notebook I gave you when you left California has the names of senators and judges, corporate people who have a lot to lose if the investigation stays open, and they have the right people on their payroll. You have one lawyer who, no matter how good she is, is in over her head." He spoke with such conviction that even though the story sounded ludicrous to me, I had no choice but to believe his words.

The words "make sure you go to jail" rang over and over in my mind.

"So what do I do?"

"Call your boyfriend."

Chapter 34

Simon didn't answer, so I left a message detailing Joey's plan. I prayed being bait wouldn't get me killed. Before I walked out of the house behind Joey, I left a note for my mom with everything she'd always wanted to know written inside.

We climbed in the non-descript sedan he'd hidden down the block. Instead of going over the details of what he wanted me to do, he turned to me and smiled. "Have you thought about what you are going to do with the club, yet?"

"No, maybe close it down or"--I grasped his arm and he jerked away-- "Maybe I'll just give it to you." I feigned excitement, forced a bubbliness into my voice not matching the gnawing in my stomach.

He hung his head down to his chest. "Aw, Dani, how did you ever get messed up with that son-of-a-bitch?" He ran onto the shoulder as he looked over at me. With a quick jerk of his arm, he pulled the car back onto the road.

I jumped and a slight squeal escaped my throat. "Joey?" Fear inched up my spine and my mind rolled in icy terror. Images of Sean killed by someone big enough to overpower him floated through my thoughts. Huge under-described Joey and puny over-described me. I'd be an easy kill for someone like him. I didn't know the name of the emotion beyond terror, but I definitely trembled from it. How did I know Joey was telling the truth? Maybe the badge was fake.

"I'm sorry, Dani."

My mouth went dry. My heart pounded and I turned my body to face him. "For what?"

"Did you find the videos?"

Videos? What videos? Then it dawned on me. There'd been a "V" next to some of the names in the notebook. God. How big an idiot could I be? "No."

"Did you read the notebook?"

From his tone, the answer mattered. "No."

"Is there anywhere you know--a storage shed maybe, or another safe room--where he might have hidden them?"

I shook my head. "I can't think of anywhere else. Our house or the club, but I assume you've been all over those, right?"

He chugged out a huffy breath and turned the car off onto a country road that hadn't seen pavement in years. We bumped along, my head smacking against the roof with each pothole he plowed over. He pulled to a stop in front of an old farmer's shack that should have met the wrecking ball several years earlier.

"Joey?"

He turned to me, grabbed my shoulders in a tight fist of bone and skin. "I need you to trust me. I won't let anyone hurt you, but you have to follow my lead." Another car pulled in behind us, and Joey curled his fingers tighter. I let out a little shriek of pain. He loosened his hold. "Wait until I let you out, and remember, I'll keep you safe. I'm one of the good guys."

Before he stepped out, I grabbed his shirt. "Shouldn't you have other good guys for back-up?"

"Don't worry. It's under control."

I nodded as a basketball sized knot of undigested fear formed in my stomach. After a moment, he came around my side and yanked me out onto the dirt road. He hauled me around the back of the car where two men stood, obviously waiting for us.

"Are they here?" Joey asked.

One of the men in black wordlessly walked to the passenger rear door of a second car, and with a cool flip of his wrist, popped it open. California Judge, Dale McHuney, stepped out first, followed by the President of Waterworks Industries, H. Morgan Smiter, and finally, Ambassador Marco Wintani. I'd read articles about them in the newspaper in LA, seen them on TV, and remembered their names from the book.

McHuney raised his glance from my shoes to my eyes, taking in all the space between. "Mrs. Turner." He smiled and held out his hand as his cronies nodded their greetings in my direction.

I crossed my arms, and he looked from me to Joey.

"Does she have it?"

"No, sir." The captains of industry and government huddled up. McHuney, a whisper of a man with salt and pepper hair, had a frame that could have benefited from suits a size smaller. Smiter, a slightly younger man, putting him in his mid-fifties with a ring of brown hair around a shiny bald cap, stood next to Wintani, a mid-thirty-ish Italian with coal black hair and blacker eyes.

Having studied the book enough to memorize their names and habits, and being this close to the trio of perverts, turned my stomach. Each had a "V" next to his name in the book that had always made me wonder.

When they turned back to us, Smiter asked, "And the videos?"

"She doesn't have them."

McHuney turned away and began walking back to the car. Over his shoulder, he tossed, "Get rid of her."

I didn't care for the sound of that and thought quickly, pulling a lame-brained idea out of the air. "Wait!"

McHuney and his posse stopped.

"I'll get you the videos." I hadn't even known they existed, but now I claimed to have them. My brain cells had sprung a leak, and the dumb ideas inside dripped out my mouth.

Joey squeezed my arm and yanked me closer to his body.

McHuney stepped away from the group and walked up to me. "You have them?"

I shrugged. "Not me, exactly, but I gave them to someone to hold for me."

"It's not the lawyer," Wintani said. "Aaron tossed her place. All he found were copies of the notebook."

"Not at her folks house, either," Smiter said, a real glimmer of evil in his eyes. Even his grin inspired a new bout of the shakes. "My guys clean up afterward."

A cold chill shot down my spine at the thought of someone rooting through our belongings.

McHuney looked from Joey to me and back again. "She's lying?"

"I believe so, sir," Joey said.

"Seriously?" I turned to Joey, thinking how badly I wanted to stomp his foot. "Sean told me all about you guys and your crazy fetishes." I jerked free of Joey's meat-fisted grasp. "And I have videos of each naughty little escapade. Unless you want the whole world to know you are a trio of perverts, you leave me and my family alone. Go the hell away and the videos never see the light of day."

McHuney laughed a full-on guffaw, holding his stomach and grabbing on to Wintani for support to stay upright. "She thinks she is on an episode of *The Sopranos*." He mimicked me in a high voice. "Just leave me alone and the videos will never see the light of day." That set him off on a fresh bubble of laughter. Then in a quick as lightening kind of move, he grabbed a gun from one of the men in black and pointed it at me.

Joey stepped in front of me. McHuney, without a second thought, shot him in the leg. "God dammit, Joseph. I really didn't want to have to do that." Joey went down in one motion to an automatic sitting position. I surveyed the wound as best I could. The blood trickled slowly without any indication of a big ooze or a spray of arterial damage, so I stood straighter, lifted my chin a notch higher. In my mind, after dragging me out here, putting me in harm's way, he'd earned a little wound.

"Leave her alone." Joey pulled himself to a standing position, the injured leg an inch or so off the ground. "She doesn't have them."

"Don't listen to him." The words just kept coming. "I'll keep your secrets if you let me and Joey go."

"An hour ago"--McHuney advanced, a vicious curl to his lips and his finger on the trigger--"he was primed to kill you, and now you're bargaining for his freedom. I find that curious." His head tilted to the side as he considered my rather erratic behavior. He looked over at his employee, then up to his friends. "What is it with this broad?" He turned to look at Wintani and Smiter. "She had one crawling all over the country to find her, she's screwing another one on the side, and now you too?"

He curled his lip, obviously not seeing what all the fuss was about.

"What can I say? I'm what all the boys are into this year."

McHuney rolled his eyes and leveled the gun at me. "I think the boys are going to have to find a new plaything." He pulled back the hammer on a shiny, pearl handled revolver.

"Just tell me this." I had to keep them talking. "Which one of you killed Sean?"

Wintani looked at me, an amused smile on his lips. "What makes you think one of us murdered him?" His thick accent accounted for his broken words. "I am hearing his angry wife killed him."

"We all know I didn't do it." I rolled my eyes. "So, it isn't rocket science, is it?" I smiled, about to impress them with my brilliant powers of deduction to stall for time. "Sean blackmailed each one of you, didn't he? How much did he get? Thousands? Hundreds of Thousands? Doesn't matter." I shook my head and started pacing back and forth, thinking of nothing more than moving targets and the chance to run.

"But the money didn't matter for you guys, right? This little piece of shit strip club owner had something on you that would ruin your sparkly little reputations as church-going, world-saving heroes. I mean, how would it look if the Honorable Judge McHuney showed up on TMZ licking cocaine off the toes of some blond bimbo he paid by the hour? Or philanthropist H. Morgan Smiter getting a whipped cream massage? And an ambassador to whatever country you"--I didn't know the word, so I winged it--"ambass for--frolicking in your pink lace panties and bustier. You guys didn't care about the money."

"Again, Mrs. Turner, this isn't an episode of *The Sopranos*. It has nothing to do with our egos." McHuney chuckled again. He had a jovial kind of attitude for a guy who shot his henchman, then pointed his gun at me. "It's all about the money."

"So, you killed Sean."

He nodded slightly. "You should have dialed 9-1-1 when you found him. Maybe the cops would have believed you." He shrugged. "Then again, maybe not." He waved his gun through the air before pointing it more directly at my chest. "A pretty little thing like you in jail? How long do you think you'd last? Your little fireman can't save you there. Trust me. This is better." He shrugged. "Joseph will clean this up, and you'll be another missing person in a world full of them."

"You just shot him." My mouth went dry and my heart hammered. I promised God I would leave all the hero business to Iron man and Thor if he got me out of this one. "Why would he clean up anything for you?"

"You're a stupid girl. He works for me. I pay him a lot of money and he'll do it because I tell him to."

A car flew up from behind them, covering us all in a cloud of dust. Before it rolled to a complete stop, Simon jumped from the passenger seat and Luke came out the other side. Each had a gun aimed at the men in front of me.

McHuney yanked me between him and the guns aimed his way.

Simon stepped closer. "Let her go or this isn't going to end well."

"You really are what all the boys want, aren't you?" He looked at Simon. "Is she really worth it?"

I wanted to turn around and tackle him as he dug his fingers into my shoulder and tightened his grip across my chest. The last thing I needed was this guy giving Simon any reason to doubt me further.

"She lied to you about your kid." He chuckled. "It's his, right?"

"That's between me and her. Now let her go."

He shifted his body from side to side. "How's your aim since your little accident?"

Joey sat on the ground behind us. "I don't know about his, but mine is great, and the chances of me missing at this distance aren't in your favor."

The events of the next few seconds happened one on top of another in such rapid fashion I couldn't focus on anything other than being pulled into Simon's arms, crushed against him as Joey fired (and missed) and McHuney took off running. Officers and agents had Wintani and Smiter in custody, and we all watched as a couple guys with guns took off after McHuney, tripping him as he almost made it to the small crossing at the creek bordering the tree line. He landed hard on his face before they pulled him up, slapped on the cuffs, and dragged him to the car.

Another agent knelt next to Joey and told him to stay still until the ambulance arrived. The blood had drained from his face, but he looked up at me and smiled. "You had me worried there for a minute. I wasn't so sure about you."

Simon walked over to talk with Luke, but every few seconds glanced over at me as though he was afraid I'd disappear.

Joey grinned. "I didn't think we'd be friends anymore after I put half of California on your tail."

I plopped down on the ground next to him. "I was rethinking it, but everything worked out."

He folded his hands in his lap. "I would never have let them hurt you."

I nodded. "So, just to get this straight, you knew all along I didn't do it?"

He nodded. "Of course I did. You're not a killer." He cracked his neck. "So, I suppose you're going home with your boyfriend now?" His eyes remained glued to his hands, but his voice cracked with a moderate note of hope.

"It's up to him, but I hope so." I spoke softly, with my own bit of optimism.

"You gonna tell him about Kieran?"

I nodded. It was time.

Chapter 35

Simon waited for me by the truck he and Luke had arrived in.

"You saved my life."

"You saved mine first." He reached out, pulled me close, and buried his head in my hair. After a few deeps breaths, he cupped my face with his palm. "After…" He pointed to the scar on his head. "I thought the way my heart beat was the way it would for the rest of my life--kind of shallow and just wrong. Then you came back and my heartbeat, my everything, was right again."

The wind picked up the scent of his aftershave and delighted my nose as it sent the powerful aroma my way. "I have so much to tell you." My heart jackhammered a path through my chest. We stood silently staring at one another. I had no power to move, to speak, to breathe. This was my chance to come clean, to let him know the reason I had kept such a big secret. Yet, I stood mute, my pulse pounding in my ears.

"I shouldn't have said those things to you about Kieran's dad. It isn't my business." He leaned with his back against the truck and his gaze on my face. "Is it?"

My eyes drifted closed. "Yes." For as matter-of-fact as my voice sounded my heart beat so loud I had to believe he could hear it. "I know you don't remember the day I left here to go to Arizona, but you were in the stable." I looked toward the woods behind him. "We had a little chat, then…" God. I didn't want to tell him this way. Honestly, in the beginning, I didn't know if I would ever even get the chance to say the words to him. "Do you remember any of it?"

He shook his head and frowned.

I investigated my shoes. "I asked you if you could think of any reason for me to stay here, and you didn't answer." I sighed. The words choked me. "I wanted to marry you, and I thought we were almost there. Then you… You broke my heart. I stuck around here for as long as I could, but seeing you hurt so bad." So I ran away with his friend.

"Dani--"

He reached out and grabbed my hand, but I ignored him and kept going. "Anyway, one minute, I was saddling a horse and the next we were…" I took a deep breath. "We were making Kieran."

"I know."

"What?" I looked at him.

"My mom and Joss were at the grocery store when Bart and Kieran came in looking for ice cream."

He hardly ever called my dad by his name.

"Joss said she knew right then. She said he looked like me when I was a kid." With a hand on each of my shoulders, he took a few steps backward. "I waited for you to tell me. I wanted you to tell me, then, the other day, when you were going to, I panicked." He cupped my face with his palm. "I was afraid. He's a cool kid and you made him that way. You taught him things and made him who he is. You got him through all the mess with Sean. I don't even know him."

I nodded, though Simon didn't see it as he had quit looking at me.

"I never knew my dad. I don't know how to be a dad. What if I do it wrong?"

My big strong firefighter was afraid of a six-year-old. I pressed a kiss to his cheek. "He likes you and you're amazing with him. I heard your little conversation the last day you were here."

"I made him cry."

I sighed and looked up at him. "Simon… " I raised a hand to his cheek. It took a minute, but finally, his eyes met mine. "Kids cry. Sometimes, it's our fault and sometimes it isn't, but they always smile again."

"Does he know?"

I shook my head. "No."

He pushed me back gently and felt around in his pocket. "For years, I haven't been very connected to my life. I always felt like I was watching everyone else live theirs, and I was lost. So much has been erased from my brain--memories you all share, or have, and I don't."

I stepped back into his personal space, wrapped myself around him.

He grinned and tilted his head. "Okay. We can do this your way. As I started to say, I haven't felt connected to anyone since the shooting. Except you. I'm attached to you in a way I can't explain, in a way that makes my sister crazy. You brought me back to life." He had one hand in my hair and the other on my hip.

I moved in closer, instinctively seeking out the boy who'd always been my forever.

"I want to grow old with you. I want to watch our kids grow up, and I want to live with you, and wake up with you, and know no matter what happens in our lives, we'll face it together. We'll make new memories. I am tired of living without you. Will you marry me?" He slipped a brilliantly sparkling diamond on my finger.

I threw my arms around him as tears of real happiness flooded my eyes. "Simon, I've wanted to marry you since our high school prom." I stood there holding the man of my dreams, looking at the ring over his shoulder. I couldn't find my voice or my ability to form a thought.

His eyes got bigger. "Are you gonna answer me or not?"

I reached up to kiss him. "The only thing I've ever wanted was to marry you."

He half chuckled on a cough. "Even now? After everything?"

"Especially now after everything."

* * * *

Later on my mother's patio as we snuggled together in a lounger, I ran a hand across his stomach and smiled as he gulped in a big breath. "How long have you known about Kieran?"

"Since about a week after you got back."

If Joss knew, then Keaton knew and probably the rest of the group, too, along with whoever was on the call tree. "And you never said anything? No one said anything?"

He chuckled. "That was a tough one to manage. Joss wanted to come over here and make you confess all of it, but I wanted you to be able to tell me when you were ready and when I was ready."

"You are going to make such a great husband."

He shrugged and lifted my hand to examine the ring. "Are we really going to do this?"

"I think if Simon says so, we have to, right?"

"Simon says."

Be sure not to miss fellow Lyrical Press author Sara Walter Ellwood's
sequel to Heartsong

Heartland

Read on for a special sneak peek of the next book in the Singing to the
Heart series!

Learn more about Sara Walter Ellwood at
http://www.kensingtonbooks.com/author.aspx/29486

Chapter 1

Emily Kendall was tired of life-changing events. She'd had enough. But God or whatever fate controlled the universe wasn't done fucking with her life. "Are you sure? Hell, it's been weeks since I've even seen my husband, let alone had sex. Maybe the test was wrong."

She'd heard many life-changing words in her twenty-two years of life. The first had come when she was only fourteen and discovered superstar country singer Seth Kendall was her biological father. A few weeks after that revelation, the man she'd grown up loving as her father had shot her real dad and planned to kidnap her to sell into sex slavery.

Since then, a lot had happened. She'd become famous. Most people would even argue she was more famous than her dad, who helped her get her first record deal when she was barely fifteen. She broke sales records set by some of the best singers in the business, won countless awards, and sponsored everything from acne creams to jeans.

When she was three months shy of turning twenty, she'd met the British pop star Fabian McPhee. They'd collaborated on a TV special for the CMT network. He was fifteen years older than she was, mega famous, and super sexy. A month later while she was on tour in Australia, he'd asked her out to a nightclub.

That night had been full of firsts. Fabian introduced her to what would become her drugs of choice--cocaine and gin. Then, she'd lost her virginity to him. She'd thought she was in love. He was like no one she'd ever known. Despite her parents' outrage over their tabloid-crazed, whirlwind relationship, only two months after that first date they were married by Fabian's drummer, who happened to be an ordained minister from some online course he'd taken.

The medical director of the facility sitting across the wide, gleaming oak desk leaned forward and clasped his hands. "Your blood test isn't wrong. You are pregnant."

"Fuck." She was on a birth control shot, but she'd forgotten to get it. The last time she'd seen Fabian had been about six weeks ago. They'd had sex, but she thought he'd used a condom. She couldn't remember much of the event, like most of their two years of married life together. They'd split up ten months ago, but neither of them had gotten around to filing for divorce or could resist an occasional tumble in the sack or getting high together.

Not able to sit still any longer, she stood to pace the length of the posh office and folded her arms tightly around herself. She'd only been here for three days and already wanted to get the hell out of the medical facility. "How far along am I?"

Dr. Barton slid his finger over the screen of the computer tablet on his desk. "According to the history you gave the nurse who checked you in and your hCG level…" When she furrowed her brows trying to remember what the letters stood for, he clarified, "Pregnancy hormone. You would have to be six weeks."

She closed her eyes and took a deep breath. Her skin was too tight and hot. A coating of sweat caused her fingers to stick together, and she wiped her shaky hands on her jeans. Turning toward the window, she stared out at the woodland park surrounding the Fernwood Rehabilitation Center. In the past three years, she'd checked into the facility's drug and alcohol program to sober up three times, and each admission had been against her will. She didn't belong here because she wasn't an addict. So what if she went a little too far this last time and was booed off stage? The venue, if the college auditorium could justify that name, sucked anyway.

This news was the very last thing she needed to hear. She turned and vigorously rubbed her arms, really needing a hit right now. The desire for a line of coke brought to mind another issue. She remembered when her mother had been pregnant with her brother five years ago she wouldn't even take Tylenol for her headaches. Did she honestly want to know the answer to what all the coke she'd snorted could have done to her baby if her mother had been afraid to take something as harmless as over-the-counter pain pills? But she had to know if she'd harmed her child. "Do you know if the baby is okay?"

Dr. Barton stood to come around his desk. He leaned his backside on the heavy oak edge and folded his hands before him. "I don't know. Emily, there is a chance your baby will be born with problems. You are an addict." He held up his hand when she started to protest. "No, I'm not listening to your rationalizations. You've got to stop the drugs."

"I can quit. I have before."

He took a deep breath that made his shoulders rise, then fall. "And yet here you are again. Why were you admitted this time?"

She needed to get the hell away. "My manager has gotten a little too big for her pants." Maybe she should fire Trish Russell for talking her into even thinking about this place again. Trish had been her manager for three years, ever since she was promoted by her father-in-law and took Emily on as one of her first clients. She considered Trish one of her few true friends, but, sometimes, the older woman was a pain in the ass.

She spun on her heels, which made her lose her balance as dizziness whipped her world out of control. Grabbing the back of the chair to keep from falling over, she tossed over her shoulder, "I think we're done here."

"Emily, I'll let you go as soon as you tell me why you are here."

She stopped halfway to the door. If she didn't answer him, he'd only follow her. Letting out a long breath, she stared at the white-painted ceiling. "I'm here because I was too high to sing."

The past five shows were a blur. Nothing fun or amazing about any of them. No fans waiting for her to autograph their T-shirts. But then again, when was the last time she took time to talk to her fans after a show? When was the last time she did anything special for her fans? Once upon a time, she'd put on massive productions in front of stadiums full to bursting with screaming, adoring fans.

Her last tour hadn't even sold out to rundown opera houses and college auditoriums. In the early days, she'd arrange spontaneous private showings for more fans than had showed up for her current tour. She'd simply leave a date, time, and place on Twitter and a hundred or so of her fans would show up for a show. When had she last sent one of her own Tweets? She knew Kelly, her assistant, did all of her social media crap for her these days.

"I'm here because my record label said if I don't sober up, they're cutting me."

"They aren't happy with you?"

She shrugged and started pacing again. The cagy feeling was getting worse. "No. My last album is six months past due its production deadline. But I can't help that all the songs suck."

"Why do they suck?"

Turning, she met the doctor's steady gaze. She wanted to tell Dr. Barton that her label and her manager had sabotaged her by giving her shit songs, but she couldn't say that. Were the songs bad? Her father's old friend, pop superstar Amanda Lang, had written four of them and had given them to Emily as a gift, despite three other singers wanting them. The other two songs she'd recorded were from an award-winning songwriter, and they, too, had been sought after by the best in the business.

She blinked when the realization hit her. The songs weren't the problem nor were the studio musicians playing on the record. She was. "I don't want to talk about my career. I want to talk about my baby. Is there any way we can determine if it's okay?" As she laid her trembling hand on her belly, she silently prayed to a God she doubted would listen to anything she asked of Him. Please let my baby be okay.

Dr. Barton looked down at his hands, then went back to his big leather chair and sat. "I'd like you to meet with a colleague of mine. Doctor Marcella Summers is an OB/Gynecologist who specializes in babies born to addicted mothers. She'd be the person who might know the answer to your question."

She faced the wide windows again, but the early summer day and the forested mountains surrounding the center weren't what she saw. "Okay."

How was she going to handle a baby? Hell, she could barely take care of herself. What if it had a major problem from all the crap she'd put into her body?

She closed her eyes and fisted her hand over her belly. Dear God, what would Fabian say about the baby? He'd warned her when they got married he didn't want any kids. Would he blame the pregnancy on her as he had so many other things over the past two years?

"Emily, I don't know an addict who easily admits they are one." Dr. Barton broke into a tirade of questions, bombarding her. "By your own admission, you use cocaine at least four times a week, but most weeks you use it every day."

She glanced over her shoulder at him. He swiped his finger over his tablet, the paused to read more of her medical record. "In August twenty-eighteen, your father admitted you to Fernwood when he found you passed out on your tour bus. According to your blood toxin levels, you were only a snort of coke away from overdosing; then in June of last year, you were admitted after falling off stage and breaking your arm. Again, your blood work showed dangerous amounts of cocaine and alcohol."

Although she snickered at the memory, the humor was short lived, and she sobered. That had been her last stadium show. Tabloid and entertainment reporters hounded her after her release from Fernwood. Fabian's own career also took a nosedive when he was arrested for drunk driving and resisting arrest. The two of them and their antics had been a favorite topic in even mainstream news since then.

He cleared his throat and folded his hands in front of him. "Your blood results weren't as toxic this time, but if you don't make an honest attempt to get clean and stay clean, not only will you jeopardize your child, you're going to end up dead."

The truth smacked her hard in the gut. She was an addict. Up until now, she never believed she was one. She used coke and drank gin because she liked them, not because she couldn't live without them. But the reality was she used drugs to deal with life and all of its shit.

Would she have become so screwed up if she'd never met Fabian McPhee? Or had she been destined to a life of drug use due to her messed up childhood and sudden super stardom? Who knew? But in that moment, she hated the man who first introduced her to drugs and destroyed so much of her life. Her country music career was dead, and the fans she'd garnered when she put out a total pop album a year and half ago at Fabian's insistence had abandoned her. She hadn't spoken to or seen her parents, except from a distance at award shows, since her marriage. Since severing her ties with her mom and dad, she hadn't seen her four-year-old brother. Now, she was responsible for developing a tiny baby who may very well end up paying for her lousy judgment.

She turned and met the doctor's patient brown eyes. The man had to be a saint to manage the care of spoiled brat idiots like her. "Okay, Dr. Barton. I'm an addict. I use coke because I can't deal with life." She squared her shoulders and let out a breath. "There, I admitted it. Set up the appointment with the OB. But there's something else I'd like you to do." One of the conditions of admission into Fernwood was no contact with the outside world except for approved visitors on an extremely short list. "I want to file for divorce before I tell Fabian about the baby."

The doctor's surprise registered in the slightest widening of his eyes. "If that is want you want."

Emily couldn't help the snort as she sat in the chair in front of the desk again. "Oh, don't be coy, Dr. Barton. I know you've been hoping I'd ditch Fabian McPhee since the first time my father dragged my sorry ass into this place a year and a half ago." She looked at her hands as a rare moment of clarity blasted away the rosy sheen she'd painted over her life with her husband. "My counselor is right. Fabian and I do have a crazy love type of relationship. He might not beat me, but he has made me dependant on him by making me an addict."

For the first time in years, she felt relief flood over her. She smiled and met the doctor's eyes again. "For my baby and for me, I have to get away from him."

Emily laid a t-shirt in her suitcase and turned at the knock on the doorframe. She smiled at the willowy woman as she entered the room. "I'm glad to see you. I'm ready to get out of here."

The eight weeks she'd been a resident of the rehab had been the longest time she'd ever stayed, but once she finally faced her demons and committed herself, she didn't want to leave until she was free of her addiction.

Trish tucked her medium-length bright red hair behind her ear and glided into the room. "Paul isn't happy about postponing your record," she said, referring to the CEO of Midland Records. "But I convinced him that you needed a break to get completely sober and to stay that way."

Emily laid another T-shirt in the case. Her reason for being at Fernwood was no secret, but the only person outside of her doctors who knew about her pregnancy was Trish. After telling her, Emily asked her to convince her record company to push her production deadline to sometime in the future. "He doesn't suspect anything, does he?"

Trish sat on the overstuffed chair in the corner of the modest room. "No. I made a convincing case about your wanting to finally quit the drugs. He's not happy, but he's also glad."

Emily moved the suitcase off to the side and sat on the edge of the bed, facing Trish. "Has Fabian signed the divorce papers?"

"Yes. Reese is filing them today, in fact." Reese Goodwin was a family friend and a Nashville divorce lawyer. "Your divorce should be final by the end of the month."

She closed her eyes and took a deep breath full of relief. Although she hadn't demanded anything of Fabian, she feared he'd delay signing the papers to end their ill-fated marriage. "Thank God."

Trish leaned back in the chair and folded her hands in her lap. "When are you going to tell him about the baby?"

With a shrug, Emily stood, opened a dresser drawer, and pulled out a stack of bras. As she set them in her bag, she said, "I'll set up a meeting with him sometime before I go home to Texas."

She planned to get out of Nashville before she started showing. At almost four months pregnant, she knew she was on borrowed time.

"How do you think he'll take the news?"

Emily went back to the drawer and took out a stack of panties. "Hopefully, he won't take the news well and will leave me and my baby the hell alone."

She swallowed at the thought of her baby never knowing her father like she hadn't known Seth, but Fabian wasn't a good man. Despite being nearly forty years old, he still partied too hard and didn't take much seriously. He'd wasted most of his own fortune and a large portion of hers on fast cars, drugs, and lavish parties.

"He didn't fight about selling the penthouse and the mansion?" Three months after they were married, Fabian talked her into moving out of her downtown craftsmen home she bought on her eighteenth birthday and into buying a twenty-million-dollar estate outside of Nashville. The place was too big and flashy and put a considerable dent into her savings. He'd convinced her by arguing that as two successful entertainers, they were expected to live in such extravagance. Besides, he swore he'd pay his share of the cost. Instead, he conned her into buying a penthouse in Manhattan. He spent a lot of time there, but she hated New York and preferred to live in Nashville.

"He wants the penthouse." Trish pulled her iPad out of her purse. The woman never went anywhere without the thing. "But he's okay with selling the Nashville property and letting you keep the money from the sale if he can keep the penthouse."

"I'm glad he wants the penthouse so badly." Emily closed her suitcase and smiled as she turned to face Trish with her hand over the slight swell of her belly. "Because then I have a bargaining chip to keep him away from us."

www.ingramcontent.com/pod-product-compliance
Lightning Source LLC
Chambersburg PA
CBHW022151260626
47155CB00017B/1798